BASILISK

*Recent Titles by Graham Masterton available
from Severn House*

The Sissy Sawyer Series

TOUCHY AND FEELY
THE PAINTED MAN

The Jim Rook Series

ROOK
THE TERROR
TOOTH AND CLAW
SNOWMAN
SWIMMER
DARKROOM

Anthologies

FACES OF FEAR
FEELINGS OF FEAR
FORTNIGHT OF FEAR
FLIGHTS OF FEAR

Novels

BASILISK
CHAOS THEORY
DESCENDANT
DOORKEEPERS
EDGEWISE
GENIUS
HIDDEN WORLD
HOLY TERROR
HOUSE OF BONES
MANITOU BLOOD
UNSPEAKABLE

BASILISK

Graham Masterton

This first world edition published 2009
in Great Britain and in the USA by
SEVERN HOUSE PUBLISHERS LTD of
9–15 High Street, Sutton, Surrey, England, SM1 1DF.
Trade paperback edition published
in Great Britain and the USA 2009 by
SEVERN HOUSE PUBLISHERS LTD

British Library Cataloguing in Publication Data

Masterton, Graham
  Basilisk
  1. Stem cells - Research - Fiction 2. Basilisks (Mythical
  animals) - Fiction 3. Coma - Patients - Fiction 4. Horror
  tales
  I. Title
  823.9'14[F]

ISBN-13: 978-0-7278-6767-4   (cased)
ISBN-13: 978-1-84751-142-3   (trade paper)

All Severn House titles are printed on acid-free paper.

Typeset by Palimpsest Book Production Ltd.,
Grangemouth, Stirlingshire, Scotland.
Printed and bound in Great Britain by
MPG Books Ltd., Bodmin, Cornwall.

'Be like the imperial basilisk,
Killing thy foe with unapparent wounds!'
Ode to Naples – Percy Bysshe Shelley

ONE

Noises in the Night

'I hear noises,' quavered Mrs Bellman. 'Two or three in the morning, mostly, when it's pitchy dark.'

Grace was standing by the window, holding Mrs Bellman's X-ray up to the light. Not that there *was* much light. It had been raining heavily since the early hours of the morning, and the sky was overcast and gloomy. Not only that, there were two ivy plants, one on either side of the window sill, which were reaching out for each other across the intervening space, like two desperate lovers.

'Noises?' said Grace. She wasn't really listening. 'What kind of noises?'

'It sounds like somebody's dragging a *sack* along the corridor, right past my door. And sometimes I hear screaming, but I don't know where that's coming from. Upstairs, maybe, or someplace way in back. Sometimes near, sometimes far off.'

'You're sure it's not your hearing aid? If you turn the volume up too high, you'll get feedback.'

Mrs Bellman emphatically shook her head, so that her jowls wobbled. 'I know the difference between hearing-aid screaming and human screaming. I was a nurse once, myself.'

'Oh, really? At which hospital?'

'You don't know the half of it. I was sent over to Europe with the Army Nurse Corps, in 1944, only two-and-a-half weeks after D-Day. The things I saw.'

'My gosh. That must have been pretty traumatic.'

'*Traumatic*? I was in the Seventy-sixth Evacuation Hospital, during the Battle of the Bulge. I had to care for men with both of their arms blown off. Men run over by tank tracks, right across the middle. So I know the difference between hearing-aid screaming and human screaming, believe you me.'

Grace tucked her X-ray back in its envelope. 'So far as I can see, your thigh bone has knitted really well. You should be back on your feet in a week or two.'

Mrs Bellman cocked her head to one side, like a querulous pullet. 'You don't believe me, do you? You think I'm hearing things.'

'Of course I don't think you're hearing things. But everything sounds different at night, doesn't it? It's probably the janitor, dragging all the sheets down to the laundry.'

'Sheets don't scream.'

'I know, Doris. But elderly ladies do, when they have nightmares, or if they're in pain. This damp weather plays havoc with a lot of women's arthritis.'

She plumped up Mrs Bellman's pillows and straightened her blankets. It wasn't her job, as a general practitioner, but for a split second she had seen in Mrs Bellman's face the brave young nurse that she must have been in 1944, when her hair was blonde and wavy instead of white and wild, and her eyes were flawless blue.

One day, thought Grace, *I'm going to be old and crabby and argumentative like this. I just hope that the young women who take care of me will see* me *for who I really am.*

'It's that Doctor Zauber,' said Mrs Bellman, in a confidential whisper. 'I never trusted him, the first day I laid eyes on him. If you ask me, he's come to some kind of arrangement with Satan.'

'Doris – you can't say things like that! Doctor Zauber is very well respected.'

'Hmph! Satan's well respected, too.'

'Yes, well. Subversive opinions like that, I think you should keep them to yourself.'

Mrs Bellman pulled her gray, loose-weave shawl closer around her shoulders, and now she looked old again. The murky light from the window reflected on her glasses, so that she appeared to be blind, and her hands were like withered claws.

On the wall behind her bed hung a mirror, with a frame made of seashells. Photographs of her family were arranged all around it – her sons and her daughters and her grandchildren.

'Lovely pictures,' said Grace.

'Oh, yes,' said Mrs Bellman. 'Pity I hardly ever get to see them in the flesh. You see that little one there, in the red-and-yellow romper suit? That's Tyler, my daughter Sarah's youngest boy. They haven't brought him to visit me since he was two years old. He's in the fourth grade now, would you believe it?'

'I'm sorry.'

'Oh – you don't have to be sorry. You grow old, you get forgotten. I'm used to it. It's like you're dead before you're dead. Sometimes I think the only person who cares about me is Harpo, and Harpo isn't even a person.'

Grace turned toward the far corner of the room, where a dome-shaped wicker cage stood on a table. Inside the cage perched a puffy white cockatoo, swinging on its swing and warbling softly in the back of its throat. She tapped gently on the bars and said, 'Come on, Harpo. Say something. Say, "good afternoon, Grace".'

The cockatoo kept on warbling to itself, regardless. Grace said, 'Come on! Even a wolf whistle would do.'

Mrs Bellman grunted. 'They don't say much, Goffin's cockatoos, even if they *do* speak. But Harpo hasn't said a word ever since I got him. I wish I could train him to say "this meat loaf tastes like an old man's rear end".'

'Doris!'

'I'm sorry. But they seem to think that just because you're old, you don't have a discriminating palate no more.'

She leaned forward, and then she whispered, 'If you ask me, that's what they keep dragging along the corridor, in that sack. They give another old geezer an overdose of xylocaine, and then they drag his body down to the kitchens, to make meat loaf.'

'You have a very macabre imagination,' said Grace. 'Are you taking those kava kava pills I gave you? They should settle you down. I'll come see you again the week after next, and maybe we can think about taking off your plaster cast.'

'That's if I'm still here. That's if Doctor Zauber hasn't done for me, too, and dragged *me* off in a sack.'

'Doris—'

Mrs Bellman flapped her hand. 'I know. I know. Keep my suspicions to myself. Sit here and eat my cream of wheat and watch *Days Of Our Lives*, and wait for Satan to come knocking.'

'See you, Doris. You take good care now, you hear?'

* * *

As she walked back along the corridor toward the reception area, Doctor Zauber came out of his office, immediately in front of her.

'Doctor Underhill!' he greeted her, in his cultured German accent. 'This is a very pleasant surprise.'

'I was on my way back to Chestnut Hill, so I thought I'd call by to see how Doris Bellman was doing.'

'And?'

'She's mending very well. She's a tough old turkey, isn't she?'

Doctor Zauber gave her a sloping smile. 'She is not the easiest of our residents, I am sorry to say. But – yes – it will take much more than a fractured femur to dispose of *her*.'

Doctor Zauber was short, but he had a disproportionately large head. His nose was curved and predatory and his eyes were so pale green that they were almost colorless. His shiny gray hair was combed sharply back from his forehead to curl over his collar. Today, as always, he was dressed in a black coat and a gray vest and striped black-and-gray pants. He looked like a mortician, rather than the director of an old people's home. Denver had said that he sounded like Jack Nicholson's evil triplet (the other evil triplet being Denver's principal at West Airy High School).

'Is Doris still on diazepam?' asked Grace, as she and Doctor Zauber walked along the corridor together.

'Why do you ask?'

'She seems to be a little anxious, that's all.'

'Oh, yes? Anxious about what?'

'She says she hears noises in the middle of the night. Screaming, and a noise like somebody dragging a sack along the corridor outside of her room.'

'Really? Maybe it's her medication, giving her delusions. I'll have a word with Sister Bennett about her.'

'I wish you would. Although I think she's lonely, more than anything else.'

'You may be right. I'll see if we can arrange a visitor for her.'

They reached the reception area and Doctor Zauber laid his hand on Grace's shoulder. 'Well, Grace,' he told her, 'I have to go in this direction. Another *langwierig* budget meeting, to decide if we can afford to give our residents anything to eat! When will we be seeing you again?'

'Not for a couple of weeks. I'm trying to persuade my husband to take time off.'

'Oh, yes! Your husband, the lion tamer.'

'Zoologist, actually.'

'Such a fascinating profession! I have always thought that animals are much more interesting than humans. What secrets they could tell us, if they could speak!'

'Nathan says that they would probably talk about nothing but food and sex. But mostly food.'

'Oh, no! Animals are much closer to God than we are. Much closer to Satan, too.'

Grace thought, *if only you knew what Doris Bellman says about you.* But she simply smiled, and said, 'See you in a couple of weeks, Doctor.'

'I look forward to it.'

Grace left the building and hurried across the parking lot. The rain was lashing across the asphalt and the trees were wildly waving their branches in the air, as if they were panicking. She pulled up the hood of her scarlet raincoat and turned her face away from the wind.

As she did so, she saw another resident staring out of a ground-floor window at her, a wan-faced woman in a plain oatmeal-colored dress. Grace gave her a spontaneous wave, but the woman didn't wave back. Maybe she hadn't seen her, or maybe she simply wasn't interested in other people any more.

TWO

Natural Disaster

I t was almost ten after eight when Richard Scryman knocked at Nathan's open door. He looked like an anxious stork – beaky, with long awkward arms and legs.

'Hey, Richard – you still here?' asked Nathan, checking his Rolex. 'Sorry, fella, I lost all track of time. I'll see you in the morning, OK?'

Richard said, 'There's no way I'm about to leave, Professor. It's the embryo's heart rate. It's gone totally berserk.'

'Shit. How bad is it?'

Richard used his fingertip to draw a wildly zig-zagging graph in the air. 'One second it's way over three, the next it's down to two thirty-five.'

'*Shit,*' said Nathan, tossing down his pen.

'I don't think we can leave it too much longer,' Richard told him. 'If it doesn't pip in the next couple of hours, I seriously doubt that it ever will.'

Nathan shrugged himself into his long white lab coat and followed Richard out of his office. '*Shit,*' he repeated. His dirty-blond hair was all messed up, and he hadn't shaved in two days. He was forty-four, but he looked like a puffy-eyed college student who has just woken up on somebody's couch after an all-night drinking session.

His two young interns, Keira and Tim, were standing in front of the glass-fronted incubating unit looking both anxious and guilty, almost as if it was their fault that the embryo was showing signs of stress.

'What's the arterial pulsation as of now?' he asked them.

Keira frowned at her computer screen. 'Two ninety-five. Two ninety-six. It's steadier than it was a few minutes ago.'

'Two ninety-six? That's high, but not critical. No sign of pipping?'

'No major muscle spasms – not yet, anyhow. Very slight shivering, but only in the legs.'

'Apart from the heart rate, any other signs of distress?'

Tim shook his head. Nathan turned back to Richard Scryman and said, 'Maybe we should give it another couple of hours. With any luck, the bpm might have settled down by then.'

Richard pulled a face. 'It's your call, Professor. But the yolk sac is pretty close to being totally depleted, and I can't see it surviving very much longer. Like, basically, it's having a heart seizure.'

'Two ninety-eight,' said Keira. Then, 'Two ninety-nine.'

Nathan stared at the egg for almost half a minute without saying anything. It was huge, at least three-quarters the size of an ostrich egg, and a very dark green, with black freckles, as if somebody had used a toothbrush to spatter Indian ink all over it. It was resting in a specially molded cup of latex foam, and it was clustered with electrodes – constantly measuring its heart rate, blood pressure and oxygen absorption.

For Nathan, this egg was the culmination of five years of intensive laboratory work – quite apart from all the fundraising dinners and the sponsorship drives and the academic wheeler-dealing. This egg was every theory he had ever dreamed up, and every genetic formula he had ever devised, made reality.

The skepticism of his fellow zoologists had probably exhausted him the most. They had never let up – not at board meetings, not at zoological seminars, not in scientific journals. Nathan Underhill is a New-Age lunatic. Nathan Underhill is a self-publicizing charlatan. Nathan Underhill is a snake-oil salesman, who has diverted much-needed funds away from far more serious research projects, just to develop a zoological freak show. More than one religious leader had accused him of doing the work of the Devil.

Even his students called him 'Doctor Freakenstein,' although with considerably more tolerance, especially the girls. They liked an oddball, especially a good-looking oddball, and even though they generally agreed that what he was attempting to do was totally insane, they also thought that it was pretty cool of him to try.

The door at the far side of the laboratory was noisily opened up, and George the janitor stuck his head around it.

'Finished yet, Professor? I'm locking up now.'

Nathan raised one hand. 'Sorry, George, we're right in the middle of something. You'll have to wait for a while.'

'Can't wait till tomorrow morning, then, this something that you're right in the middle of?'

'No, George, it can't. It's only slightly less important than the birth of Jesus.'

'Oh, that's OK, then. I'll check back later, when I've finished my hoagie.'

'Bet the Three Wise Men never said that,' Tim remarked, under his breath.

Nathan unhooked his stethoscope and held it against the eggshell. He could hear the heartbeat, soft and frantic, and he checked it against his wristwatch. Over four times faster than a human heartbeat, but only slightly quicker than a chicken's.

He checked the latest acoustic scans on his computer screen.

The embryo *looked* OK. He could clearly see its head, its body and its wings. He could see the egg tooth, too: the sharp projection on its beak with which it was supposed to pierce the air sac inside its shell. This would start it breathing, and then it would break open the shell itself, and hatch out into the open air.

But to start hatching, it needed to give one convulsive jerk with its neck muscle, and so far it had shown no signs that it was strong enough. Based on its size and weight, Nathan had calculated that it would start to pip after thirty-five days, compared with twenty-one days for a chicken, but after thirty-eight days it was still folded up inside its shell, and it hardly ever stirred.

'Blood pressure's dropping,' said Tim. 'Oxygen saturation – that's going down, too.'

'It's dying,' said Richard.

Nathan knew that he was right. He had hoped so much for a natural hatching, but it was obvious now that the embryo was far too weak.

Tim said, 'Blood pressure's down to twelve.'

'Heart rate's dropping, too,' said Keira. 'Two sixty-five. Two sixty-three. Two fifty-one.'

Richard looked at Nathan and even though Nathan didn't want to admit it, he knew that he had no choice. He opened the deep drawer under the laboratory bench, and took out the picture-framing hammer that he had bought especially for this moment – this moment that he had not believed would ever come.

He tied a surgical mask over his face, and snapped on a pair of purple latex gloves.

'Two twenty-one,' Keira intoned. 'Two-one-seven. Two-one-two.'

'Video cameras running?' asked Nathan.

Tim gave him the thumbs-up. Quickly but very carefully, Nathan peeled the electrodes off the speckled green shell. He listened again with his stethoscope, to satisfy himself that the embryo's heart was still beating. Then he carefully tapped the top of the egg with his hammer.

He tapped it once – twice – three times – but it didn't crack. It was obviously much thicker and stronger than he had calculated.

He looked at Richard but all Richard could do was shrug. Keira and Tim looked equally helpless.

'OK,' he said. 'Here goes nothing.'

He struck the egg as hard as he could, and it broke into three large pieces, although they didn't fall apart. He put down his hammer, and gently lifted the uppermost piece. Inside, there was a thin translucent membrane which stretched and then tore. A gray feathered head appeared, glistening with mucus, and a single orange eye which stared at him, unblinking.

'Holy *Ker*-ist!' said Tim.

An appalling stench poured out of the egg, so foul that Keira made a retching noise and clamped her hand over her nose and her mouth, and even Richard coughed and took two steps back. The smell was sulfurous, like a rotten chicken's egg, but it also had a strong undertone of chicken meat that was turning green, and a sinus-burning corrosiveness. It reminded Nathan of a blocked kitchen sink filled with Drano – hair and fat dissolving in sodium hydroxide.

'Oh God,' said Richard. 'Look at it! It's still alive, but it's half decomposed.'

Nathan turned his head away, took a deep breath, and held it. He turned back and tugged away the second piece of shell, and then the third. The embryo's wing feathers were slimy, and its body was like a soft, half-collapsed sack. It had all the component parts that he had expected – the head, the beak, the legs and the claws – and there was no doubt that its heart was still beating.

But it took one sticky breath, and then another, and then it choked, and stopped breathing altogether. Nathan carefully scooped both hands underneath it, trying to lift it up.

'Tim – bring me the nest! Like, *now*! Keira – get ready with the oxygen!'

Tim carried over a red plastic bowl filled with fine sand and feathers and shreds of soft purple wool. Nathan had designed it himself, based on the scrapes that were hollowed out on cliffsides by peregrine falcons, to rear their young.

With trembling hands, Tim held the bowl close to the incubator unit.

'OK, now, easy,' said Nathan. 'We've put too much love and effort into this little guy to see him die now.'

'He's eighty per cent necrotic already,' said Richard. 'He. *It*. Maybe it's a she.'

Nathan raised his hands, and as he did so, the embryo fell

apart. The wings dropped off, on to the floor, and the head rolled into the nest. The rest of the body collapsed into a mush of skin and bones and putrescent slime.

'Oh God,' said Keira, and walked off toward the other side of the laboratory, one hand raised in utter revulsion. 'That is *totally* disgusting.'

Nathan let the embryo's remains fall back into the incubating unit, scraping the gelatinous green flesh off his fingers. Then he peeled off his latex gloves, and went to the sink to wash his hands with antiseptic gel.

He said nothing. He couldn't find the words. Tim watched him, still holding the nesting bowl. Keira stayed in the corner, by the door.

With undisguised distaste, Richard picked up the embryo's wings and restored its head to the top of its body. He coughed again, and said, '*Feurrgh!*' and spat into a tissue. Then, 'What happened, Professor?'

Nathan finished drying his hands before he answered. 'Some kind of bacterial infection is my first guess. Group A Streptococcus, most likely.'

'But how did its heart go on beating for so long? No human could have survived that degree of necrosis.'

'Of course not. But we're not dealing with a human here, are we? We're not even dealing with any recognized species of bird or beast.'

'So what do we do now?' asked Tim. His cheeks were even more flushed than they usually were. 'Jesus . . . I've been working on this one cryptozoology project ever since I left the Academy.'

Nathan laid a hand on his shoulder. 'We refrigerate the remains and first thing tomorrow we start a detailed necropsy. And – listen – we don't tell anybody what's happened, not yet. I had a call from the Zoological Society's funding department yesterday afternoon, and so far we've managed to go through two-point-seven.

'*Million*,' he added, when he received no immediate reaction. 'Dollars.'

Richard looked down at the wretched tangle of bones and feathers lying in the incubating unit. 'Wow,' he said.

'You're damn right, *wow* – when all we have to show for it is one putrefying embryo.'

'Still,' said Richard, 'we might be able to salvage something from it. If we can discover how the embryo managed to live for so long, in such an advanced state of decomposition . . . the zoo might get *some* return for its investment in Cee-Zee research. You know, somebody like Pfizer might be interested.'

Nathan didn't answer. Richard was probably right, but he felt much too upset. After a while, Richard went over to one of the refrigerators and returned with a stainless-steel tray. He picked up one of the embryo's wings but Nathan said, 'No, Richard – it's OK. It's my fricking disaster, I'll clean it up. I'll see you guys early tomorrow, OK?'

'You're sure?' said Richard.

Nathan nodded. 'I could do with some thinking time. Right now, I'm feeling kind of bereaved, to say the least.'

At that moment, the laboratory door opened again, and George stuck his head around it. 'Jesus born yet?'

THREE

Feathers Fly

I t was nearly midnight before he made it back home. He walked into the bedroom and stood beside the bed, exhausted, saying nothing, as if he had reached the end of a very long journey. Grace was sitting up, reading *Northern Liberties*, a romantic novel about early Philadelphia, when it had been the largest city in America.

'My God, Nathan,' she said, putting down her book. 'You look *pooped.*'

'Bad day at Black Rock,' he told her. He pulled off his dark green sweater and started to unbutton his shirt. 'I think God is giving me a hard time for playing God.'

'So what went wrong?'

'What *didn't* go wrong?'

'Not the gryphon. You thought it might be hatching today.'

He sat down on the end of the bed. 'It died. Its heart was still beating, but it obviously didn't have the strength to break out of its shell. So I cracked it open. And – *yuck*. You should have smelled it. Or rather, you were lucky you didn't. It was eighty per cent putrefied. Almost liquid, parts of it.'

'Oh, Nate. After all your work.'

'I'm going to get myself a beer,' he told her. 'You don't want one, do you?'

She shook her head. 'I'm so sorry,' she said.

'Well, it's always been totally out there, this project. But I really thought that this was going to be the one.'

He went downstairs to the kitchen and came back with a can of Dale's Pale Ale. He sat back down on the bed and popped it open. 'Somehow, the embryo got infected. I don't know how, or what with. But it looks like some kind of necrotizing fasciitis.'

Grace pulled aside the bedcovers, climbed out of bed and sat down close to him, wrapping her arms around his shoulders. 'You must be shattered. I don't know what to say.'

'I feel totally numb, to tell you the truth. Feel my hands, I'm freezing. I was convinced that by this time next week, there I'd be, on the front cover of *Scientific American*, grinning at all those skeptical bastards who said that I couldn't even breed hamsters.'

'What will you do now?'

Nathan swallowed beer, and sniffed. 'In the short term, try to find out what the hell went wrong. It could have been a bacterial infection – it could have been something more fundamental.'

'And in the long term?'

'In the long term – I guess it all it depends on Henry Burnside. If he doesn't cut off my research budget, I'll try again. But he's been making some pretty grumpy noises lately. As of yesterday we've spent over two-point-seven million, and I haven't even given him a ratfish, leave alone a fully grown gryphon.'

'Maybe you hyped it up too much,' said Grace. 'It's an amazing idea, and I can see why Burnside bought it. But you never really told him how difficult it was going to be.'

'Difficult? That's the understatement of the twenty-first century. More like fricking impossible. For me, anyhow.'

'Oh, come on, Nate. Give yourself some credit. If the embryo was fully grown, the basic genetics must have been sound, mustn't they?'

'Maybe. Maybe not. I won't find out for certain until we've carried out a full necropsy. I would have started it tonight but I was too damn tired and too damn pissed.'

'Have you told him yet?'

'Burnside?' Nathan shook his head. 'No. It's much too late to call him now. And I'm not *about* to tell him, either. Not until I know exactly what went wrong, and how to make sure that it doesn't happen again.'

'Are you hungry?' Grace asked him. 'There's some vegetable chowder in the pot, if you feel like some. Or some cold chicken.'

'Chicken – no, thanks,' said Nathan. He could still smell the gryphon's egg breaking open. He could almost *taste* it. 'I'm fine, really. I think I need some sleep, more than anything else.'

Grace kissed him, very lightly, on the cheek. He turned to look at her. He suddenly realized that he hadn't been seeing nearly enough of her lately. She had changed her hair and he hadn't even noticed. It was very short now, and she had lighter brown streaks in it. He had almost forgotten how alluring she was, with that perfect oval face, like a medieval saint; and how greeny-gray her eyes were, like the ocean on a very dull day.

'You do really believe that I can do this?' he asked her. 'I'm not really a New-Age lunatic, am I?'

She took hold of his hand and squeezed it. 'I've never doubted you, Nate, you know that. But maybe you should try something less ambitious. Maybe you *should* try a ratfish.'

'Well, maybe. But the genetics are just as complicated. And what do you end up with? Either a fish that can run up a drainpipe or a rat that can play water polo.'

Grace pressed her forehead against his, as if she wanted him to share her sympathy by osmosis. 'You're not going to give up, though, are you?'

'No, I'm not going to give up. But I need to think this whole thing through, all over again, right from the basement upward. I keep feeling that I'm missing something.'

'Such as what?'

'Well – I'm sure that the biology is good. The genetic coding, the cell development, everything. But maybe it takes more than biology to create a mythical creature. Maybe – I don't know – maybe it takes a certain amount of *myth*.'

Grace blinked at him. 'Now you've lost me.'

'Think about it,' said Nathan. 'All those medieval sorcerers who first bred gryphons, and hippogryphs, and chimeras, how did *they* do it?'

'Nobody knows, do they?'

'Well, one thing's for sure. They didn't know squat about IVF or egg transplantation. They didn't have CT scanners or ballistocardiograms. But they still managed to breed all those monstrosities. So before I try to fertilize another gryphon's egg, maybe I should find out how they did it in the Middle Ages.'

'I think you're right,' said Grace.

'You do?'

'Yes – I think you *do* need some sleep. Let's talk about it tomorrow.'

He came back into the bedroom after his shower, with a thick white towel wrapped around his waist. He had washed his hair, and shaved, and slapped on some Acqua di Gio, and he felt human again.

'I didn't ask you, sweetheart, I'm sorry. How was *your* day?'

'Busy, but pretty ho-hum. That stomach bug doesn't show any signs of letting up. But I had a *very* spooky conversation with old Mrs Bellman, at the Murdstone Rest Home.'

'Mrs Bellman?'

'You remember – that dotty old lady who tried to slide down the banisters and broke her thigh bone? She told me that she's been hearing people dragging sacks along the corridor, in the middle of the night. And *screaming*. She's convinced that Doctor Zauber is killing off his patients and grinding up their bodies for meat loaf.'

Nathan leaned over and peered at himself in her dressing-table mirror. 'Maybe she's right. Maybe they're running that place like *Soylent Green* – you know, that sci-fi movie when they turned old folks into food.'

'She's lonely, that's all, and delusional.'

Nathan peered at himself even more closely. 'God, I'm handsome.' He plucked a hair out of his left nostril between finger and thumb, and said, '*Ouch.*'

'I just wish I could do more for women like her, that's all.

Her family never visit her. She's sitting in that room, day after day, with nobody to talk to. It's not surprising she gets weird ideas. And there must be millions of old people in the same predicament.'

Nathan climbed into bed, and kissed her shoulder. 'The only answer is, not to get old. Why do you think I'm doing all of this research? The Egyptian bennu bird was supposed to live for over a thousand years. If we could share its genetic coding, then who knows how long *we* could live?'

'Uh-uh. I don't think I could bear to be married to you for another nine hundred and eighty-two years, thank you.'

'Hey –' he said, whacking at her with his pillow.

Just as he did so, though, he heard the front door slam, downstairs. He frowned at Grace and said, 'Is that Denver?'

'I forgot to tell you. He went out. He said he'd be back by eleven.'

Nathan checked his bedside clock. 'It's ten after one. Where the hell has he been?'

'I don't know. You'll have to ask him. He said he was going bowling with Stu Wintergreen and that Evans boy.'

They heard clattering in the kitchen. Nathan climbed out of bed again, and took his bathrobe down from the back of the door.

'Nate –' said Grace, anxiously. 'Don't be too hard on him.'

'I'm not going to be hard on him. What makes you think I'm going to be hard on him?'

'Because you usually are, that's why. Come on, Nate, he's seventeen years old now. Think what *you* were doing when you were seventeen.'

'Exactly.'

He went out on to the landing, just as Denver was climbing the stairs, with a can of beer in each hand. Denver looked almost exactly like Grace, with a pale oval face and dark shoulder-length hair. But he had inherited his default expression from Nathan – always serious, and interrogative, as if something was troubling him, but he couldn't decide what.

'Well, well!' said Nathan. 'The wanderer returneth! What the hell time do you calleth this?'

Denver swayed, and blinked. 'I don't know, Pops. Sidereal time?'

'You've been drinking, for Christ's sake.'

'I sure hope so. I'd hate to feel like this if I hadn't.'

'You're seventeen years old, Denver. Drinking alcohol is illegal until you're twenty-one. Where the hell did you get it? You didn't *drive* in this condition, did you?'

'I had to, Pops. I was too drunk to walk.'

Nathan made a grab for the cans of beer. He managed to snatch one of them out of Denver's right hand, but Denver hid the other one behind his back.

'Give me that beer, Denver. There's absolutely no way you're drinking any more.'

By now, Grace had come to the bedroom door. 'Denver, look at the state of you!'

'Look at the state of me? Look at the state of me? I'm seventeen years old and I went bowling with my friends. I drank three cans of Miller and I pissed over a fence. I horsed around and I laughed and I had a stupid, ordinary time doing nothing but stupid, ordinary things. I didn't steal anything, I didn't vandalize anything, I didn't rape any girls. Why are you being so goddamned cen-snorious?'

Nathan held out his hand. 'Give me that can of beer.'

'Oh, no.' Denver shook his head. 'This can of beer is your compensation to me for being such a dick. You know what I have to put up with, every single day? Has your dad hatched any good dragons lately? He sure succeeded in breeding a gargoyle, didn't he? Just take a look in the mirror!'

'Give me that can of beer, Denver, or else you're grounded for the rest of the month, and I'm not kidding you.'

Denver swayed and almost toppled backward down the stairs. 'I know you're not kidding me. You *never* kid. You're always so goddamned serious. But how can you be so goddamned serious when you spend all day trying to breed creatures that don't even exist? That's you, Pops! That's you! You don't care about reality! You don't give a flying fuck about your own son! The trouble with me is, I'm *real*! I exist! I'm not a unicorn or a gryphon or a three-headed what-do-you-call-it! I'm just a boring, real, ordinary, stupid person!'

Nathan grabbed Denver's sleeve, and heaved him forcibly up to the landing. Denver's eyes were glassy but he raised his chin in defiance and said, 'What? What are you going to do now? You going to hit me?'

Grace said, 'Nate, *don't*.'

Nathan stared back at Denver, trying to face him down. But then shook his head and said, 'Why don't you just get to bed, kid, and sleep it off? I can't hurt you nearly as much as your head will, in the morning.'

'Is that a joke?' Denver challenged him. 'Don't tell me you've cracked a joke! Mom – did you hear that? Pops just cracked a joke! Must have been all that practice you've been getting, cracking eggs!'

Nathan seized Denver's sweatshirt and pulled him so close that their noses were almost touching. He was trembling, but he knew that it wasn't Denver's fault. It was his own rage that nearly five years of painstaking laboratory work had come to nothing. Instead of a shining, preening gryphon, all he had was a trayful of sticky feathers and a few lumps of liquefying flesh.

'Get to bed,' he said, releasing Denver's shirt.

'You suck,' said Denver. 'You really, really suck.'

'I said, get to bed. I'll talk to you tomorrow.'

Denver lurched along the landing toward his bedroom door. As he passed Grace, he stopped for a moment, and said, 'Give Pops some of your St John's wort, Mom. That'll calm him down. Natural medicine for ever!'

'Don't you talk to your mother like that!' Nathan snapped.

'Or what?' Denver retorted. He staggered against the wall, knocking a picture crooked. Then he held up the can of beer and said, 'Here! Take it back! I don't need any compensation from you! Doctor Freakenstein!'

He threw the can of beer at Nathan, as hard as he could. It missed, and struck the antique china vase at the end of the corridor, chipping the rim.

Nathan didn't say anything, and he didn't move. He had taught himself several years ago not to let his temper overwhelm him. All the same, he had to grip the banister-rail very tightly as Denver spun around and staggered into his bedroom, slamming the door behind him.

Grace took hold of Nathan's arm and led him back to bed. 'He's drunk,' she said. 'We all say things we don't mean when we're drunk. He'll apologize tomorrow.'

'Why should he? That's exactly what I am – Doctor Freakenstein. I'm not even good at it, either. In five years, what have I actually managed to produce? Twenty-eight unfertilized eggs, and one dead gryphon. He's absolutely right. I suck.'

They heard a loud crash, which sounded like Denver tripping over his own jeans as he tried to take them off. This was followed by the banging of a toilet seat, and then the unmistakable sound of Denver being torrentially sick.

At last Denver fell into bed, and the house was quiet. As exhausted as he was, however, Nathan couldn't sleep, and lay with his arms around Grace, feeling her ribcage and listening to her breathing.

He kept seeing the gryphon's orange eye, staring at him helplessly from the gray jelly of its own putrefaction. He thought about the wizards and the sorcerers who had first created such hybrids – not just rats crossed with salmon, or hawks crossed with cats, but much larger beasts, like dragons and hippogryphs – half gryphon and half horse.

He thought of the poem by Ludovico Ariosto, which he had quoted in his first presentation to the Philadelphia Zoological Society, when he was asking them for funds.

No empty fiction wrought by magic lore,
But natural was the steed the wizard pressed;
For him a filly to a griffin bore;
Hight hippogryph. In wings and beak and crest,
Formed like his sire, as in the feet before;
But like the mare, his dam, in all the rest.

It sounded so bombastic now, so full of shit. How could he have thought that he could really breed a gryphon, leave alone a hippogryph? How could he have been so arrogant?

Grace murmured, and turned over. Nathan turned over, too. The illuminated clock on his nightstand said two seventeen. His eyes closed, and he started to slide into sleep. But then he heard Denver stumble into the bathroom again, and the toilet seat clattering, and the groaning of a young man who swears by all that's holy that he will never drink alcohol again, like *ever.*

FOUR

Post Mortem

I t was still raining the next morning, and a blustery wind was blowing from the north-west. Nathan's designated parking space had been taken up by a delivery van from Emsco Scientific Supplies, so he had to park his black Dodge Avenger under the trees on the opposite side of the parking lot, where it would inevitably get covered in wet leaves and bits of branches and bird droppings.

He had nearly reached the laboratory steps when he heard footsteps hurrying up behind him, and the jostling of a waterproof coat.

'Professor Underhill! *Professor Underhill!*'

He turned around. A pretty blonde girl in a puffy red squall was jogging across the parking lot toward him. She was wearing bright red rubbers with sparkles on them, and a red knitted hat with bunny's ears on top of it.

'Professor Underhill! Sir! May I talk to you, please?'

'It depends what about.'

The girl bit off one of her gloves with her teeth and dug into her pocket for an identity card. 'Patti Laquelle, from *The Philadelphia Web*,' she panted. 'I'm *so* glad I caught you!'

'*The Philadelphia Web*? You mean the online newspaper?' Nathan wasn't impressed. The *Web* was the digital equivalent of *The National Enquirer*, full of stories about the marital indiscretions of minor TV celebrities and bungling local bank robbers and budgerigars that could whistle 'Pennsylvania, Pennsylvania, Mighty is your name.'

Most of the media had been deeply skeptical about Nathan's cryptozoological project when the zoo had first announced it, but the *Web* had mocked him more than most. 'Dragon's Eggs Could Be Miracle Cure For Everything That Ails Us, Claims Philly's Would-Be Wizard.' After that, he had responded to all media inquiries about his progress with only the dullest and most technical of answers, and over the years the media had gradually lost interest. Until today, anyhow.

'I'm sorry, Ms Laquelle. But I'm busy right now, and I'm a half-hour late already.'

'But I need to ask you about your gryphon!'

'My what?'

'Your *gryphon*, Professor. Come on, I know that you managed to fertilize a gryphon's egg.'

'OK,' said Nathan, defensively. 'I never made a secret of it.'

'No. But you haven't exactly shouted it from the rooftops, have you?'

'It's difficult, complicated stuff, that's why. Not exactly *Web* material. If you're really interested, I published a three-thousand-word article about it in *The American Journal of Genetics* – November seventeenth last year.'

'You did? Wow – I don't know how I could have missed that.'

'You and about three hundred and three million other people. Don't worry about it.'

'So how's the little monster getting along?'

'It's growing, and we're keeping a close watch on its development. That's all. It's taking a little longer to hatch out than we thought it would, but – well – there's absolutely no precedent for what we're doing here, is there?'

'You mean it hasn't hatched already?'

Nathan opened the laboratory door. 'Listen, Ms Laquelle. As soon as anything happens, you'll be the first to know about it. I promise you.'

'You're *sure* it hasn't hatched already?'

'No, it hasn't. Now I really have to get going.'

'How come I heard from a very reliable source that it *did* hatch, but it was stillborn?'

He hesitated, still holding the door open. 'I can't imagine why you should think that.'

'Meaning that it *did* hatch, and it *was* stillborn?'

'Meaning that I can't tell you anything, because there's absolutely nothing to tell you.'

Patti Laquelle came up the steps and stood very close to him, frowning up at him as intently as if she could read his mind. She had a spattering of freckles across the bridge of her nose and her blonde fringe was sparkling with raindrops. She reminded him of a girlfriend he used to go out with, when he was only fifteen.

'That's not true, Professor, is it?' she asked him.

'Ms Laquelle—'

'Please, call me Patti. I know what's happened, Professor. I know it's all gone wrong. And I have to file *something* about it. You can't expect me not to.'

Nathan was silent for a very long time. Then he said, 'Who leaked it?'

'You know I can't tell you that. But if you explain to me exactly how the gryphon died, and why, I won't have to speculate, will I? I won't have to write "How Did Philly's Would-Be Wizard Get Egg On His Face?" Don't forget that all the other media are going to be after you, too, as soon as this story breaks. "Breaks" – sorry! But you know I'm right. It's going to be a feeding frenzy.'

Nathan hesitated. Then he said, 'Come along inside,' and opened the door wider.

He led her into his office. Richard hadn't arrived yet, to open up the refrigerator and take out the gryphon's remains. All the same, Nathan sniffed, twice, and he was sure that he could still smell it.

Patti took off her squall. Nathan took it from her and hung it up on the coat stand. 'Kind of big for you, this coat.'

'It belonged to my last boyfriend. *Lars*, would you believe? He was a skiing nut. Me – I always hated skiing. Trudging up hills, sliding back down again. I could never see the point.'

'You want some coffee?'

'Sure. Black. No sugar.'

Nathan spooned coffee into the cafetière on top of his filing cabinet. Without turning around, he said, 'You're right about the gryphon. It died yesterday evening, just after eight. It was fully grown, but it never made any attempt to pip – that is, to hatch itself. Too feeble, I guess.'

'So what did you do?'

'I cracked the egg myself, with a hammer. But when I opened it up, I found that the gryphon was in what you might call an advanced state of decomposition. In other words, it had putrefied.'

'Oh, my God.'

'It died a few seconds later. There wasn't a hope in hell that we could have revived it.'

He poured boiling water on to the coffee grounds. 'It's too early to say what went wrong. It could have been a bacterial infection, it could have been some kind of chromosome disorder. It could have been some genetic problem that I can't even begin to understand.

'All I know is that the people who want to see this project shut down are going to have a field day.'

Patti said, 'I'm sorry, Professor. Truly.'

'Why should you care?'

'Well – what a *gas* it would have been, wouldn't it, if you had managed to pull it off? A real live walking talking gryphon! Well, maybe not talking, but *squawking*. You could have made a fortune! *I* could have made a fortune! Think of the syndication rights!'

'For Christ's sake. I'm a molecular biologist, not P.T. Barnum.'

'So what do you want me to post on the *Web*?'

'Why are you asking me? You'll write whatever you feel like. "Gryphon's Egg Is A Big Fat Zero." "Gryphon Egg Project Goes Pear-Shaped." Who knows?'

'No, seriously.'

Nathan poured them each a mug of coffee. 'Why don't you just remind people of what I'm working on here?'

'OK. Why not?'

He smiled and shook his head. 'I'm not sure I trust you.'

'Try me, why don't you? I won't call you a "would-be wizard", I promise you. Nor a "zany zoologist" either. Although you *are* a zoologist, aren't you? And what you're doing here, it is kind of zany, you have to admit.'

'Ms Laquelle – Patti – I'm not breeding these so-called mythical creatures for their entertainment value. I want them for their embryonic stem cells. Hopefully I can use them to cure people who have diseases that are currently incurable – like Alzheimer's, and cystic fibrosis, and motor neurone disease, and Huntington's.'

'That's such an incredible idea,' said Patti. 'But if these creatures are mythical, they're like *imaginary*, aren't they? They never really existed.'

Nathan said, 'Some paleontologists absolutely refuse to

believe in them, yes. But there's a whole mountain of documentary evidence that they *did* exist, going right back to Sumerian times. Descriptions, drawings, accounts of their habits and behavior. All from highly reliable sources.

'They were amazing, some of these creatures. Jackals with enormous wings, that could fly. Birds that lived for hundreds of years. Lizards that could heal themselves, even when their skins were burned to a cinder. Aristotle, the Greek philosopher, he was a zoologist, too, although not many people know that. He was supposed to have owned a three-headed dog that could remember *everything*. What one head forgot, another head remembered.'

'That sounds exactly like my grandma,' said Patti.

Nathan opened a drawer, took out a file, and handed her a woodcut of a gryphon sitting on its nest. 'You know who drew that? Albrecht Dürer, in 1513. His drawings of exotic animals were so accurate that they were still being used in schoolbooks three hundred years after his death.

'There are plenty of remains, too. Only last October they found a gryphon skeleton at the foot of the Altai Mountains, in the Gobi Desert. The official interpretation was that it was the bones of a young protoceratops. Hardly anybody had the nerve to say what it really was. In fact only one paleontologist came out and said that it was almost certainly a gryphon. The head of an eagle and the body of a lion.'

Patti stared at the woodcut for a long time, and then handed it back. 'I still find it hard to believe. You actually bred one of these.'

'Well, I did, yes, even if it *did* die. And if the zoological society doesn't decide to cut my funding, I'm sure that I can do it again. And – in time – I think I can breed any other kind of hybrid you care to mention. Gargoyles, wyverns, hippogryphs. Maybe a cuegle, even, which can grow extra limbs for itself. Imagine that, you lose a leg, you can grow yourself another one.'

'Can I *see* it?' asked Patti.

'The gryphon? Not unless you want to lose your breakfast.'

'I didn't eat breakfast. Only grapefruit juice. Come on, let me take a look at it.'

'OK . . . but no photographs, mind. Not until after the necropsy – and, even then, only maybe.'

Nathan led her across the laboratory to the stainless-steel refrigerators. Patti stood a little way away while he slid open the drawer with the gryphon's embryo in it. Even though it had been chilled, it still smelled just as foul.

He used a glass stirring rod to point out its head and its beak and its claws. He lifted its feathers so that she could see how wide its wingspan would have been.

'It's fantastic,' said Patti, with her hand cupped over her face. 'If I didn't know it was for real, I would have thought you just sewed them together, a bird and a lion cub.'

At that moment, the door banged open, and Richard came into the laboratory, closely followed by Keira and Tim.

'Professor?' he asked, hanging up his limp khaki raincoat. 'What's going on?'

'Impromptu press conference,' said Nathan. 'This is Ms Patti Laquelle, from *The Philadelphia Web*. She's going to make us famous.'

'*The Philadelphia Web*?' asked Tim. 'As in, "My Grandmother Ate My Schnauzer"?'

'That's the one,' said Patti. 'Only it wasn't "schnauzer", it was "chihuahua".'

FIVE

Sack-Dragger

Denver was still sullen at suppertime, toying with his chicken-and-pepper stew and hardly saying a word.

'I won't ask how your necropsy went,' said Grace. 'Not while we're eating, anyhow.'

Nathan poured himself another glass of white wine. 'Let's just say that I still don't have the first idea what went wrong. It was very a virulent infection, that's for sure, but what kind of bacillus it was and where it came from—'

Denver threw down his fork. It bounced across his plate and landed on the tablecloth. 'Didn't you hear what Mom said? Do you really think we want to hear about bacterial infections while we're trying to eat our supper?'

Nathan said, 'OK. OK. I'm sorry. But you don't have to toss your cutlery around.'

Denver pushed back his chair so that it tilted and fell over. 'Forget it. I'm not hungry now. I'm going out.'

'Sit down and finish your supper.'

'What? And listen to you talking about pus and infections and decomposing gryphons? Don't you *ever* give it a rest? Don't you ever think that we don't want to hear about it?'

Nathan looked down at his plate. He was trying hard not to lose his temper, and he took a very deep breath to steady himself.

Grace said, 'Denver . . . you need to apologize. Your dad's had some really difficult problems to deal with. His whole future at the zoo could depend on this. The last thing he needs is you stamping your feet like a two-year-old.'

'Oh, he's had some really difficult problems to deal with, has he? So we have to sit here and listen to all this disgusting stuff about dead creatures that should never have been alive in the first place, is that it? While we're *eating*, for Christ's sake!'

'Denver,' said Nathan, in a very quiet voice. 'Shut up.'

Denver jabbed his finger at him. 'You think you're the only person in this house who's allowed to have an opinion, don't you? I don't count for anything! Do you know what I've been doing at school lately? Do you have any idea? Of course you don't! Did you know that I was thrown off the basketball team?'

'No,' said Nathan. 'I didn't know because you didn't tell me.'

'You want to know why? Look at you – you don't even want to know why!'

'Of course I want to know why.'

'No you don't. You're totally not interested. So why don't you just go back to your disgusting conversation about rotting creatures? I'm going out.'

'I said – shut up, sit down, and finish your supper. You're not going anyplace. You're grounded until you can learn some respect.'

Denver shook his head. 'Respect? You know why they threw me off the basketball team? For fighting. And do you know what I was fighting about? *You.*'

Nathan sat back in his chair. 'Did somebody say something?'

'Yes, somebody said something. And whatever I think about you, nobody insults me or my family. As if you cared. As if you'd ever do the same for me.'

'So what did they say?'

'I'm not telling you. It was just as disgusting as all this infection stuff you've been talking about.'

'Denver—'

'Forget it, Pops. Just forget it. I'm going out.'

'What did they say?' Nathan demanded.

'I scored three slam dunks, one after the other. Alver Dunsmore said you must have injected Mom's eggs with kangaroo sperm.'

Grace felt her cheeks flushing, and she had to press her hand over her mouth.

Nathan said, 'Don't you think it could have been a joke?'

'Alver didn't say it for a joke. It sure didn't *sound* like a joke.'

'Don't you think you might have overreacted? Come on, Denver, it's a knockabout world out there. Sometimes you have to roll with the punches.'

'OK – if you think I was wrong to stand up for you and Mom, then all I can say is that you have no family values whatsoever. And I'm going out.'

'All right,' Nathan conceded. 'You go out. Maybe it will help you to cool off.'

Nathan's anger had subsided now. He remembered that he had been just as aggressive and frustrated as Denver, when he was seventeen. The whole world had appeared to be stupid and illogical and back to front, like looking-glass land, and he had never been able to understand why his parents had so blithely accepted it.

Denver pushed his hair out of his eyes. 'Sorry, Mom. This isn't anything to do with you.'

'You want me to keep your supper for you?'

Denver picked up his tipped-over chair. He hesitated for a long moment, and Nathan could tell that he was sorely tempted to sit down and continue eating. In the end, however, he turned around and left the dining room, and they heard him opening the cloakroom door to get his windbreaker.

'I'll tell you what!' Nathan called out. 'I'll talk to your coach tomorrow – see if we can get you back on the team! I don't know how they could have dropped a player with kangaroo genes! I mean – what are they, crazy?'

The front door slammed. Grace got up from her chair and came around the table and put her arms around his neck and kissed him. 'You know something? In spite of himself, I think he's beginning to come round. Thank you for not shouting.'

Nathan kissed her back. 'I couldn't shout. I was trying too hard not to laugh.'

At that moment, the phone warbled. Grace went to answer it.

'Doctor Underhill? Is that Doctor Underhill?'

'That's right. Who is this?'

'It's Doris Bellman, Doctor Underhill. I hope you don't mind me calling you so late.'

'Of course not, Doris. It's only seven thirty. How can I help you?'

'I've heard it again, Doctor Underhill. The screaming. And somebody dragging a sack past my door.'

'Have you told your carers?'

'I don't want to do that, Doctor Underhill. I don't trust them. The only person I could think of calling was you.'

Nathan raised his eyebrows, to ask Grace who was calling her. Grace raised her hand and mouthed, 'Won't be a minute.' Then she said, 'Listen, Doris, why don't I call by to see you tomorrow morning? You can tell me all about it then.'

'I'm frightened, Doctor Underhill. I'm terribly frightened.'

'I'm sure there's nothing for you to worry about. Take a couple of kava kavas . . . they should calm you down. I'll come to see you first thing tomorrow.'

'Can't you come to see me now? I know it's a great deal to ask of you.'

Grace closed her eyes for a moment. She had been operating from eight a.m. to four thirty p.m., with only a twenty-minute break, and then she had come home to cook supper. She had also drunk a glass and a half of wine.

'I'm so sorry, Doris. I can't make it tonight.'

'But I can hear them outside my door! They're coming for *me* next, I'm sure of it!'

'Doris, I promise you. Everything's going to be fine. All you have to do is get a good night's sleep.'

Mrs Bellman didn't answer. Grace said, 'Doris? Are you still there? I'm sure you have nothing to worry about.'

'What if they try to break into my room?'

'Who, Doris?'

'The sack-draggers. What if they try to break into my room?'

'Doris, I'm sure that they won't. But if they do, you just give me another call, OK?'

'I'm terribly frightened, Doctor Underhill.'

'I know you are. But try to relax. Is there anything you want me to bring you? A cake, maybe, or some cookies? Some magazines for you to read?'

Mrs Bellman hung up without saying anything more. Grace put down the phone and said, 'Mrs Bellman, from the Murdstone.'

'You gave her your home number?'

'I wish I hadn't now. I just felt sorry for her, I guess. She's convinced that she's going to be dragged away in a sack, and she wants me to come and rescue her.'

She sat down. Her chicken stew was congealing now, and she didn't feel hungry any more. Although Mrs Bellman was obviously suffering from the early stages of senile dementia, she still felt guilty that she wasn't driving straight over to see her. But the Murdstone Rest Home was nearly ten miles away, in Millbourne, and she didn't really know what she could do to help Mrs Bellman even if she went there.

Denver returned home, very quietly, a few minutes after midnight. Nathan heard the front door close, and the alarm switched on. Tonight, it didn't sound as if Denver had been drinking, because he managed to creep up the stairs and tippy-toe along the landing. Nathan heard him switch on his TV, at very low volume, and climb into bed.

'Is that Denver?' asked Grace, blurrily.

'Hey – I thought you were asleep.'

'I'm a mother. Mothers never sleep. Not completely, anyhow.'

They lay there in silence for a while. Then Nathan said, 'Maybe he's right. Maybe I don't pay him enough attention. I've been so obsessed with this goddamned project.'

Grace said, 'Stop beating yourself up about it. He's growing up, that's all. He needs somebody to rebel against, and that somebody just happens to be you.'

'I know – but I should leave my work where it belongs, in the laboratory, and not bring it home with me. I'll try to have a talk to him tomorrow. You know, man-to-man stuff.'

'My God. You'll be taking him fishing next.'

'Not a hope. But I might take him to see the Seventy-sixers.'

'That sounds great. So long as you don't expect *me* to come along.'

Grace fell back to sleep. Around two twenty-five a.m., Nathan heard Denver switch off his TV. He would definitely talk to him tomorrow, and he wouldn't mention mythical creatures once. A new beginning, father and son, the way it used to be when Denver was little, and they used to play football together, and go cycling to the store.

Nathan closed his eyes. Almost immediately, he opened them again. The bedroom was very dark – much darker than it had been before. He could hear breathing but it wasn't Grace. It was thicker and much harsher, more like an animal. He lay there for a few seconds, listening to it, and then he sat up.

In the corner of the room, barely visible in the gloom, he saw a large black shape. It appeared to have bristling horns on top of its head, or a crown made out of dry branches, and it reached almost to the ceiling. He thought he might have seen its eyes glittering, too, but he couldn't be sure.

The sack-dragger, he thought. Instead of going to help Mrs Bellman, Grace had stayed at home, and now the sack-dragger had dragged itself all the way here, looking for her, sniffing her out.

He eased back the bedcover. He kept his own breathing shallow, to suppress his fear. He couldn't imagine how the sack-dragger had managed to get into the house, and climb up the stairs to their bedroom, but here it was. It lurched to one side, so that the floorboards creaked, and then it took a single shuffling step toward him.

He groped down underneath the bed for his baseball bat. He found the handle and pulled it out. The sack-dragger took another step toward him, and then another. Its breathing was louder and harsher, and he was sure that he could see its curved black claws.

'Grace,' he said, urgently. He climbed out of bed and stood facing the sack-dragger, gripping the baseball bat tight. *'Grace, wake up!'*

The sack-dragger was almost on top of him now, brushing up against him. It felt as if it were wrapped around in layer upon layer of frayed black burlap, like a medieval leper trying to conceal his noseless face. Now that it was so close, he could smell it, too, and it smelled of dust and sacking and rotting chicken.

'Grace, wake up! For Christ's sake, Grace, you have to wake up!'

The sack-dragger uttered a throaty, gargling noise, and lunged at him. He swung the baseball bat as hard as he could, and he felt it collide with heavy layers of fabric. He swung it again, and again, and shouted out, 'Get out of here, you bastard! Get the hell out!'

With a soft rumbling sound the sack-dragger collapsed in front of him. He beat it with hard, criss-cross chops, never letting up. The sack-dragger seemed to diminish with every chop, as if he were smashing up its ribcage and its pelvis, and reducing it to nothing more than broken bones and dusty black hessian.

He stopped, and held his breath, and listened. He couldn't hear it breathing any longer. He prodded it with his baseball bat, two or three times, but it didn't stir. He had either killed it, or beaten it into unconsciousness.

He dropped back on to the bed, gasping. It was then that Grace switched on her bedside lamp and sat up straight, with her hair tousled and her cheeks flushed pink.

'Nate? What's going on?'

He blinked at her. 'The sack-dragger. Look.'

She peered over the side of the bed. Their dark brown comforter was lying on the floor in a crumpled heap.

'The sack-dragger? What are you talking about? And what are you doing with that bat?'

'It, ah – I don't really know. I kind of thought that—'

'Whatever you thought, darling, how about putting that comforter back on the bed? It's freezing!'

Nathan lowered the baseball bat and pushed it back under the bed. Then he picked up the comforter. There were no broken bones inside it, and it was covered in damask cotton, not burlap. If it smelled of anything, it was Grace's perfume, and his own fresh perspiration.

'I guess I had a nightmare. But it wasn't at all like a regular nightmare. I was sure that I was awake. I could feel it. I could *smell* it.'

Grace dragged the comforter over to her own side of the bed. 'It's that gryphon. I think you're more upset about it than you realize yourself.'

'Well, maybe.'

Nathan punched his pillow back into shape and buried himself in the bedcovers. Grace switched off her bedside lamp and he closed his eyes and tried to get to sleep. After only a few minutes, though, he opened them. He was sure he could hear breathing again, and it wasn't Grace. It was harsh, and thick, and very close.

He was sure that there was something in the bedroom with them. A sack-dragger, or the shadow of a sack-dragger.

If I don't move, if I don't acknowledge it, then maybe it will stay in the corner, and gradually fade away when the sun comes up. All the same, I'm going to keep my eyes open, and I'm going to keep straining my ears for the slightest hint of a shuffle. If this sack-dragger is more than a nightmare, if it really has claws and horns or a crown of twigs, I don't want to be fast asleep if it decides to show me.

SIX

Death Stare

When Grace came out of the shower the next morning Nathan was still deeply asleep, breathing through his mouth. She opened the drapes, so that the bedroom was a little lighter, but all he did was bury himself deeper under the comforter.

Usually she would have woken him, but today she decided to let him sleep. He had tried to be philosophical about his gryphon project, but she knew how bitterly disappointed he was, and how much it had taken out of him, both mentally and physically. A couple of hours' extra rest would do him good.

After she had dressed, she closed her closet door as quietly as she could, but it still made a sharp clicking noise.

'*Quick*,' Nathan mumbled. Then, '*Don't want to – no!*'

'Nathan?' she said, but he didn't open his eyes. She bent over and kissed his stubbly cheek, and then she went downstairs.

'*Hurry*,' Nathan repeated. '*For God's sake, hurry!*'

In the kitchen, Denver was already sitting at the counter with a bowl of Cap'n Crunch, swimming in almost a half-pint of milk. He was wearing a black T-shirt with *I'm Only Wearing Black Until They Invent Something Darker* printed on the front. He hadn't yet brushed his hair so his face was almost completely hidden, except for his nose.

'Hi,' she said. 'Do you want a ride into school today?'

''S . . . OK. Taser's picking me up.'

'Taser?'

'You don't know him. They call him that because he's always shocking the teachers.'

'Oh.'

She took a carton of pomegranate juice out of the fridge and poured herself a large glassful. 'Are you going to be late for supper tonight?'

'I don't know yet. We might have a band practice. I'll call you, OK?'

'How's the band coming along?'

'It's OK, but we need a new drummer. I don't know what's happened to Chesney. He's total crap.'

'Chesney's parents are getting a divorce. You can't blame Chesney if he's got his mind on other things, apart from drumming. Like you shouldn't get so upset if your father doesn't give you as much attention as you think you deserve.'

Denver tossed his spoon into his half-finished cereal. 'I don't think I deserve *any* attention, as a matter of fact. At least, that's what Pops has always made me feel like. I sometimes wish I was a dragon or something. Maybe then he'd *look* at me, at least. Maybe he'd even ask me how my day was.'

'Your father loves you. You don't even realize how much.'

Denver stood up and tipped the remains of his bowl into

the InSinkErator. But he dropped his spoon into it, as well as his cereal, and said, '*Shit.*'

'Here,' said Grace, opening up one of the kitchen drawers and taking out a pair of tongs. 'Fish it out with this.'

But Denver reached his right hand into the InSinkErator as far as his wrist.

'Denver – take your hand out! You should never do that!'

'What, in case I accidentally switch it on, and grind my hand off? Do you think Pops would pay me some attention if I did that? Like, I'd probably scream, wouldn't I? And think of the blood! He'd have to repaint the entire kitchen. Bummer.'

'Denver, take your hand out of there right now. You shouldn't even joke about it.'

Denver gave her a wide-eyed, exaggerated stare, like a mad person, and reached toward the 'on' switch. Grace snapped, '*Don't!*'

She remembered a friend of hers at high school, Jill Somersby, who had given her that same pretend-crazy stare, the morning before she had taken an overdose of paracetamol. Grace had found out two weeks later that Jill had been sexually abused by her stepfather ever since she was five. And in later years, during her medical training, she had come to realize that teenagers often pretend to be joking because they don't know how else to show the world how deadly serious they are.

Denver took his hand out of the InSinkErator and triumphantly held up his cereal spoon. 'Did I scare you?' he grinned.

'No. You just annoyed me.'

'Oh, well. At least I got *some* reaction out of you, yeah?'

It was raining hard as Grace drove down to the Murdstone Rest Home, and her windshield wipers flapped hysterically from side to side. A school bus had collided with a glazier's van on the City Avenue on-ramp, and there was a tailback of more than a mile. As she passed the scene of the accident, Grace had to drive at less than five miles an hour over twenty yards of crunching glass, while the children in the school bus stared at her mournfully.

The rain and the broken glass and the pale children's faces gave her a strange feeling of disquiet, as if she had fallen

asleep and woken up in one of those disturbing Japanese
movies like *The Ring*.

She reached Millbourne just after nine thirty a.m. and turned
into Glencoe Road. As she parked outside the rest home, she
heard a collision of thunder, somewhere off to the north-west.
She tugged her mini-umbrella out from underneath the
passenger seat, and struggled to put it up. Three of its spokes
were broken, so that it looked like a wounded crow.

She hurried across the parking lot. The Murdstone Rest
Home was a sprawling collection of depressing buildings,
some dating from the 1920s, and others from the mid-1960s,
when prefabricated concrete was in fashion. The main building
was a mock-medieval castle, with a formstone fascia and a
grandiose pillared porch. On the crest of the porch sat a
concrete gargoyle, its head and its shoulders darkened with
rain. The gargoyle was holding its chin in both hands and
staring down at whoever entered the rest home with undisguised amusement, as if it knew that they would only ever
leave here in a casket.

Grace entered the swing doors at the front of the building
and was immediately met by Sister Bennett and two Korean
carers. Sister Bennett was a large woman, thirty-fiveish, with
a florid face and fraying red hair. She had a glassy blue squint,
as if she had recently had her eyes replaced at a dolls' hospital.
One of the Korean carers was very beautiful, in a flat-faced,
impenetrable way, while the other was squat and ugly but
always smiling and nodding. All three of them wore purple-
striped blouses and black skirts and rubbery black shoes.

'Doctor Underhill?' said Sister Bennett, as if Grace had
already asked her a question.

'I came to see Doris Bellman,' Grace told her. 'She called
me last night and she sounded distressed.'

'*Distressed*?' asked Sister Bennett.

'Yes. She had the impression that somebody was trying to
force their way into her room.'

Sister Bennett pouted and shook her head. 'I don't understand. Mrs Bellman's room would never have been locked.
None of the rooms are *ever* locked, for health and safety
reasons. And who would be trying to get into her room, even
if it were? Only her carers, to check on her.'

'Well, yes,' said Grace. 'But she called me, all the same,

so I thought I'd drop by to reassure her that she doesn't have anything to worry about.'

'That much is very true,' said Sister Bennett. 'She *doesn't* have anything to worry about. Not any more.'

'Excuse me?'

'Mrs Bellman has passed, Doctor Underhill. She passed last night, shortly after midnight.'

'She's *dead*?'

'Shortly after midnight. It was very quick. AMI.'

'But she called me at eight and she sounded fine. She was distressed, yes, like I say, but she used to be a nurse herself. I think she would have known if she were just about to have a heart attack.'

Sister Bennett had found a stray white thread on her cuff and she was tugging at it. 'AMI, that's what Doctor Zauber said. Could have been an embolism, maybe, from her broken leg.'

'So where is she now?'

'They took her to the Burns Funeral Home, around seven o'clock this morning.'

Grace said, 'I can't believe it. She's *gone*, just like that?'

Sister Bennett lifted her cuff to her mouth and bit off the offending thread. 'It's always the toughest ones who take you by surprise, don't you think? You get some doddery old dear who has everything wrong with her you can care to mention, and she lives to see her hundred-and-second birthday. Then you get a sharp-tongued survivor like Doris Bellman, and what happens? You turn your back for half a minute, and when you turn around again, they're staring at you like they're still alive, and just about to say something to you, but they're dead as a donut. Gone, *poof*, and there you are! Standing in their room, right next to them, but in actual fact you're all alone.'

The squat and ugly nurse smiled, and nodded.

Grace checked her watch. 'It looks like I didn't need to come here, after all.'

'I'm sorry,' said Sister Bennett. 'If I'd known you were coming, I would have called you.'

No you wouldn't, thought Grace. But then she didn't totally blame her. The carers at Murdstone were no different from the nurses at any other institution for the very old and the very sick. Everybody they cared for was going to die, most

of them very soon, so they never allowed themselves to become
attached to them. They couldn't be expected to live their lives
in constant mourning. On the other hand, that was no excuse
for them to be indifferent to their charges, or cruel.

'Do you think I could take a look at her room?' Grace asked
her. She didn't really know why she wanted to, but maybe it
would give her a last sense of Doris Bellman's presence: the
young nurse who had gone out to Europe, in the closing stages
of World War Two; and the old woman who had been neglected
by her family, and had passed her closing years with nobody
except a cockatoo for company, and no view but a parking
lot, and some blue-painted drainpipes, and a small pentagram
of cloudy sky.

'Be my guest,' said Sister Bennett. 'Just be warned that we
haven't had time to service it yet.'

Grace walked along the corridor to Doris Bellman's room.
On the way, she encountered an old man staring out of one
of the windows. He wore a drooping brown bathrobe with his
pockets crammed with crumpled tissues, and brown corduroy
slippers, and he had a wild white shock of hair like Albert
Einstein. As he turned toward her, she saw that one lens of
his spectacles was covered up with silver duct tape.

'Didn't you bring the car round yet?' he snapped at her, as
she approached.

'I'm sorry?'

He frowned down at a wristwatch that wasn't there. 'We're
going to be late, at this rate! We can't afford to be late! We'll
miss the overture!'

Grace stopped. 'It's OK. You don't have to worry. We have
hours yet.'

He stared at her with one milky blue eye. 'Are you sure?
I don't want to disappoint her. She's been looking forward to
this for months.'

'You won't let her down, I promise you.'

'Ah! Well, that's all right, then. But you won't forget to tell
me when you bring the car round?'

'Of course not. Do I ever?'

She was about to continue on her way toward Doris
Bellman's room when the old man snatched at her sleeve. He
smelled sour, like the inside of a cupboard that hasn't been
opened in years. 'You will be super careful, won't you?'

'I always am.'

He glanced furtively along the corridor, right and then left. 'I've seen it for myself. They try to pretend that I'm losing my marbles, but they can't fool me. I've seen it.'

Grace gently pried his hand away. 'I really have to be going. I hope everything goes well tonight.'

'I didn't see it face to face,' the old man continued, as if he hadn't even heard her. 'Lucky for me that I didn't, if you ask me. But I opened my door and looked out of my room and I was just in time to see it disappearing around that corner.'

'I'm sorry,' said Grace, 'I don't follow you.'

The old man narrowed his one visible eye. 'You're not one of them, are you? One of the gang of witches that run this place?'

'No, I'm a doctor. I came here today to see Doris Bellman, but they tell me she passed in the night.'

The old man furiously shook his head – so furiously that Grace was almost afraid that it was going to fly right off his shoulders. '*Pass*? Doris Bellman didn't *pass*. She was *taken*. It came for her, when the dark was at its darkest.'

'*It* being . . .?'

'Who knows? Who knows what it is? But I swear to you on a roomful of Bibles, I saw it. Not face to face, no ma'am. Lucky for me that I didn't, if you ask me. But it was disappearing around that corner and it was huge and it was black and it was all hunched over, and there were kind of jaggedy bits on top of its head.'

Grace thought: *my God, that sounds just like Nathan's nightmare about the sack-dragger*. But then she thought: *no, how could it*? Nathan had been dreaming about his mythical creatures, but who could tell what terrors this old man had been dreaming about? Nobody shares their nightmares, whatever Jung had said about all of us having a collective unconscious.

She looked at her watch. Time was ticking by, and she had a meeting with the hospital acquisitions board in less than three-quarters of an hour.

'Listen,' she said, 'maybe we could talk about this some other time, when I'm not in so much of a hurry. Do you want to tell me your name?'

The old man narrowed his eye again. 'You're not going to snitch on me, are you? You're not going to rat on me to those witches?'

'Of course not. Why should I do that?'

The old man glanced along the corridor again, just to make sure that nobody was listening. Then he said, 'Michael Dukakis'.

'Michael Dukakis?'

'That's right. Michael Stanley Dukakis.'

'Not by any chance the same Michael Stanley Dukakis who ran against George Bush in the 1988 presidential election?'

The old man grinned with pleasure. 'That's right! You recognized me! Not too many people do! It's been a few years, though, hasn't it? Quite a few years, you know, and time takes its toll.'

He suddenly stopped grinning, and looked reflective. 'Should have beaten him, though, Bush. Should have licked him good and proper. Asshole. *Him*, I mean. Bush, not me.'

'Well, OK, Michael,' said Grace. 'Next time I visit, I'll ask for you, OK, and we can sit down and you can tell me all about this *it* that you saw.'

He seized her sleeve again and pulled her very close to him, so that when he spoke his spit prickled her face. 'It was *hunched over* and it was black and it was all covered up in these raggedy sacks. And it had horns on top of its head. Or maybe a crown of sorts. And I prayed that it wouldn't turn around and see me. I prayed, believe me. But lucky for me it didn't. It disappeared. But I could still hear it.'

Grace took hold of his hand, trying to ease herself loose. His fingers felt like chicken's leg bones.

'It made this kind of *shuffling* sound,' the old man told her. 'Like it was tired, and old, and weary, but it wasn't going to let nothing stop it, not for nothing.'

'I really have to go,' said Grace.

The old man abruptly released her. 'Sure you do. Don't want to waste your precious time, listening to me blather. What time are you going to bring the car around?'

'I'll come get you, I promise.'

The old man nodded, and noisily sucked his dentures. 'Know what my father used to say? "If life was a bet, slick, I wouldn't take it".'

Grace left him and walked along to Doris Bellman's room. She noticed that Mrs Bellman's name had already been removed from the slot beside the door. She opened it and stepped inside.

The room was exactly as it had been the day before yesterday, except that Doris Bellman had gone. Her bed was still unmade, and her gray loose-weave shawl was lying on the floor beside it. A tumbler of water stood on the night-stand, with bubbles in it. Her little leather-covered travel clock had stopped at twelve after twelve.

The first thing that Grace noticed was that the two ivy plants on either side of the window were shriveled up, as if they hadn't been watered for months. She went across and felt their leaves. They were totally dry, and they crumbled between her fingers. Yet only yesterday they had been flourishing.

She stood by the window for a while, watching the rain-drops dribbling down the glass. Then she suddenly realized that, apart from the sound of the rain, and the distant drone of vacuum-cleaning, Doris Bellman's room was silent.

She turned around. A frayed beige pashmina was draped over Harpo the cockatoo's cage, but Harpo was making no noise at all: no squawking or scratching or pecking at his bars. Grace went over and lifted the pashmina off. Harpo was lying on the bottom of his cage, one claw raised, his puffy blue eyelids closed.

Grace stood in the middle of the room. She had come here to feel the last echoes of Doris Bellman's life, but instead she felt another kind of resonance, like the dying chord of a full-size church organ. She couldn't exactly understand how, but she felt a strong sense of *panic*. Even the photographs of Doris Bellman's family seemed to be staring at her in desperation, as if they had witnessed something terrible, but had been powerless to stop it.

She looked at her own face, in the mirror with the frame made of seashells. 'What happened, Doris?' she whispered. 'Give me some clue, will you?'

She turned around and gasped. The squat and ugly nurse had appeared in the doorway, and was standing there grinning at her.

'Excuse me, yes please, I have to service this room now.'

'Have you informed Mrs Bellman's relatives?'

'Excuse me?'

'Her relatives.' Grace repeated, and pointed to the photographs. 'Has anybody told them that Mrs Bellman has passed?'

The carer shrugged but didn't stop grinning. 'I do not know about this. Ask Sister Bennett.'

'All right,' said Grace. 'But you shouldn't touch or move any of Mrs Bellman's things until her next of kin gets here.'

'Yes,' said the carer, although Grace didn't think that she had the faintest idea what she was talking about.

'What's your name?' she asked her.

'Phuong,' said the carer.

'Well, Phuong, do you have any idea of what happened in this room last night?'

'Yes. Mrs Bellman die.'

'I know that. But – look – her pet cockatoo is dead, too, and so are her plants.'

The carer nodded. Grace thought: *I really don't know if I'm getting through here.*

'Phuong – everything that was living in this room yesterday is now dead. *Everything.*'

The carer blinked at her, but obviously couldn't understand what she was trying to say. Grace turned to the window to show her the curled-up ivy, and it was then that she saw four or five bottle-green blowflies lying on their backs, behind the drapes.

'Did you see anything last night? Did you see a man, all dressed up in black, with maybe some kind of spiky hat on?'

'No man, no.'

'He would have been very big, and hunched over. Like Quasimodo, you know? Or, obviously, you *wouldn't* know. Or maybe you heard a noise, like somebody dragging a heavy sack.'

The carer shook her head and continued to shake it.

Grace hesitated for a moment, and then she said, 'Did you hear Mrs Bellman scream?'

It was then, though, that the door was pushed open wider and Sister Bennett appeared. 'Doctor Underhill? I'm sorry, but we really have to get on and service this room. We have a wait list, you know, and a new resident will be arriving here tomorrow morning.'

'What about Mrs Bellman's things?'

'I gather that her son is flying in from Houston tomorrow. All Mrs Bellman's possessions will be cataloged and locked away in our property store. They'll be perfectly secure.'

'I'm sure they will. But before you do that, don't you think the police ought to take a look at this room, just the way it is?'

Sister Bennett stared at her as if she had said something in a foreign language. 'The *police*? What on earth for?'

'Well ... Mrs Bellman called me at home and said that somebody was trying to break into her room. And the last time I saw her, she was sure that somebody was walking up and down the corridors at night, like a prowler. And one of your residents told me that he saw some kind of intruder, right outside his room.'

'Oh, really? And which particular resident would that be?'

'I met him in the corridor,' said Grace. 'He was wearing a brown bathrobe. He said his name was Michael Dukakis but I don't suppose for a second that it really is.'

Sister Bennett laughed – an abrupt, humorless scurry of laughter. But her glassy blue eyes remained totally hostile.

'Mr Stavrianos is suffering from senile dementia,' she said. 'He sees gorillas in the woods around the grounds. He sees giant lizards in his bathtub. He thinks he's some world-famous conductor, and he's always late for his next big concert.'

'I see.'

Sister Bennett stooped down and picked up Doris Bellman's shawl. 'Don't let it worry you, doctor. You get used to it, after a while, working in a rest home. All the delusions, all the paranoia. These people's brains are coming unraveled, and all we can do is try to keep them as calm as possible and protect them from harming themselves.'

'Yes,' said Grace. She still thought that the police ought to be notified of Doris Bellman's death, and the terrors that she had expressed, only hours before she died. But Sister Bennett was probably right. The black, hunched-up sack-dragger was nothing more than an old woman's nightmare, the same kind of nightmare that frightens little children, and there was a strong possibility that she had told 'Michael Dukakis' about it, so that he was convinced that *he* had seen it, too.

Besides, thought Grace, I really need to get going. I can't afford the time to hang around here for hours, talking to bored and skeptical detectives, while Sister Bennett gives me her death stare in the background.

'OK,' she said. 'I'll leave it all to you.'

When she emerged from the Murdstone, she found that it had stopped raining. The rainclouds had passed over the Delaware

River, toward Camden, trailing their dirty gray skirts behind them, and now the sun was shining.

In the corner of the parking lot there was a large green dumpster. She dropped her broken umbrella into it, and promised to buy herself a new one. As she walked back to her car, she turned around and looked back, although she didn't know why. The Murdstone's roof was dazzling, almost as if the building were on fire. But it was the gargoyle on the crest of the porch which caught her attention. It was grinning at her mockingly, as if it knew that she had just conceded defeat to Sister Bennett.

So you chickened out, did you? Couldn't be bothered? But what if that sack-dragger is really real, and is going to go shuffling along those corridors night after night, claiming one old person after another?

She climbed into her car and started the engine. Her eyes looked back at her out of the rear-view mirror, expressionless. For the first time in years, she felt a complete lack of certainty. She had absolutely no idea what she ought to do next.

SEVEN

The Black Book

At the same time that Grace was leaving the Murdstone, Nathan was arriving at the research wing at the Philadelphia Zoo. As he drove in through the entrance gates, he saw two TV vans, one from WHYY and one from the public broadcasting system WCAU, as well as a small crowd of TV and newspaper reporters.

Without slowing down, he circled around a huge reflecting pool of rainwater in the middle of the parking lot, and sped back out again. He drove around to the rear of the laboratory block and parked his car next to a battered green truck that stood outside the maintenance department.

One of the maintenance staff immediately waddled out, in green zoo coveralls. He had a bulbous nose and a gingery buzzcut and near-together eyes like a mandrill. 'Can't park there, fella.'

'What's it to you where I park?' Nathan demanded. 'You're maintenance, not traffic management. Go maintain something.'

He climbed the steps and pushed open the double doors. The maintenance man said, *'Hey!'* but Nathan ignored him. He walked along the corridor to the very end, with the man repeating *'Hey!'* and *'Hey, fella!'* at regular intervals. He didn't answer to 'fella', especially today.

When he turned the corner at the end of the corridor, he found Patti Laquelle standing outside his laboratory, wearing her red squall and a very short skirt and Ugg boots, chatting on her cell.

Patti said, 'Millie? Have to call you later, babes. Professor Underhill has finally showed up.'

'So how did *you* get in here?' asked Nathan, as she followed him into his office. 'This whole building is supposed to be restricted.'

'I used my amazing charm, of course. And my identity badge.'

Nathan took hold of the plastic card that was safety-pinned to her windbreaker, and peered at it. It was a genuine Philadelphia Zoo Visitor ID, but on close inspection it was obvious that Patti had glued her own photograph on top of the original.

'OK, I picked it up from your desk,' she admitted. But then she said, 'Did you see my article? I thought it came out really, really great.'

'I haven't had time yet, Patti. To tell you the truth, I overslept.'

'It came out really, really great. At least, I thought it did. *My Rotten Break: By Dragon's Egg Egghead.*'

Nathan sat down at his desk, and switched on his computer.

'That was the headline? "My Rotten Break: By Dragon's Egg Egghead"?'

'You really need to read it,' Patti insisted. 'It's totally *simpatico*. I put in all that stuff you told me about Alzheimer's and cystic what's-it's-name and Parkinson's disease.'

'Good. Great. Thank you.'

He checked his emails. Patti stayed where she was, on the opposite side of his desk, smiling.

He looked up. 'Did you want something else?' he asked her.

'Not really. I wanted to tell you that the story came out good, that's all. And maybe I could do a follow-up.'

'A follow-up?'

'Absolutely. You are going to try again, aren't you? You are going to grow another gryphon's egg? I'd like to cover it right from the moment of *concepción*.'

'I don't know. I don't know what went wrong with this one yet. And it all depends on my funding. The Zoo isn't going to give me a blank check to go on breeding mythical creatures if none of them survive.'

'But they *must*. Like – this research that you're doing, it's much too important for them to pull the plug on you.'

'Well, I agree with you, Patti. But tell that to the funding department.'

Richard knocked at the door. He had fastened his lab coat with the wrong buttons, which made him look even more lopsided than usual, and the parting in his hair was a zig-zag. 'Morning,' he said, looking suspiciously at Patti. 'Traffic bad, was it?'

'Like I was telling Ms Laquelle here, I slept late. Did you make a start on the necropsy yet?'

'You've had about a zillion phone calls, but I didn't pick up. I guessed it was probably the media, you know.'

'I'll deal with the media later. What have you done so far?'

'OK . . .' Richard took a crumpled Kleenex out of his sleeve and fastidiously wiped his nose. 'I've taken DNA samples. I've taken soft-tissue specimens from the muscles and internal organs, including the liver and the spleen. I've also taken bone-marrow samples from the skeleton, and keratin from the feathers and the beak. I've started growing seven different bacterial cultures from the various body fluids.'

'Good work,' said Nathan. He was impressed.

'It's kind of early to tell what the primary COD was,' Richard told him. 'But so far I think that you're probably right. Or *mostly* right. We *are* dealing with a Group A Streptococcus. But maybe something else, too.'

'Did *you* read my article, Richard?' Patti interrupted him. She was sitting on the corner of Nathan's desk and her skirt was hiked up so high that he could see her pink polka-dot panties, so he immediately looked away.

Richard wiped his nose again, and sniffed. 'On the *Web*? Sure. I read it.'

'And what did you think? Didn't you think it was great?'

Richard thought for a moment, but then he said, 'I have to admit it, yes, it was reasonably accurate. Apart from the headline, that is. We've never actually tried to breed dragons as such.'

'Well – dragons, gargoyles, gryphons,' said Patti. 'They're all the same kind of thing, aren't they? It's just that your average *Web* reader wouldn't have a clue what a gryphon is.'

Nathan's phone rang. He picked it up and said, 'Cee-Zee Lab.'

'Oh, hi! This is Kevin McNamara, senior science editor on *The Philadelphia Inquirer*. Can I speak to Professor Nathan Underhill, please?

'I'm sorry, Mr McNamara. Professor Underhill isn't here today.'

'Oh. Pity. I just wanted to ask him a couple of questions about his work on mythical creatures. In particular, the gryphon that just hatched.'

'The gryphon was stillborn. You can read all about it on the *Web*.'

'Yes, I know that. But I wanted to ask Professor Underhill if he intends to continue his research, of if he's ready to admit that it's never going to come to anything, and throw in the towel.'

Nathan said, 'My impression is that Professor Underhill is pretty much determined to carry on.'

'Oh, really? He told you that?'

'That's the impression he gave me. But of course the ultimate decision rests with the zoo, whether they're prepared to fund him or not. You'll have to ask Doctor Burnside about that. He's in charge of the purse strings.'

'I already did.'

'And?'

'I don't think that Doctor Burnside has said anything to Professor Underhill yet, but I don't think that Professor Underhill is going to like it, when he does.'

'Oh, really? What did Doctor Burnside have to say?'

'He didn't mince his words, let's put it that way. He said

that Professor Underhill has spent five years and more than two million dollars and yet he still hasn't produced a single viable hybrid. He said that the zoo isn't prepared to invest a single penny more into Professor Underhill's project. He called it a "wild gryphon chase". A complete waste of valuable resources. And I quote.'

Nathan looked across at Richard and Patti. He could feel a muscle in his left cheek begin to twitch. He said, as calmly as he could manage, 'For your information, Mr McNamara, Professor Underhill is recognized as one of the most imaginative and ground-breaking research zoologists since Thomas Hunt Morgan.'

'Well, that's as may be. But he's trying to recreate creatures that lived hundreds of years in the past, isn't he? That's if they ever lived at all.'

'You're right, yes. You're absolutely right. But if he's successful, he could single-handedly take medical science hundreds of years into the future, overnight. He could cure multiple sclerosis, for Christ's sake.'

There was a pause on the other end of the phone. Nathan could almost hear the *Inquirer* reporter grinning.

'I'm *talking* to Professor Underhill, aren't I? Come on, Professor, admit it!'

Nathan grimaced. He should have kept his mouth shut.

'Come on, Professor! Tell me how you feel about your project being deep-sixed.'

'I told you,' said Nathan. 'Professor Underhill isn't here today. He won't be here tomorrow, either. Or the day after.'

'Professor – all I want is one short quote. "Dr Burnside is a short-sighted reactionary bastard," that'll do.'

Nathan slowly and carefully hung up, and then sat back in his chair.

Richard was furiously blinking. 'What's wrong?' he asked. 'Has something gone wrong?'

'It's all over,' Nathan told him. 'Burnside is closing us down. You might as well toss everything into the incinerator bin, what's left of it. Then we can all go home.'

Patti said, 'That's it? It's all over? No more dragons? No more gryphons?'

'No,' said Nathan. 'I'll be lucky if they put me on chimp-sexing duty. That's if they decide to keep me here at all.'

'But they can't *do* that, can they?' Patti protested.

'Oh, they can, and they have. And do you know what the most frustrating thing is? I shall never know how close I came to recreating a mythical creature. Or how far away I was.'

'Well, *I* think you were very close,' said Richard. 'Very, very close indeed.'

'Thanks. But we'll never have any way of knowing it, will we? Not for sure.'

Richard said, 'Maybe I should put the embryo back in the chiller. You never know.'

'What's the point?'

The phone again. This time, it was Dr Burnside himself. His voice was as dry as Saltine crackers.

'Nathan? I need to see you in my office. As soon as possible, please.'

'It's all right, Henry,' Nathan told him. 'I've heard the news already. You can spare me the crocodile tears.'

'We need to discuss your future, Nathan, here at the zoo.'

'So what are you going to offer me? Engineer, on the PZ Express? –' that was the kiddies' train ride that circled around the zoo – 'everybody over forty-eight inches has to be accompanied by a small child.'

'Come on, Nathan. I know you're upset about this. I fully appreciate all of the research work you've done. You've made some outstanding progress in the field of cryptozoology, you know that. It hasn't all been wasted.'

'Not what you told *The Inquirer*.'

'Come see me. Please. We need to see what we can profitably salvage from your research, and we need to decide which direction you're going to go in now.'

Nathan took a deep breath. 'There's only one direction I'm going in now, Henry, and that's to Fado's, for a very large Irish whiskey.'

'Nathan—' said Dr Burnside, but Nathan hung up.

He put on his coat, and took a look around his office. 'You coming?' he asked Patti. 'I could do with a shoulder to cry on.'

'Sure,' Patti said, and picked up her bag.

'Richard? How about a drink?'

Richard said, 'No thanks, Professor. A little too early for me. I'll stay here and clear everything up.'

Nathan left his laboratory and walked back along the

corridor, with Patti hopping and skipping to keep up with him. 'Maybe you can find somebody else to finance you,' she suggested. 'You know, a big corporation like Coca-Cola or Macdonald's. Or even the Pep Boys.'

'Don't you get it?' said Nathan, as he pushed open the doors. 'I've spent all of that time and all of that money and I've failed to come up with the goods. Nobody's going to throw good money after bad. Especially the amount that I'm going to need.'

He stepped outside, just in time to see a big red tow truck dragging his car around the corner of the maintenance block. The maintenance man in the green coveralls was standing at the bottom of the steps, his arms folded in satisfaction.

He whistled, and ran after the tow truck, and managed to flag down the driver just before he reached the exit gate.

'You want to unhook my goddamned car, please?'

'Fifty bucks,' said the driver, relentlessly chewing gum. He looked like another member of the mandrill family, except that his hair was wiry and gray.

'Fifty bucks? What the hell are you talking about? I work here. I'm a research professor.'

'Listen – you could be St Francis of Assisi, for all I care. Fifty bucks. That's the tow charge. We're a private contractor, no connection to the zoo.'

'If you think I'm going to pay you to get my own car back, then you're out of your mind.'

The tow truck driver shrugged. Then he switched off his engine and picked up a copy of the sports section. 'Bad Call, Sloppy Ball Costs Phils Against Cubs.'

Nathan turned away. It took all of his self-control not to pick up the concrete-based sign saying NO PUBLIC PARKING and smash it against the tow truck door.

Patti came up and said, 'Hey – they're, like, towing your car? That's *so* not appreciative.'

Just then, her cellphone played 'Oops . . . I Did It Again.' She flipped it open and said, 'Yes? Who? Really? You're kidding me! You're *kidding* me! OK, then.'

She came up to Nathan and said, 'That drink . . . I'll have to take a rain check. Some seventy-year-old woman in Fishtown has just been arrested for strangling her spaniel. And cooking it. Spaniel cheesesteak, can you imagine?'

'OK, whatever,' Nathan told her. He wasn't really listening. He took out his wallet and counted out fifty dollars. He walked back to the tow truck and held the money up in front of the driver's open window. His hand was shaking. 'Here you go. Here's your fifty bucks. I surrender.'

The driver climbed down from his cab. He took the money and counted it, licking his thumb to separate the bills.

'Do you know what my motto is?' he said, as he tucked it into his pocket. 'Never beat your head against a brick wall. You know why? Because it's brick.'

Instead of going to Fado's, Nathan drove home. He was depressed, but he didn't relish drinking whiskey on his own, staring at his unkempt reflection in the mirror of a noisy Irish bar. Besides, it was raining again, heavily, and he didn't feel like driving around and around with his windshield wipers flapping, looking for someplace to park.

As he arrived outside his house, he heard loud music coming from Denver's bedroom. He opened the front door and it was almost deafening.

He went upstairs and knocked on Denver's door. There was no answer, so he opened it. Denver and his friend Stu Wintergreen were standing in the middle of the room, their knees bent, their eyes screwed tight shut, flinging their hair from side to side and thrashing wildly at two invisible guitars.

Nathan watched them for a while. But then Stu opened his eyes and saw him standing in the doorway. He pushed Denver so hard that Denver almost lost his balance.

Denver turned around, and his cheeks flushed in embarrassment.

'Who's this?' Nathan shouted, over the music.

'What?'

'Who's this? Which band?'

Denver looked baffled for a moment, especially since Nathan hadn't asked him what the hell he was doing out of school.

'Pig Destroyers!' he shouted back, in his hoarse-teenage voice.

'Pig Destroyers, huh?'

'They're a deathgrind band from Virginia! This track is called "Rotten Yellow"!'

'I see! They're pretty good, aren't they?' He paused. 'Pretty loud, anyhow!'

Stu blinked at him from behind his thick-rimmed eyeglasses. 'They're totally awesome!'

Denver gave *him* a push, as if to warn him not to be so friendly to his dad. But Nathan said, 'OK. See you guys later,' and closed the door.

So Denver wanted to take a day off school, and jump around in his bedroom pretending to be a Pig Destroyer? Suddenly it didn't seem to matter any more.

It stopped raining around three p.m. The sun started to glitter on the pavement outside, and Denver and Stu put on their windbreakers and sneakers to go out. Nathan was sitting on the living-room couch with his laptop and a cold can of pale ale, and *Diagnosis Murder* was playing on the television with the sound turned off.

'Pops? We're going over to Stu's house to play *Halo 3*.'

'OK.'

Denver hesitated. 'Tell Mom I'll be back around six, OK?'

'OK.'

An even longer hesitation. Then Denver said, 'Like, ah – what are *you* doing home?'

'I'm taking some well-deserved downtime. Any objections?'

'No, of course not. I thought things were crazy at the lab, that's all.'

Nathan looked at him. How could he explain to Denver that everything he had been trying to achieve for the past five years had come to nothing at all? Hundreds of tests, thousands of experiments. Hours of squinting into a microscope, until his head thumped and his eyes went blurry.

He wasn't concerned that Denver would mock him about it, or be triumphal, because he didn't believe that he would be. But he was worried that he might come to the conclusion that study and hard work were not ultimately worth the effort, because there was always some bureaucrat who could pull the plug on you, even if you might be inches away from success.

'Don't be too late, OK?' he told Denver; he didn't even add 'because you have school tomorrow.'

Grace arrived home only twenty minutes later. As she was parking her car, Nathan opened the front door for her.

'Hey – what are *you* doing home?' she asked him, as she collected up her shopping.

'Denver asked me the same question.'

'*Denver* was here?'

'I surprised him. Him and his friend Stu. They were doing a little home study. I think the subject was Intolerably Loud Music, Grade Three.'

'That boy. I swear to God.'

'Hey,' said Nathan, as he followed her into the kitchen, 'you're the one who's always saying we should make allowances.'

She put down her shopping sacks on the kitchen table. 'What are we having tonight?' he asked her, peering inside.

'Jambalaya,' she said. 'You still haven't told me why you're home so early.'

'You want it straight? I'm home early because I'm out of a job. Henry Burnside has decided that the zoo is no longer prepared to finance the breeding of mythical creatures.'

'Oh, you're kidding me! Oh, *Nathan*, I'm so sorry.'

'It's OK,' he said. 'I should have seen this coming months ago. Like you said, I probably overhyped it. I gave the zoo all kinds of unrealistic expectations. I bet they believed that they'd have baby gryphons running around by now. Maybe they even thought they could put them on public display. You know – Gryphon World. You can't really blame them for cutting my funds off.'

'So what are you going to do now?'

'I haven't given it a whole lot of thought, to tell you the truth. I've been too busy feeling sorry for myself.'

Grace unpacked her shopping – celery, and green peppers, and hickory-smoked pork sausages. 'Something happened to me today, too. Something really strange.'

'Oh, yes?'

She told Nathan about her visit to the Murdstone Rest Home, and 'Michael Dukakis', and Sister Bennett.

'But what was strangest of all was that everything in Mrs Bellman's room was dead. Not just her, although they'd taken her away by then. But her cockatoo, and her ivy plants, and even the blowflies on the window sill. *Everything*.'

Nathan frowned at her. 'And this "Michael Dukakis" . . . he said that he'd seen a big black creature, with kind of like horns, or a crown, something like that?'

'That's right. He said it was black, and it was hunched over, with "jaggedy bits" on top of its head. I thought it sounded so much like your nightmare. But it couldn't have been, could it?'

'Wait up a minute,' said Nathan. He left the kitchen and went to his study at the back of the house. His desk had long since been buried by an avalanche of cardboard files and newspapers and magazines, but he knew exactly where to find the books he was looking for. On the shelf next to the door there was a thin paperback copy of *Natural History*, by Pliny the Elder, and a thick volume bound in cracked black leather, *Czarny Ksiązka – The Black Book*, by the Blessed Wincenty Kadlubek.

He brought them back to the kitchen and opened them up.

'What?' asked Grace.

'This creature . . . it killed everything in the room, right? Look what Pliny wrote about a serpent called a basilisk: "There is not one looketh upon its eyes, but hee dyeth presently".

'And see here: "He killeth all trees and shrubs not only that he toucheth, and that he doth breath upon also. As for grasse and hearbs, those hee sindgeth and burneth up, yea and breaketh stones in sunder, so venimous and deadly is he".

'"He creepeth not winding and crawling by as other serpents doe, but goeth upright and aloft from the ground with the one halfe part of his bodie." It also says he wears a coronet or a diadem, on his head.

'And what did your "Michael Dukakis" tell you? The creature he saw had horns on his head.'

Grace said, 'I don't know. He frightened me. The whole thing frightened me. If you hadn't had that dream, or whatever it was, I would have said that he had senile dementia, and left it at that. But – I don't know. Maybe you're right. Maybe there *is* some kind of creature. But I don't know how there can be. It's unreal.'

But Nathan opened the black-leather book and said, 'You only have to read this. It was written by Saint Wincenty Kadłubek, who was Bishop of Kraków, in Poland. In the year 1218 he unexpectedly resigned and went to live with the Cistercian monks in an isolated monastery at Jędrzejów. Nobody knew *why* he had resigned, not until this book was published, about thirty-five years after his death.

'It says here that one April night he was holding a Midnight Mass in St Andrzej's Church when "the darkest of creatures appeared from the shadows, all swathed in many black robes, and with a black crown of thorns upon its head". This creature "breathed upon the assembled worshippers with the foulest and coldest of breath, and stared at them with eyes that shone like two terrible lamps".

'According to this, the congregation all fell to the floor, more than thirty of them, but the bishop was dragged out through a side door by three of his priests, and he escaped. "The next morning, when they dared to venture back inside, they found no sign of the creature, but that all of the congregation still lay where they had first fallen, and that the church floor was strewn with dozens of dead swallows that had been nesting in the rafters, and hundreds of dead flies".

'Not only that, listen – "all of the flowers with which the church had been decorated had dried up and shriveled, as if they had been scorched by a fire".'

Nathan closed the book. 'The way you found Doris Bellman's room, that was pretty much the same, wasn't it? Everything was dead. The flowers, the birds. Even the flies.'

'But a *basilisk*, creeping around the Murdstone? How can that be?'

'I feel the same way as you, Grace. I don't know what to believe. But that thing I saw in my nightmare, and that hunched-up monster that "Michael Dukakis" saw, going around the corner, and that "darkest of creatures" that Bishop Kadłubek saw in Kraków – they're all so similar, don't you think? And they're *all* just like Pliny's description of a basilisk.'

Grace came around the kitchen table and laid her hands on his shoulders. 'Nate, let's be serious. You only *dreamed* about this creature, you didn't see it for real. And "Michael Dukakis" is suffering from senile dementia, so you can hardly call *him* a reliable witness. His real name's Stavros, or something like that. As for your Polish bishop – well, they were all very superstitious in the Middle Ages, weren't they? Not only that – April? It was probably Lent, and he hadn't eaten for days, and he simply imagined it.'

Nathan looked away. Grace was probably right.

'Suppose for a moment that it really *is* a basilisk?' Grace asked him. 'Where could it have come from? The world's leading expert on mythical zoology is *you*, and you haven't been able to hatch even one living gryphon.'

Nathan looked down at his books. Next to Bishop Kadłubek's account of the creature in St Andrzej's, there was a thirteenth-century woodcut of a basilisk. The creature had the head of a cockerel, with razor-sharp teeth in its beak, and a scaly body that was hideously swollen in the middle, like a boa constrictor that has just swallowed an entire goat.

He said, 'OK . . . but just suppose that I'm *not* the world's leading expert on mythical zoology. What if there's some zoological genius who knows a whole lot more about it than I do?'

'Oh come on, Nathan. That's not very likely. There can't be more than three people in the whole world trying to breed mythical creatures. If one of them had actually managed to hatch a basilisk, don't you think you'd know who they were?'

'Maybe they're keeping it a secret.'

'But why would they? It would have to be the greatest zoological breakthrough *ever*. They wouldn't want to keep it to themselves. They would be world-famous. They would be rich. Just like *you* expected to be.'

Nathan shrugged. 'How should I know why they're keeping it a secret? Maybe they're simply not ready to announce it yet. And if it's killed people, like Doris Bellman, maybe they're scared that they're going to be held liable.'

He thought for a moment, and then he said, 'Maybe they have some kind of evil master plan, to dominate the world with mythical creatures. Or maybe they tried to hatch out dozens more basilisks, but only one of them survived. Maybe it was born deformed, and that's why they cover it up in blankets.'

Grace gave him the gentlest of shakes. 'Earth to Nate! Earth to Nate! You just want to believe that somebody has managed to hatch a basilisk, don't you, never mind the reason? Because if somebody *has* managed to hatch a basilisk, that means that it might still be feasible that *you* could hatch a gryphon.'

'Well? Why not? It makes sense, doesn't it?'

Grace kissed him. 'Sweetheart, let's try to be reasonable. You had a nightmare about a big black shadowy thing, and "Michael Dukakis" thought he saw a huge hunched-up monster with horns. I agree that was kind of a weird coincidence, for sure. Doris Bellman heard dragging noises outside of her room, although she never saw anything. All the same, she died, along with her cockatoo and her ivy plants. It all sounds very scary. But it doesn't really add up to much, does it? It doesn't add up to a real live mythical creature.'

'So you don't really believe that there *is* a basilisk on the loose?'

'I'm not saying that. You know me. I always have an open mind about everything. I'm a doctor, remember?'

'But?'

'But, to be perfectly frank with you, it's just about the least plausible explanation that I can think of.'

'So?'

'So we use Occam's razor and we look for the simplest theory first. Somebody needs to investigate the Murdstone Rest Home. If not the police, then the Philadelphia health authorities. After all, Doris Bellman must have been frightened by *something,* or she wouldn't have called me. And even if his mind is wandering, "Michael Dukakis" must have seen something, too.'

'But not a basilisk?'

Grace shook her head. 'You remember that retirement home in Virginia, where the manager warned all the residents that there was a monster prowling around the corridors after lights out? All he wanted to do was scare the old folks into staying in their rooms, because they used to keep wandering around in the middle of the night. But one old woman thought she saw the monster coming up the stairs, and she died of a heart seizure.

'And there was another rest home – in Maine, I think. The trustees persuaded their residents to include them in their wills, and then a couple of months later they filled up their bedrooms with carbon monoxide. The old folks died, and their pets died, too.'

Nathan said, 'Sure. I remember that case in Maine. But even if Doris Bellman was killed by carbon monoxide, and her cockatoo, too, it wouldn't have had any effect on her ivy plant.'

'OK. Fine. That's a very reasonable point. But like I say, let's start by thinking simple.'

Nathan dry-washed his face with his hands. 'You're right, as usual. What it is to be married to an MD.'

Grace kissed him. 'At least you're not married to a professor, like I am.'

EIGHT

The White Face

G race cooked her famous jambalaya with smoked sausage and green peppers and marinated chicken, and they sprawled on the couch in front of the TV with their plates on their laps, which they never did when Denver was home. Nathan thought that Denver had inherited enough of their bad habits already.

They didn't talk about Doris Bellman any more, although Grace could tell that Nathan was still thinking about the basilisk, even when he was pretending to laugh at David Letterman.

The phone rang twice, but each time it was for Denver. The first caller was a boy who even *sounded* as if he had raging acne; and the second was a breathy girl with a very strong South Philly accent. She called herself Whimzy ('that's with a zee . . . he'll know who it is, aayt?)

Nathan put down the receiver. He had been expecting a call from Richard, with the early results of his necropsy; and he had secretly been hoping that Dr Burnside might ring him, suggesting that if he was more disciplined with his budget, he could carry on with his breeding program.

'Does Denver have a girlfriend called Whimzy with a zee?'

Grace shook her head. 'I didn't know that Denver *had* a girlfriend. Not since Marian Mellenstein, anyhow.'

'Marian Mellenstein wasn't a girlfriend. She was a three-toed sloth, with curly hair and glasses.'

'Oh, *don't*. She couldn't help it, poor thing.'

'I didn't say she could. But just because *I* breed creatures from different species, that doesn't mean my son has to try it.'

They went to bed around eleven thirty p.m., and a few minutes later Denver came home. They heard him come upstairs, and knock at their door.

'Pops?' he said, in a throaty voice, holding up the note that Nathan had left him. 'What did Whimzy want?'

'She didn't say. She just said you'd know who she was. Least, that's what I *think* she said.'

'OK.'

'There's jambalaya in the Dutch oven,' said Grace. 'You may need to warm it up a little.'

'So who is she, this Whimzy?' asked Nathan. 'Is she pretty? Will we ever get to meet her?'

'Just some girl I know, that's all. Thanks, Mom.'

Denver closed the door and went downstairs. Nathan and Grace looked at each other.

'Did you see that?' said Nathan. 'He definitely blushed.'

'At least it proves he's not gay.'

'I'm not worried about him being gay. But I *am* worried if he's going out with girls with accents like that, *aayt*?'

Grace laughed, and switched off her light.

Two hours later Nathan was still awake. The bedroom was airless and far too warm, and the wind must have been blowing from the south-west, because planes were turning and decelerating almost directly overhead as they made their approach to Philadelphia International Airport. Every time one of them came over, the low thunder of their engines made the window frames buzz like trapped blowflies.

He heard a man angrily shouting in one of the houses opposite, and then he heard accordion music, and laughter, and doors slamming. He heard a car slowly trundling down West Airy Road, as if its tires were all punctured and it was rolling along on its wheel rims. He was sure that Grace murmured something, but he couldn't be sure what it was.

'Grace?' he said, and leaned closer to her. 'Grace, are you awake?'

'*Never,*' she said. '*Never looks once. Never.*'

'Who are you talking about?' he asked her. He waited for her to explain what she meant, but she turned over and started to breathe steady and even, and it was obvious that she was deeply asleep. Nathan lay back on his pillow but he couldn't close his eyes. His bedside clock said seven minutes past two.

At the top of the bedroom drapes, there was a small tri-angular gap where Grace hadn't quite drawn them together tightly enough, so that the moonlight shone in a wide fan pattern across the ceiling. Where the plaster was uneven, the moonlight cast irregular shadows; and as Nathan stared up at them, he began to distinguish patterns, and shapes. He saw a curve that looked like a man's cheek, and another curve that could have been the side of his nose. Then he made out a ripple that formed the shape of his mouth.

A rough semicircle of plaster made him look as if he had a high forehead with his hair brushed back.

'*It can't be,*' Grace insisted.

'Grace? You're talking in your sleep, sweetheart.'

'*I don't care what you say about it, it can't be. It simply isn't possible.*'

While Grace was talking, the man's face in the ceiling began to grow more and more distinct. His eyes were closed, as if he were a death mask, but as the minutes passed, his features appeared in greater depth and greater detail – his eyebrows, his cheekbones, the curve of his lips. Nathan was tempted to pull back the bedcover and stand up on the bed, so that he could actually touch the face with his fingertips, but he was sure that it was only a trick of the moonlight. The moon must be sinking, that was all – and as it sank lower, it was casting longer and longer shadows, which made the man's face look increasingly three-dimensional.

He stared at the face for more than twenty minutes. When it was daylight, he would probably look at exactly the same place on the ceiling and see nothing but lumps and bumps. He remembered that when he was six years old, he had been convinced that there was a wolf in his closet door, but it had only been the pattern of the walnut veneer.

'*You won't leave me, Nate, will you?*' said Grace, and turned over, so that her hand accidentally struck his shoulder.

'No,' he reassured her, even though she was fast asleep. 'I won't leave you. I promise.'

At last his eyes began to close. His mind was still churning over and over, but his exhaustion was gradually dragging him off to sleep. He kept seeing flickering images of the gryphon, and the resentful way in which the gryphon had stared at him with its single orange eye. And he could hear Dr Burnside's voice in his ears, whispery and harsh. *'We need to discuss your future, Nathan, here at the zoo.'*

'Future?' said a thick, guttural voice. 'You have no *future.'*

Instantly, he opened his eyes, and raised his head. He looked around the bedroom, frowning. He thought for a split second that it had been Grace talking to him, but then he lifted his eyes toward the man's white face on the ceiling. The man had opened *his* eyes, too – eyes that were totally white and apparently blind.

I'm dreaming, Nathan told himself. *I'm having another nightmare.*

'You think so? How can you possibly be dreaming, with your eyes open?'

The man's lips moved, but somehow his words and his lip movements didn't quite synchronize, as if his voice had been dubbed. His eyes opened and closed in a mechanical way, like a ventriloquist's dummy.

I'm dreaming because you can't be real. You're nothing but shadows, on a badly plastered ceiling.

'What? *You* of all people should know the difference between dreams and reality. You're the one who wants to breed gryphons, and gargoyles, and bennu birds.'

Yes, but those creatures, they're not dreams They all existed, once, and I can bring them back to life.

'Like the basilisk?'

If there is *a basilisk, yes.*

'You doubt it? How do you think that Doris Bellman died? What do you think it was that old Mr Stavrianos saw outside his room? And what kind of a beast did *you* see, when you had that nightmare?'

I'm having a nightmare now.

'You think so?' the man challenged him, and his eyelids blinked even more rapidly. 'Then what do you make of *this*?'

Nathan looked down toward the foot of the bed. A black shape was rising up from the floor. It was huge, and hunched, with a complicated array of twigs or horns on top of its head. Like before, it was covered in layers of tattered sacking, and out of the sacking two claws emerged, gleaming in the moonlight.

Oh shit, said Nathan. *This time it's real, isn't it.*

'Maybe it is. Maybe it's not. As I say, my friend, *you* are the expert on the difference between dreams and reality.'

The black creature began to drag itself around to the side of the bed. With every breath it was wheezing and whistling, as if its lungs were clogged with phlegm, and Nathan could smell again that nauseating combination of dust and decaying poultry.

He leaned over the side of the bed and groped frantically around for his baseball bat. But even as he did so he thought: *stop, don't, this really isn't real. It wasn't real the last time and it isn't real now.*

'Look at the beast,' the man told him. 'Look into its eyes. Then you'll know for sure.'

With a harsh grunt, the black creature tossed its head, so that it threw back the stringy rags that half-covered its face. The bedroom was still too dark for Nathan to be able to see clearly what it looked like, but he thought he could make out a beak, of sorts, and rounded white cheeks. He was frightened, but at the same time he was mesmerized. Could this really be a genuine basilisk? If it was, where had it come from, and how had it managed to get into his house?

'Look into its eyes,' the man repeated.

Nathan cautiously raised his hand in front of his face. If the myths were true, a real basilisk could kill him stone dead with one stare. But how could it be? It was madness. It was nothing but a nightmare.

The creature's eyes glowed very dimly at first, like two white lights seen behind layers of grimy net curtains. But very quickly they began to shine brighter, until they were blinding. Nathan closed his eyes tightly and turned his face away.

He felt a cold corrosive sensation that started on his scalp and then crawled slowly but inexorably down the back of his neck and his shoulders and his chest. It was more painful than anything that he had ever experienced in his life – like being frozen and scalded, both at once. As it burned his stomach and started to creep down toward his genitals, he opened his mouth to scream, but the cold was so stunning that he couldn't find the breath. It felt as if a flask of liquid nitrogen was gradually being poured all over him, freezing his skin and penetrating right through his flesh to his bone marrow.

Stop, he cried out. *It hurts too much. Call it off.*

'Now do you believe that it's real?'

What? What do you mean?

'Tell me if you believe that it's real. That's all I'm asking.'

Yes, anything. Yes, it's real. Call it off, for Christ's sake, it hurts.

'Nathan!'

He opened his eyes. Grace was shaking his shoulder and shouting out, 'Nathan! *Nate!* Wake up! What's the matter?'

He stared at her. Then he reached across and switched on his bedside lamp. The black creature had gone, if it had ever been there. When he looked up, the white face on the ceiling had disappeared, too.

'Did you have another nightmare?' Grace asked him.

He nodded. 'The same nightmare, only it was ten times worse. And so goddamned *real*.'

'The creature with the horns?'

'It's a basilisk, I'm sure of it.'

'Nathan—'

'It's a basilisk, Grace! I don't know why the hell I've been having nightmares about it. I'm not even sure that they *are* nightmares. They're more like – I don't know – *visions*. It's *alive*. And it's like somebody's trying to tell me that it's real, and it's out there someplace. And I'm sure that it killed Doris Bellman.'

He swung his legs out of bed, went across to his closet and took out a pair of jeans.

'What are you doing? It's twenty after three.'

'I'm going to the Murdstone Rest Home. If that creature is actually there, I'm going to find it.'

Grace said, 'Nate, this is totally crazy. You can't go wandering around the Murdstone in the middle of the night, you'll get yourself arrested.'

'I have to go, Grace – even if it's just to satisfy myself that it doesn't exist.'

'Leave it till the morning, at least. I'll come with you. We could go together and talk to Doctor Zauber about it.'

'Unh-hunh. If there *is* a basilisk there, we won't be able to find it tomorrow morning. It's totally nocturnal. During the day, it hides itself in the darkest crevice it can find, and sleeps.'

Grace climbed out of bed, too, and watched him in frustration as he pulled on his dark blue sweater. 'You've had a nightmare about it, that's all.'

'Two nightmares.'

'OK, you had *two* nightmares. But lots of people have recurring nightmares. I've had recurring nightmares since I was three years old, about being chased through Strawbridge's furniture department by the wolf from *Little Red Riding Hood*. You can have a nightmare a thousand times but that doesn't make it any more real.'

Nathan pointed upward. 'I just saw a man's face, right there on the ceiling.'

'You saw *what*?'

'A man's face, molded right out of the plaster.'

'Nate, for goodness' sake. You're tired, you're stressed, your project's just been canceled. How about I get you a couple of Somnapril and you come back to bed?'

'I'm going to the Murdstone. I have to. The man spoke to me.'

'The man on the ceiling?'

'That's right. He knew who I was, and all about my mythical creature project. He told me that Doris Bellman was killed by a basilisk, and that your senile old friend in the bathrobe saw a basilisk, too. He *showed* me a basilisk, for Christ's sake. It came rearing right up from the end of the bed. It was black, and it had horns, and it had eyes like headlights.'

'You had a nightmare about a monster and a man's face on the ceiling and that's why you're going to drive ten miles at three thirty in the morning and break into an old folks' rest home?'

'Not a nightmare. Not a dream. A vision. And, yes.'

Grace came up to him and brushed his hair with her hand. 'Come on,' she said. 'Come back to bed.'

She was trying to calm him down but Nathan was too fired up. 'Everybody said I was out of my mind when I first suggested my Cee-Zee program. But I was proved right, wasn't I? I did actually breed a gryphon, even if it died. And I could do it again. And next time, I'm going to make sure that it survives.'

'Nathan, I have total faith in you, and I'm not the only one. Remember what Professor Jung Choi said about what you were doing? "Daring," he said. "Cutting-edge zoology." But that's why you *have* to stay focused. So many people have so much respect for you. Even Henry Burnside.'

'Burnside? You're kidding me.'

'Believe me, Nate, you should have heard what he said about you at that fundraiser last month. If he had only had the resources, he would have gone on financing you. But he simply doesn't – and the zoo's trustees have all gotten cold feet.'

Nathan shook his head. 'Maybe I'm totally off beam. I mean – I don't have any empirical evidence whatsoever. But something's come alive out there, and it's so close to what I've been working on for so long that I can practically *feel* it.'

Grace thought for a while, and then she said, 'OK. So you want to go to the Murdstone and take a sneaky look around?'

'I want to see this sack-dragger that Doris Bellman told you about. I want to see this hunched-up monster that "Michael Dukakis" saw in the corridor.'

'And if you get caught, what do you say then?'

'I don't know,' Nathan admitted. 'But I'm sure that I can think of some plausible explanation for being there. Maybe I could say that I'm checking the place out with a view to sending my old man there, but he's practically blind, so I thought it would be a good idea to see what it's like in the dark.'

Grace shook her head. 'You're mad, you know that? The archetypal mad scientist, from *The Twilight Zone*.'

'Grace – if somebody has successfully bred a basilisk – I *have* to see it. I have to know for sure. It would be the single most significant scientific breakthrough since DNA.'

'OK, OK. Go. But I'm coming with you.'

'You can't.'

'What do you mean, I *can't*? I know the Murdstone like the back of my hand, and I can show you how to find Doris Bellman's room, and I can show you exactly where "Michael Dukakis" saw his hunched-up figure.'

Nathan said, 'Weren't you listening, when I was reading out that stuff from Bishop Kadłubek's *Black Book*? The basilisk can kill any living thing just by staring at it.'

'So why is it OK for *you* to go looking for it, but not *me*?'

'I'm taking some precautions.' He went to his nightstand, opened it, and took out the black SK automatic that he had never used, not even once.

'You're going to trespass in an old people's rest home in the middle of the night and you're going to take a *gun?*'

'That's not all.' He went into the bathroom and came out with his circular shaving mirror.

'A gun, and a shaving mirror?'

'In old Polish legends, the way that people beat the basilisk was to hold up a mirror and the basilisk's stare was turned right back on it.'

He went to his closet, took out the black necktie that he only ever wore to funerals, and knotted it around the mirror's folding stand. Then he hung it around his neck and buttoned his shirt up over it.

Grace said, 'I think we should call the police.'

'And tell them what? That there's some kind of medieval monster prowling around the Murdstone Rest Home, and you know that for sure because your husband had two nightmares about it?'

'No – that my husband is thinking of breaking into a home for seniors, and he's armed and unhinged.'

Nathan lowered his head. 'Grace, I *know* this sounds nuts. But it's my whole life's work. Recreating these creatures – it's what defines me. It's what they're going to put on my headstone, when I die. *He Made Mythical Monsters.*'

Grace came up to him and kissed him. 'OK, Nate. But you're not going alone. We're husband and wife, remember? *Hart to Hart.* If you absolutely insist on doing this, then I absolutely insist on coming along with you to watch your ass, because your ass is very precious to me, as well as the rest of you.'

It took them less than twenty-five minutes to drive to Millbourne. There was hardly any traffic around, apart from a mechanical street sweeper and three buses crowded with tired-looking shift workers.

'Now *that's* a rare sight in Philly,' said Grace, as they over-took the street sweeper. 'Even rarer than a basilisk, probably.'

Nathan said, 'You don't have to mock me. If there's nothing there, I'll admit that I'm ready for the funny farm. But at least let's check it out, OK?'

'I'm not mocking you, Nate. I'm trying to lighten the mood, is all.'

They crossed the Schuylkill River. The moon was sinking toward the horizon, and the smoggy atmosphere had turned it blood-red. Another blood-red moon was rising from the river to meet it.

They reached the Murdstone Rest Home and Nathan parked on the opposite side of the street, beneath an elm tree. He took a flashlight out of the glovebox and shone it under his chin to make sure that it was working. 'That makes you look like a vampire,' said Grace.

'You do believe me, don't you?' Nathan asked her. 'I mean, about the face on the ceiling? I genuinely feel like somebody's trying to make contact with me. I don't know whether they're trying to warn me, or whether they're trying to scare me off. I haven't felt like this since I was a kid about ten years old, when my grandfather died. I actually heard him say "go fly your kite, Nathan", right inside my head.'

Grace took hold of his hand and squeezed it. 'Let's go take a look, shall we? Then we'll know for sure.' She put up the hood of her short black duffel coat. 'Maybe I should have worn a stocking mask, too.'

They climbed out of the car and crossed the street together. The sky was gradually beginning to grow lighter, with smeary gray clouds. A skein of geese flew overhead, in eerie silence.

Grace said, 'I think they lock the main doors at night, but they have to keep the back door open in case of emergencies.'

They walked around the left-hand side of the buildings, staying deep in the shadow of the high yew hedge that separated the rest home from the residential property next door. Nathan could see lights in some of the upstairs rooms, and on the main staircase, but most of the ground floor was in darkness.

As they skirted around the rear of the kitchen block, Grace tugged at his sleeve and said, 'Careful . . . the staff quarters are just around this next corner, and there's always somebody in there, twenty-four seven.'

Keeping close to the ivy-covered brickwork, Nathan made his way to the end of the wall, and cautiously peeked around it. Immediately, he raised his hand and said, '*Ssh!*'

Two members of the Murdstone's nursing staff were standing outside the back door, talking and smoking. Nathan could smell their cigarettes from twenty yards away. One was a heavily built black orderly, in purple scrubs, and the other was a Korean nurse, in the purple-and-white striped blouse that all of the nursing staff wore.

'Maybe we should try again tomorrow,' said Grace. 'After all, it's going to be light soon.'

Nathan looked up at the sky. He was half inclined to agree with her. If there was one characteristic that was mentioned in every narrative that he had ever read about the basilisk, it was that it never ventured out during the day. Daylight would do it no harm – unlike vampires, which were famously supposed to catch fire if they were ever exposed to the sun, and burn to ash. But the basilisk's eyes were highly photosensitive, and it was almost completely blinded by natural light. That was why it always sought out cellars and caves and crevices to hide in, and only emerged when the sun went down. As late as the 1850s, some French vintners refused to go down to their wine cellars during the day, in case they disturbed a basilisk hiding in the darkness.

'What do you think?' asked Grace. 'I don't mind coming back tomorrow, if you want to.'

At that moment, however, the orderly flicked his cigarette butt into the bushes, and the nurse dropped hers on to the ground and stepped on it. The orderly said something to the nurse and both of them laughed. Then they went back inside, closing the door behind them.

'Come on,' said Nathan. 'We should still have time, if we're quick.'

'I'm not so sure now,' said Grace.

'Please – you know the layout.'

Grace hesitated, with her hand covering her mouth. Then she said, 'OK, then. But as soon as it starts getting light, we're out of there.'

They made their way along the back of the kitchen block to the staff quarters. The first-floor window was lit, but it was covered by a yellow calico blind. Behind the blind, Nathan saw the orderly cross from one side of the room to the other, like a character in a shadow theater. The nurse followed, although she was further away from the window, and her shadow appeared shrunken and misshapen.

He went up to the back door, which had two wired-glass panels in the upper half, and peered inside. Inside, on the left-hand side, over a dozen overcoats and hats were hanging on pegs, like a crowd of strap-hanging monks. There was no light in the hallway, but the door to the staff quarters was directly opposite, and the nurse had left it a few inches ajar. Nathan could see the arm of a red-upholstered couch, and part of a coffee table, and a bookshelf crammed with dog-eared paperbacks. On the wall hung a framed poster for Bartram's Garden, with a flowering tulip tree.

He tried the door handle. Its spring made a scrunching noise as he pulled it downward, but the door was unlocked. He turned to Grace and said, 'OK? When we get in there, which way should we go?'

'Straight ahead, to the end of the corridor, then left. Then immediately right, and up four or five stairs.'

'You ready?'

'Ready as I'll ever be.'

Nathan opened the door wider and they stepped inside. Behind the door to the staff quarters they could hear some crackly old horror movie playing on the TV, with the sound turned right down. The orderly was complaining about the hours he had to work. 'Never even gave me no notice – thinks I can change my shift just to suit *him* – I got kids to pick up from school.'

'You should not tolerate it, Newton,' the nurse replied. Her voice became louder as she approached the door, and for a heart-stopping moment Nathan and Grace thought that she was going to open it and find them right outside. Instead, however, she closed it, leaving them in almost total darkness.

Nathan took out his flashlight and switched it on. He shone it down the corridor in front of them, and Grace said, 'Come on, let's go. You know what some of these seniors are like. They only sleep for a couple of hours. We don't want one of *them* raising the alarm.'

They hurried down the corridor, turned left and then right, and then up the stairs.

'Here,' said Grace. 'This was Doris Bellman's room, right here. And if you go that way, that's where I met "Michael Dukakis".'

'Did he tell you exactly where he saw that hunched-up monster of his?'

'It would have been *there*, coming round that corner, heading this way.'

'So it could have been coming to attack Doris Bellman?'

Nathan shone his flashlight up and down the corridor. The pale brown carpet was wearing out in places, and its pile had been furrowed by a vigorous going-over with a vacuum cleaner, but there were no signs of any claw marks. There were stains and scratches on the wallpaper, although there was nothing that couldn't have been caused by wheelchairs bumping into the walls, or coffee being spilled.

However, when he pointed the flashlight upward, it *did* look as if something had scraped the ceiling – and quite recently, too. There were four or five parallel ruts in the plaster, nearly a quarter of an inch deep. They ran all the way from the corner where 'Michael Dukakis' had glimpsed his hunched-up monster, ending up abruptly in a wild cross-hatch pattern about four feet away from Doris Bellman's door.

'Will you take a look at that?' he said, hoarsely. 'I mean, what do you think caused all of those grooves?' He reached up with his left hand, and stood on tiptoe, but he couldn't even touch the ceiling, let alone scratch it.

'That thing I saw in my nightmare—' he began, but Grace said '*Listen!*' and lifted up one finger. 'There,' she said. 'Did you hear that?'

Nathan strained his ears. From one of the upper floors, very faintly, came the plaintive cry of some old man calling out vainly for assistance. '*Nurse! Nurse!*' Apart from that, though, all he could hear was the endless, irritating grinding of the outdated air-conditioning system.

Grace said, 'That's funny. I thought I heard a kind of a scraping noise.'

'Scraping?'

'I don't know. It's hard to describe exactly.'

'I don't hear anything.'

They listened some more, but there was nothing. Even the old man had stopped crying for help. Nathan turned his flashlight on to the door of Doris Bellman's room.

'Let's take a look inside, shall we? There won't be anybody in here, will there?'

'No. Sister Bennett said the next resident won't be coming till tomorrow – well, later today.'

Nathan tried the handle. The door was unlocked. He eased it open and shone his flashlight inside. The bed was made, and ready for its new occupant. The birdcage had been taken away, as well as the ivy plants. All of Doris Bellman's photographs had gone, as well as her crucifix, although there were shadowy marks on the wall where they had hung for so long.

The room smelled strongly of Dettox.

'Nothing here,' said Nathan. But he hunkered down and shone his flashlight into the corners of the room, and under the bed.

'What are you looking for?' Grace asked him. 'Come on – I really think we need to get out of here.'

'Basilisks were supposed to have been like lizards, they were constantly shedding their scales. I was just hoping that this baby might have left one or two of them behind.'

'Hurry up,' Grace urged him. 'I'm sure I can hear somebody coming.'

Nathan was about to leave the bedroom when he saw what looked like a black stick, protruding two or three inches from the back of the nightstand. He bent down and picked it up, and examined it closely. It wasn't a stick, but a fragment of black horny material, like an antler. He showed it to Grace and said, 'What do you make of this?'

Grace peered at it closely but she wouldn't touch it. 'It could be anything. I don't know. Piece of a broken walking-stick?'

'I don't know. I'll take it back to the lab and analyze it.'

He dropped the black stick into his shirt pocket, and quietly closed the door of Doris Bellman's room. It was then that they heard another scraping sound, much louder this time, much sharper, and followed by a complicated shuffle.

'What's that?' said Grace. She was frightened now.

'Whatever it is, it sounds like it's coming closer.'

'Nate, I seriously think we should go.'

There was yet another scrape, and then a harsh, high-pitched whine, like somebody trying to breathe with clogged-up lungs. Grace started to head back toward the stairs, but Nathan caught hold of her arm.

'Grace – wait up – it sounds like it's just around the corner. Come on, sweetheart, if it's really here, I need to see it.'

'No – we need to go. I'm sorry. This is crazy.'

She tugged herself free, but as she did so, a shadowy figure appeared around the corner of the corridor. It stood there, swaying slightly. It was hunched, and it appeared to have spines on top of its head, but it didn't look nearly as bulky as Nathan had expected it to be. After all, whatever had made its way along this corridor to Doris Bellman's room had been tall enough to scrape furrows in the ceiling.

He shone his flashlight at it, and he saw at once that it was an elderly man in a sagging brown bathrobe, with his hair sticking up. One lens of his eyeglasses was covered up with silver duct tape, but he lifted his hand to shield his other eye. 'What's going on?' he demanded. 'What time is it? Didn't you bring the car round yet?'

'Michael?' said Grace. 'Michael Dukakis?'

'That's right. Who is that? You want to take that flashlight out of my face?'

'It's OK, Michael. We're just making sure that you're safe.'

'Michael Dukakis' came shuffling toward them in his worn brown slippers. 'None of us is safe. Not one of us. Not while that creature's still here. It took Doris and it'll take the rest of us, if we give it the chance.'

'Have you seen it again?'

'Michael Dukakis' shook his head. 'Haven't seen it, but I've sure heard it. Late last night, dragging its way down the corridor. Went past my room, and paused awhile, and I swear that I could hear it breathing. I was lying there, and I was sure that it was going to come for me, but in the end it moved on. But who knows, it could be my turn next time around.'

'What time did you hear it?' Nathan asked him. 'Can you remember?'

'Exactly. I was waiting for them to bring the car round. I was late. The overture was supposed to start at eight o'clock, and they were five hours and eleven minutes late.'

'So, one eleven?'

'Five hours and eleven minutes late, exactly. Saw it on my bedside clock.'

Outside the windows of the Murdstone Rest Home, the sky was growing paler and paler. Nathan said, 'We'd better leave before anybody sees us. It's too late now, in any case. Not dark enough for a basilisk.'

'What time are you bringing the car around?' asked 'Michael Dukakis'.

'After breakfast, I promise you,' said Grace. 'Meanwhile, why don't you go back to bed and catch yourself a few more zees?'

'Michael Dukakis' thought about that, and then nodded. 'You're a good woman, Belinda. Always said you were. You always took care of me, didn't you, even when Ruby passed over, God rest her poor bewildered soul.'

Nathan and Grace left 'Michael Dukakis' still talking to himself. They made their way down the stairs and along the corridor to the back of the building. The door to the staff quarters was still closed, and the television was still playing loudly – *Gilligan's Island*.

'*That hair, I could run my fingers through it – up to the elbows,*' and then a burst of studio laughter.

They let themselves out of the back door, into the gradually lightening day.

NINE

Test of Loyalty

As soon as they got home, Nathan took a long hot shower. He stood in the shower stall with his head bowed and the water turned on full, trying to wash the madness out of his brain. But he couldn't wash away the image of the white blind-eyed face that had appeared on the ceiling, and the huge black creature that had reared up at the end of his bed, with eyes that had frozen him right through to his backbone.

'*Look at the beast. Look into its eyes. Then you'll know for sure.*'

He came into the kitchen after his shower to find that Grace had made some espresso coffee and wholemeal toast. He tore off a piece of paper towel and laid the black stick on top of it.

'That is *disgusting,*' Grace complained. 'I wish you'd take it off the counter. Come on, Nate, you don't know where it's been. It could be dried feces, for all you know.'

Nathan picked it up and examined it closely. It was a little over five inches long and about three-quarters of an inch in diameter. It was dry and brittle, and only weighed a few grams.

'It's not shit, I promise you. I've been studying zoology long enough to know shit when I see it. This is definitely *bone* – the broken-off point from some animal's antlers, if I'm not mistaken.'

'You're talking about a deer, something like that?'

'I won't know for sure until I take it into the lab and analyze it properly. But the incredible thing about antlers is that they are the only known regeneration of a complete and anatomically complex appendage in a mammal. It's like losing your hand, but then growing another identical hand, just like that.'

'Well, surprise, surprise, I happen to know that,' said Grace. 'But whatever it is, can you please put it someplace else?'

Nathan scraped the stick with the edge of his knife, and peered at it again. 'Definitely bone. Almost certainly antler.'

'Nate—'

'The thing is, right up until early last year, nobody knew how antlers regenerated. Deer and moose and elks, every twelve months, their antlers drop off. But how do they grow another rack, exactly the same as the rack they grew the year before, and so darn *fast*? Sometimes they grow as much as one centimeter in a single day. But Hans Rolf at the University of Göttingen has just discovered that the regrowth of antlers is caused by the activation of resident stem cells.'

'Well, I didn't know *that,*' Grace admitted.

'Neither did I, until last year. That's because the whole antler-research thing is still in its infancy. But if this is a piece of basilisk antler, and it contains resident stem cells, then it's not beyond the bounds of possibility that these stem cells can be activated to help people to grow back fingers they've had amputated, or toes, or even their arms or their legs . . . Well, come on, Grace, who's the mad scientist now?'

Grace looked at the black stick without much enthusiasm. 'You *still* think it came from a basilisk?'

'What else? It didn't come from any species of deer that I

recognize. If anything, it looks like a piece of a stag beetle's antler, except that it's way too big.'

'I don't know. It's not that I don't believe you, Nate. It's not that I don't *want* to believe you. It's just that I don't think you ought to jump to conclusions.'

Nathan carried the black stick across to the window and set it down on the sill. He rinsed his hands and then he returned to the counter. Grace poured him a cup of coffee while he spread a thick layer of boysenberry jelly on to his toast, and cut it in half.

'I'm not going to get my hopes up, Grace, I promise you – not until I've taken it to the lab and run some basic tests. But *something* has been prowling around the Murdstone Rest Home, hasn't it? whether it's human or animal or God alone knows what. And that something left this piece of bone behind.'

Grace was silent for a moment. Then she reached over and laid her hand on Nathan's arm. 'Nate . . . Supposing they don't let you?'

'Supposing they don't let me what?'

'Go into the lab. Analyze it.'

'They haven't sacked me yet, sweetheart. They've pulled the plug on my funding. But I'm still contractually beholden to those bastards, and so long as I am, I'm going to use their facilities.'

Denver appeared, pale-faced and puffy-eyed, with his hair sticking up like a parrot's crest. He was wearing a crumpled khaki T-shirt with *Get The F Out of Iraq* printed on the front, and a droopy pair of mustard-yellow boxer shorts.

'Good morning, favorite and only son,' said Nathan. 'How did you sleep?'

Denver opened the fridge door and stared into it for almost half a minute, blinking. Then he took out a carton of orange-juice and poured himself a large glassful. Had Nathan and Grace not been here, he would have glugged it straight from the carton, but he knew what they would say, and his brain couldn't take nagging at eight fifteen in the morning.

'You want some toast?' Grace asked him.

Denver climbed up on to one of the stools and shook his head.

'What are you doing today?' Nathan asked him. 'Anything special? Band practice?'

Denver shook his head again. He was silent for a long while, trying to focus on his glass of orange juice, but then he said, 'Did you guys go *out* last night?'

Grace glanced at Nathan. Nathan said, 'Yes, as a matter of fact.'

'What did you go out for? It must have been three thirty in the morning.'

'Nothing. We couldn't sleep, that's all. We went for a drive and we saw the moon set.'

Denver frowned at them. 'You went for a drive, at three thirty in the morning? Like, I know you guys aren't exactly normal like normal parents, but when did you ever do anything like that?'

'Last night,' said Nathan. What else could he possibly tell him? That he and Denver's mother had gone basilisk-hunting in an old people's rest home?

Denver said, 'OK. I guess you're old enough to do whatever you want. But I thought I heard somebody walking around the house while you were out.'

'You must have dreamed it,' said Nathan.

'Unh-hunh. I was totally awake, man. Somebody came up the stairs and along the corridor and stopped outside my bedroom door. I thought it was you, but it couldn't have been, because I heard you come back later.'

'I'm sure you dreamed it,' Nathan told him. 'I put the alarm back on when we went out, and nobody could have gotten into the house while we were away without setting it off.'

Denver shrugged. 'I heard what I heard, that's all I can say. Whoever it was, they stopped right outside my bedroom door, like they were listening, or waiting, or something. I could hear the floorboards creaking. I could hear them *breathing*, man, like they had a headcold or something.'

Grace glanced up at the railroad clock on the kitchen wall. 'I'd better take a shower. I have a practice meeting at nine thirty.'

Denver said, 'How about a ride to school, Mom?'

'OK . . . but aren't you going to have any breakfast?'

'Sure. As soon as my teeth wake up.'

Nathan sat and watched him while he poured himself a bowlful of Cocoa Crunchies and then drowned them in milk.

'Denver – if you hear anything like that again, you'll

call me, OK? You won't open the door, you'll just shout out "Pops!"? Or if I happen to be out, call me on my cell.'

Denver blinked at him. 'Why? What was it?'

'I don't know exactly. But some pretty outré things have been happening. They're probably harmless, but I'm not really sure yet.'

'Outré? What's outré?'

'Like, weird. Things like your hearing somebody outside of your bedroom door when there's nobody there. Things like—'

Nathan hesitated. He wasn't sure if he ought to tell Denver about his nightmares, or his visions, or whatever they were. Denver had heard something, too, and maybe he needed to be warned that something was prowling through their consciousness, even if it wasn't actually prowling through their home. But he didn't understand himself what it was that he had seen, or *imagined* that he had seen, and he didn't want to alarm Denver for no good reason.

'Things like *what*, Pops?' Denver was waiting with milk dripping from his cereal spoon.

'I'm not too sure. Maybe you could call them phenomena.'

'What's phamononama?'

'Like when you see things and hear things but they're not really there.'

'Like being high? You and Mom – you haven't been, like, *smoking* anything, have you?'

Nathan managed a slightly twisted smile. 'Not recently. But yes, it's a little like that.'

'I get it,' said Denver, and nodded, and nodded. 'Don't worry, Pops. I won't tell anybody, I promise. Especially the cops.'

After Grace and Denver had left the house, Nathan poured himself another cup of coffee and walked through to the sunroom. He picked up that morning's *Philadelphia Inquirer* and was about to sit down and read it when he noticed three birds lying on the patio right outside the sunroom windows.

He went up to the windows and looked at them more closely. There were two gray jays and a crow, lying only a few inches away from each other. They didn't appear to have any superficial injuries, but there was no doubt that they were stone dead.

Their eyes were closed and the morning breeze was ruffling their feathers.

Nathan unlocked the sunroom door and stepped outside. It was then that he saw that the entire back yard was strewn with dead birds – at least half a dozen more jays, and a scattering of warblers, and another two crows. They looked as if they had simply fallen out of the sky. He felt distinctly unnerved, as if he had walked into one of those 1960s science-fiction movies.

He prodded one of the jays with a stick. It rolled over on to its back but neither of its wings appeared to be broken and it hadn't lost any of its tail feathers.

Nathan had heard of flocks of birds being brought down by lightning or by sudden downdrafts. But there had been no electric storms around West Airy last night, and although the wind had picked up since daybreak, and it was now quite blustery, the birds that he could see in the sky above him were soaring, not falling.

Maybe these birds had been poisoned, but he couldn't imagine how, or by what. Crows and jays and warblers didn't feed together. Jays were notorious for their boldness, and often walked into human habitats – houses or tents or trailers – looking for scraps. But if they were out in a field or a garden, crows would almost always chase them away; and warblers would never come anywhere near either of them.

He went back into the house to fetch his camera. He walked around the yard, taking twenty or thirty photographs of the dead birds, from every angle. Then he put on a pair of rubber household gloves, and picked up the bodies of a jay and a warbler and a crow, placing them carefully into a small cardboard box lined with crumpled-up newspaper.

He looked around. He couldn't help thinking of *The Black Book*, by Bishop Wincenty Kadłubek. '*The church floor was strewn with dozens of dead swallows that had been nesting in the rafters, and hundreds of dead flies.*'

Maybe Denver *had* heard something, creeping around the house last night. Maybe something was walking this world that didn't take any notice of locked doors, or alarms – something that could strike other creatures dead just by staring at them – like these jays and these crows and these warblers.

He gathered up the rest of the bodies, and dropped them

into the trash. He didn't want Grace to find them, if she came home before he did; and if they had been killed by poisoning, he didn't want any of the local cats to eat them, or take them back to their owners, as trophies.

Nathan arrived at the zoo shortly after ten fifteen a.m. The wind was still gusty, and the clouds were tumbling overhead like mongrels, chasing each other.

As he turned into the gates, he saw a silver private bus parked outside, and a group of fifteen or twenty people standing around talking. He could see Henry Burnside there, too, tall and patrician, with his white lion's-mane hair and his large nose and his heavy tortoiseshell spectacles, wearing a red-and-green plaid coat. Nathan had forgotten that today was the day that Dr Burnside was going to be hosting a presentation for the zoo's principal investors.

Dr Burnside was just about the last person in the world that he wanted to talk to right now, so he stopped, backed up, and drove around to the maintenance area where he had parked on his previous visit. This time, there was no sign of the mandrill-like maintenance man. He left his car close to the retaining wall, by the steps, right in front of the NO PARKING sign.

When he walked into his laboratory, carrying his cardboard box, he found that Richard and Keira were already at work. *Bat Out Of Hell* was playing on the sound system, while Richard was preparing microscope slides of the decomposed gryphon, and Keira was busily typing on her laptop.

'I'm updating all of our results,' Keira told him, before he had even had time to ask her.

He leaned over her shoulder and looked at the columns of figures that she had entered under *Embryonic Circulation: Second Stage*.

'We're not beaten yet, Keira,' he told her. 'We might have lost the skirmish, but the campaign goes on. And – hey – I like that perfume you're wearing.'

'Gucci Rush.' She smiled at him.

He laid the cardboard box on the workbench next to her. 'There's something you can do for me. There are three dead birds in here. I found them in my yard this morning, along with a whole lot more. I'd like to know why they died.'

Keira peered into the box, and said, 'Does this have anything to do with the Cee-Zee program?'

'I don't know. I'm not sure. Maybe. But if you could do it just as a favor to me.'

'Okay . . . anything's more exciting than blood-pressure statistics.'

'Thanks, Keira, I won't forget you for this, when I'm accepting my Nobel Prize.'

He went over to Richard. 'Richard – how's our late lamented gryphon coming along?'

'I should finish up the necropsy today, apart from the last of the bone-marrow tests.'

'*Today*? You're not going to rush it, are you? I want you to test for staphylococcus, too.'

Richard looked embarrassed. 'Dr Burnside came in to see us. He said I should wrap it up as soon as possible, and send the results over to Dr Bream. He said the Cee-Zee program was officially terminated.'

'I see. He's going to find you another project to work on?'

Richard was cultivating an angry red zit on the end of his nose, which Nathan found it hard not to look at.

'As a matter of fact I've been negotiating a research position with somebody else,' he said, without looking at Nathan directly.

'Really? Who? Do they pay better? I sure hope they pay better.'

'Yes. They do. They pay pretty good.'

'What kind of research is it? Nothing as cutting edge as this, I'll bet. Well, nothing as wacky.'

Richard gave him a disconnected shrug, but said nothing.

'Well . . . good luck to you, Richard,' said Nathan. 'You did some terrific work for me here. Maybe we didn't quite manage to finish what we started, but we made some amazing progress, didn't we? We really broke the mold.'

He looked around. 'Where's Tim, by the way?'

'Job interview,' said Keira. 'He'll be back first thing tomorrow, to finish up his notes.'

'Something zoological, I hope?'

'Kind of. The Wistar Institute. Research assistant for Dr Hui Hu.'

'Well, *he* didn't waste any time.' Nathan didn't want to

make any remarks about 'rats' and 'sinking ships', although he felt like it. On the other hand, he could hardly blame Richard and Tim for looking for new and better-paid employment. Laboratory assistants in almost every other animal research program earned more than they did – even the technicians who worked for Super-Dog Foods, in Leola. They used to joke about it: you get paid twice as much to feed 'em as you do to breed 'em.

He went into his office, took off his brown-leather Indiana Jones jacket and changed into his lab coat. On his desk, he found a long message from the zoo's human resources manager, Norman Berliner. 'Now that your cryptozoological project is being wound down, could you please supply the Zoo management with an up-to-date inventory of all unused chemicals, as well as a complete list of writing paper, envelopes, print cartridges and paperclips.' He rolled the message up between the palms of his hands and tossed it toward the wastebasket on the other side of the room, and missed. Norman Berliner could put *that* request where he didn't need Ray-Bans. And why were HR managers always called Norman?

However, there was also a note from Patti Laquelle, saying simply, 'Sorry to hear what happened, *muchacho*! Give me a call anytime and I'll take you to Fado's and buy you that very large Irish whiskey.'

He took the black stick fragment from his pocket and carried it through to the laboratory.

'What do you make of this?' he asked Richard.

Richard took it, and inspected it closely. 'It looks like a piece of horn, of some kind. Where did you get it?'

'Let's just say that I came across it by happenstance.'

Richard held the stick under a magnifying lens. 'There's some abrasion, on the tip. Natural wear and tear, by the look of it. I'd say that it's a broken-off tusk, or an antler. But I wouldn't like to guess what species of animal it came from.'

'Me neither. But I'm going to run some tests on it.'

He took the stick over to the other side of the laboratory. To start with, he took a small surgical saw out of his drawer and sawed the stick into inch-long sections, so that he could see if there was any difference in its chemical composition from its tip to the point where it had broken off, as there usually was with deer antlers.

By mid-afternoon, they had played all of *Bat Out Of Hell* and all of *Dead Ringer* and they were halfway through Santanas' *Abraxas*. Even Richard had to pause in his work to perform 'Samba Pa Ti' on his air guitar, his eyes squeezed tight shut and his teeth clenched together.

Nathan had tested the antler for dry matter such as collagen, ash, calcium, phosphorus and magnesium, as well as proteins and lipids. He had isolated uronic acid and sulfated glycosaminoglycan, along with chondroitin sulfate and keratan sulfate.

Chemically – as he had first suspected – the black stick was very similar to a deer antler. Nathan began to think that Grace was right, and that his 'basilisk' had been nothing more than a nightmare, after all. Maybe the stick had been exactly what Grace had first suggested: the broken-off tip from some moose antler that somebody had used as a walking-cane. Outside the laboratory window, the rain began to fall, lightly at first, then heavier and heavier, and he heard indigestive rumbles of thunder.

A little after three thirty p.m., Keira came over. She had untied her hair and let it fall loose.

'Professor? I've run preliminary tests on all three birds. None of them have suffered any physical injury that I can detect. Like, they didn't fly into a plate-glass window, or get hit by the blades of a wind turbine, or an airplane.'

'What about toxicology?'

'I haven't screened them for everything yet. But they haven't ingested Avitrol or any proprietary bird poison. They weren't gassed or asphyxiated and they didn't inhale any airborne pollutants over and above the average for Philadelphia County.'

'So what *did* kill them?'

Keira said, 'Almost certainly, they died from multiple-organ failure. Their hearts hemorrhaged, and then their lungs, and then their livers. Shortly afterward, their brains.'

'That sounds like shock.'

Keira nodded. 'The symptoms are absolutely typical.'

'So . . . what kind of shock? Any ideas?'

'Not so far. Like I say, they weren't physically injured and they weren't poisoned. I would say that something frightened them – so much so that they simply dropped down dead. It happens, especially to sensitive birds like cockatiels. You can handle one too much and it dies. You don't have a neighbor with a very scary cat, do you?'

'My neighbor has a cat, yes. But *scary*? That fat furball wouldn't scare a mosquito, let alone a whole bunch of birds.'

'I'll run some more tests, if you want to, but I'm ninety-nine per cent certain that's your cause of death. Subendocardial hemorrhage, induced by catastrophic nervous trauma.'

'Thanks, Keira. I appreciate it. You can go home now, if you like.'

'I'm not in a hurry, Professor. Besides, I didn't finish logging our statistics yet.'

'Don't bother. You can leave them. If Dr Bream wants a five-year profile of systolic blood pressures, he can work it out for himself. Listen – I'm real sorry about the way this turned out, this whole project. Do you have any idea what you're going to do now?'

'In the long term, no. I might take some time off and visit my sister in San Francisco.'

She peered at the screen of his spectrometer. 'What are you doing there? Can I help you?'

'I'm analyzing what I'm pretty sure is a fragment of some animal's antler.'

'An antler? Like a deer antler? You know that they use deer antlers in Chinese medicine? They grind them up and they're supposed to make men more virile.'

'And do they?'

'I don't know.' Keira blushed. 'I never had a boyfriend who tried it.'

'Well, if it *does* work, I guess it gives a whole new meaning to the word "horny".'

TEN

Hidden Message

A s the day went on, the sky grew darker and darker, and Nathan grew increasingly frustrated and disappointed. He had been hoping that the antler would prove to belong to some mythological creature – if not a basilisk, then a gargoyle, or a wyvern. At least it would have given him some ammunition to take back to Henry Burnside and make a last-ditch effort to rescue his Cee-Zee program.

Keira came over and gave him a hug. 'I'm going to go now, Professor. But thanks for everything. It's been wonderful.'

'Thanks,' he told her. 'If they ever give me funding again, you'll be the first person I come looking for.'

She smiled up at him, and he was surprised and touched to see that she had tears in her eyes. She sniffed and laughed and said, 'I'm just being sentimental. But it seems such a pity, doesn't it, after we've done so much hard work.'

Outside, lightning flickered, and the laboratory was shaken by another burst of thunder. At the same time, his CE machine suddenly blinked and whirred into life and printed out the first of his DNA results.

He tugged out the sheet of paper, and carried it across to the coffee machine. He refilled the machine with his right hand while he held the DNA results in his left. He wasn't expecting the printout to show him anything special. *Doh, a deer, a female deer.*

As he studied the DNA pairings, however, and as the coffee machine started to gurgle, he began to feel a shrinking sensation in his scalp. It was the same sensation that he had experienced when his gryphon had first begun to show stir inside its egg. His scalp was shrinking, his skin was shrinking. His whole life was shrinking, as if by comparison with what he had just discovered, it had less and less significance.

He left the coffee machine and went back to his bench. He printed out the DNA results a second time, to make absolutely sure that he wasn't making a mistake. But there was no doubt about it.

According to the test, this piece of bone may have been chemically close to a fallow deer antler, but its DNA showed that it had broken off a creature that was not only part mammal and part bird – like his gryphon – but part reptile, too. All three genetic codings, tangled together in one living being.

He stood up. Keira had left about ten minutes ago, but Richard was still here.

'Richard! Take a look at this!'

Richard swung around on his chair and pointed to the phone that he was holding to his ear. 'Won't keep you a moment, Professor!'

Nathan studied the DNA printout again. He was so over-whelmed by what he had found out that his hand was shaking. It was like suddenly understanding how God had created the world, and everything in it.

Richard snapped his cell shut and came across the laboratory.

'Professor? Did you find out what it is?'

'Yes,' he said, but then he stopped himself.

He suddenly found that he didn't want to share this discovery, not just yet. It was too overwhelming, and he hadn't had time to consider all of its implications. It was going to change lives, maybe millions of lives. It was going to change *his* life, for sure. He felt the same way he had on the day that Denver had been born: he had left it until early evening before calling his parents or Grace's family and telling them the good news. He had just wanted to keep it to himself, for a few hours.

Not only that, Richard was going, and he hadn't yet told him where. Nathan had no reason at all not to trust him, but if he was no longer working on a cryptozoological project, there was no reason why he needed to know.

He tried to sound disappointed and offhand. 'It's exactly what it looks like,' he said. 'A piece of fallow deer antler.'

'Oh. OK. I thought you were going to say it came from something really rare, like a muntjac. All the same . . . antler is pretty interesting stuff.'

'Sure. But it's not going to save the Cee-Zee program for us.'

Richard said, 'I guess not. It's a darned shame.' He took out a crumpled handkerchief and blew his nose. 'I'm just about finished now. I ran a second test for super-strep. But I still don't think that bacterial infection was the primary COD.'

'So what was?'

'I wish I could tell you. I'll give you all of the results that I've completed so far, but it's still hard to say why the poor little guy didn't make it. Maybe we need to re-examine its DNA. It has so much jabberwocky – much more than any other creature I've ever tested.'

Nathan said, 'OK. Thanks, anyhow. I'll take everything home tonight and go through it.' 'Jabberwocky' was what they called DNA codings that didn't appear to play any obvious part in developing a creature's growth – genetic junk mail – and all creatures had a certain amount of it. It was like creating a human being by specifying 'fingersballoon-searscakeslegstoespencils.' But 'jabberwocky' sometimes contained hidden messages that revealed exactly why a particular species always turned out the way it did.

Richard said, 'I really want to thank you for all of the help you've given me, Professor. Without you . . . without this project . . . I'd probably still be in Kutztown, analyzing pig semen for the Farm Bureau.'

'You still haven't told me where you're moving to.'

Richard looked embarrassed. 'I'm not one hundred per cent sure that the job's in the bag, that's why. They're supposed to be getting in touch with me today.'

'Well, good luck. And you *will* keep in contact, won't you? We're not finished with Cee-Zee yet. Not by a long way.'

As Nathan was hanging up his lab coat, George the janitor knocked at his office door.

'Leaving us, then, Professor?'

'News travels fast.'

'Well, they're going to rent this laboratory to some cat-worming company. I have to get it all spruced up by Monday morning.'

'I'm going to miss you, George.'

'Can't say the feeling's mutual, Professor. Maybe the next person to take over this office will make sure that their coffee cups are empty before they toss them in the trash.'

'Sorry, George. What else can I say?'

He left the laboratory and walked out of the building. The wind had dropped but it was still raining – that fine, persistent drizzle that can soak you right through in minutes. He took out his car keys but when he reached the place where he had parked his car, he discovered that it had gone.

He stood there for a few moments, breathing deeply. *That bastard. That mandrill-faced bastard. I'll bet he was watching me out of his window when I was first parking here.* Now the maintenance department was closed, and in darkness, and the zoo's administration office would be closed now, too, so he couldn't even find out the name of the tow-truck company.

He took out his cell and called All City Taxi. They could come to pick him up but not for forty minutes, because of the traffic. He was just about to call Star Taxi when his cell warbled and it was Grace.

'Do you want Mexican chicken for supper or chili?'

'Where are you?'

'I'm in Genuardi's, shopping. Where are you?'

He told her what had happened. He used four swear words: one for his car, one for the tow-truck driver, and two for the maintenance man.

'That's OK,' she soothed him. 'I can pick you up on the way home. I'm almost done.'

He went back to his office, opened up his battered brown briefcase, and took out Richard's necropsy results.

George came back in, carrying a mop and Nathan's empty trashcan.

'Can't get enough of the place, huh?'

'My car got towed. That gorilla in maintenance snitched on me.'

'Hey, ex-squeeze me, that person you're calling a gorilla, that's my cousin Teddy.'

'In that case I feel sorry for you, sharing your genes with a throwback like him.'

'He has his own. He doesn't have to share mine.'

Nathan stared at George narrowly, for any hint that he was pulling his leg. But George started mopping, and tunelessly whistling between his teeth, and Nathan decided not to take this conversation any further.

*　　*　　*

Grace took nearly a half-hour. When she came into the laboratory, her hair was bedraggled and she looked tired, with pale
purple shadows under her eyes.

'The traffic!' she said. 'What a nightmare.'

'I could have called for a taxi.'

'No, never mind. I was practically passing here anyhow.'

They left the building. As they went down the front steps,
Grace looked around and said, 'Oh . . . they've gone. I was
going to go over and say hello.'

'Who's gone?'

'Richard, and Doctor Zauber.'

'Richard Scryman?'

'That's right. They were sitting in Doctor Zauber's car, right
over there. I knew it was Doctor Zauber because of his regis-
tration plate, DOCZ.'

They climbed into Grace's SUV. Nathan said, 'Did you
know that they knew each other?'

Grace shook her head. 'I had no idea. You wouldn't have
thought they had much in common, would you?'

They drove out of the zoo and headed north-east. The
expressway was a river of red stop lights, and although West
Girard Avenue was clogged up, too, at least the traffic appeared
to be inching its way forward. It was raining too hard to set the
windshield wipers to interval-wipe, and not hard enough to prevent
the wiper blades from making an annoying rubbery squeak.

Nathan said, 'Richard told me this morning that he'd found
himself another job. Well, he wasn't cast-iron certain that he'd
got it, but he seemed to be confident enough. And he said
that the pay was pretty good. Maybe he's going to be working
for Doctor Zauber.'

'But what would he *do*? He's a biologist, not a care worker.'

Nathan was silent for a while, as they waited to turn on to
North Thirty-Third. Then he said, 'What's he like, this Doctor
Zauber? Do you know anything about his background?'

Grace shrugged. 'He's German. Well – he has this very
strong German accent, anyhow. I don't know how long he's
been running the Murdstone. Maybe three years, four. So long
as I can remember, anyhow.'

'But think about it: Doctor Zauber knows Richard, and
Richard knows as much about the Cee-Zee project as I do,
and there's a basilisk roaming around the Murdstone.'

'Come on, Nate. You *suspect* that there's a basilisk roaming around the Murdstone. You don't know for sure.'

Nathan reached into his inside pocket and took out a clear cellophane envelope with the sawn-up pieces of antler in it. 'Oh, I'm sure, sweetheart. And this is the evidence.'

Grace glanced over at him. 'You analyzed it?'

'I did, and it's a piece of horn, very similar to a deer's antler. But I tested its DNA and what do you know? It has *three* types of DNA. Mammal, bird and reptile, combined.'

'So what kind of a creature is that? A flying deer, with frogs' legs?'

Nathan smiled – amused, but triumphant, too. 'There is only one living animal which combines all three types of DNA, and that's the duck-billed platypus. The platypus has fur, and it lays eggs, and the male platypus has venom, too, like a snake. Its genetic make-up goes way back more than one hundred and seventy million years, to a time when almost every creature on earth was some variety of reptile.'

'But platypuses don't have horns, do they? Or is it platypi?'

'No, they don't. And as far as we know, there was only ever one creature which possessed all three types of DNA, as well as horns, and that was the basilisk.'

Grace edged in front of a truck, and the van driver blasted his horn at her, and gave her the finger. In return, Grace gave him the sweetest of smiles.

'Somebody's done it, Grace,' said Nathan. 'Somebody's created a Cee-Zee hybrid, and it's survived.'

'And you're thinking—'

'Of course I am. It must be Doctor Zauber. Who else could it be?'

'But Doctor Zauber isn't a biologist.'

'How do you know? You don't know anything about him, except that he runs the Murdstone Rest Home.'

'I can't get my head around this.'

'There's no other explanation – well, none that I can think of. Maybe he's been using the rest home as a front for a Cee-Zee project. You need a license for this kind of research, unless nobody knows that you're doing it.'

'You really believe that?'

'It fits the evidence, doesn't it? Maybe the Murdstone is *more* than a front. Maybe that's where Doctor Zauber gets his

funding. There's a shitload of money in rest homes, especially
from old folks who go to meet their Maker before their time,
like Doris Bellman. Legacies, unclaimed investments, jewelry,
real estate, you name it.'

'It just seems incredible, the whole thing.'

'I know, but the first biologist who creates a viable mythical creature, he's going to be rich and famous. He's going to
go down in history.'

Grace drove in silence for a while. Then she said, 'You
really think that Richard has been feeding Doctor Zauber with
all of your results?'

'I don't know. I sure hope not. But it wouldn't be the first
time that a lab tech has sold his soul, would it? He bought
himself a new car a couple of months ago, do you remember
me telling you? A Saturn Sky. It wasn't brand new, but I
always wondered how he managed to afford it, on what I've
been paying him.'

'Nate – you can't be certain about this. You don't want to
start making accusations unless you're sure.'

'Can you think of any other reason why Richard should
have been talking to Doctor Zauber? Why should Doctor
Zauber have been there at the zoo at all? It was only by sheer
chance that my car was towed and you came around to pick
me up. Richard must have thought that I had left already. But
even if I had seen him together with Doctor Zauber, I wouldn't
have known who Doctor Zauber was, would I?'

Grace was silent for a while, thinking. Then she said, 'I
have to admit that it all sounds horribly convincing. What do
you think we ought to do now?'

'Go back to the Murdstone. Find the basilisk. Confront
Doctor Zauber with the living evidence that he's stolen my
research.'

'Then what?'

'I don't know. Call the cops, I suppose. Have him charged
with whatever crime it is to lift somebody else's lab results.
Zoological espionage, I don't know.'

The traffic began to ease and ten minutes later they were
turning into their own driveway. Grace switched off the engine
but she didn't immediately get out of the truck.

'What?' Nathan asked her.

'I don't know. I have a very bad feeling about this, that's

all. I think we ought to talk to the police first, instead of trying to find the basilisk ourselves. If there *is* no basilisk, we'll look like a couple of idiots. If there *is* – and it can really do what you say it can do – kill you just by looking at you – well, it could kill us just by looking at us.'

Nathan took hold of her hand. 'Grace – I have to see it for myself.'

'OK, then,' she said, although she didn't look happy. 'But don't blame me if Denver ends up as an orphan.'

'By the way—' Nathan began. He was going to tell her about the dead birds that he had found in the yard.

'Yes?' she asked him.

'Nothing. I was wondering what you'd decided to make for dinner, that's all.'

'Do you want to go back to the Murdstone tonight?'

'The sooner the better.'

'In that case, order yourself a pizza. I'm going to take a shower, and change, and pour myself a glass of wine. I'm going to be way too tense to think about chopping up capsicums.'

They reached the Murdstone almost dead on midnight. The skies had cleared and the moon was high and disconcertingly bright, so that the street looked like a stage set. They had to keep very close to the hedge as they made their way to the rear of the buildings, because there was scarcely any shadow.

The blind that covered the staffroom window was drawn down only to halfway. Inside, they could see a Korean carer watching TV and sewing, while a white orderly with a shaved head was sprawled on the couch with a large pack of cheese Doritos in his lap.

Nathan ducked down below the level of the window ledge and crouched his way along to the back door. Grace followed him. She was wearing a black knitted hat to cover her shiny light-brown hair, a black rollneck sweater and tight black jeans. Nathan had said that she looked more like a James Bond girl than a family doctor. She said that *he* looked like Brad Pitt, in *Fight Club*, only scruffier.

'This time, we'll start off upstairs,' Nathan whispered.

'OK. The upstairs corridors are like an H. Two long ones, joined by a short one in the middle. But at the top of the H, there's also an extension going off to the right – a single long corridor leading to the linen stores and the sanitarium, and there are some other rooms, too, but I don't know what's in them. Supplies, I expect.'

Nathan took hold of the door handle, and gently squeezed it downward. 'Remember what I told you . . . if you see something big and black, with shining eyes, don't look at it, whatever you do. Turn your face away, hold up your mirror toward it, and get the hell out of there, *prontissimo*.'

'What if it catches me?'

'I won't let it catch you.'

'But what if it does?'

'I won't let it. But keep your eyes tight shut.'

He opened the door and they stepped inside. They listened for a moment, and then they crept past the strap-hanging monks. *Wheel of Fortune* was playing on the television inside the staffroom, very loudly. The back door clicked behind them, and at the same time the orderly suddenly shouted out, 'Make it a habit! That's the answer! Make it a habit!'

They froze for a moment, pressing themselves close to the coats, but the orderly didn't shout out anything else. Even if he had heard the door clicking, he was obviously too comfortable on his couch to get up and investigate.

Once they had passed the staffroom, they switched on their flashlights. Grace led the way along the corridor toward the stairs. There was a strong smell of boiled fish in the building, which must have lingered since suppertime.

They reached the foot of the staircase. Halfway up the first flight of stairs there was a tall leaded window, so the hallway was filled with moonlight. They both stopped, and listened. Somewhere on the second floor, a woman was weeping: not loudly, but hopelessly. The weeping of somebody who knows that life is never going to get any better.

'You're still sure you want to do this?' Grace whispered.

Nathan nodded. 'I have to, sweetheart. This means everything. This is the Holy Grail, as far as I'm concerned.'

'All right, then. But God knows what I'm going to say if we get caught.'

'Doctor Mark Sloan never gets into trouble, when *he* investigates crimes.'

'Doctor Mark Sloan from *Diagnosis Murder*? Dick Van Dyke? You're crazy. You know that?'

Nathan mounted the stairs, with Grace close behind him. The moonlight was so bright that they didn't need their flashlights, and Nathan switched his off. He had almost reached the second-floor landing when he heard the deep creaking of floorboards, followed by a sharp scraping noise.

He stopped, with only two stairs left to climb.

'Did you hear that?'

Grace nodded. Her face in the moonlight looked very white, as if she were a ghost of herself.

Nathan hesitated. For nearly half a minute, all he could hear was the hissing of water in the Murdstone's plumbing. Presumably somebody had flushed a toilet somewhere, or run a bath, and the cold-water tank was filling up. The weeping woman was silent now, although some old man had started to cough.

'Come on,' said Nathan. He stepped up on to the landing and switched his flashlight back on, pointing it along the corridor. At the very far end a door opened, and a figure appeared. Grace gasped, but it was only an elderly resident, with white hair and red-rimmed eyes and a red plaid dressing gown. The old man raised his hand to shield his eyes from the flashlight, and then he disappeared back into his bedroom, closing the door behind him.

Grace said, *phewf*! in relief. 'For one moment there—'

Nathan took hold of her hand. 'Let's take a look down here first. If Zauber has been doing any lab work, my guess is that he'll have used the sanitarium, and the stock rooms.'

'As long as we don't get any more surprises like that. I don't think my heart will take it.'

They walked along the corridor as soft-footedly as they could, until they reached the extension. Nathan took a quick peek around the corner, but the extension corridor was deserted, too. All he could see was the moonlight, shining in squares through the windows.

The first door they came to was marked *Cleaning Supplies*. Nathan tried the handle but it was locked. He tried the next door, which was unmarked, but that was locked, too. The third door was labeled *Laundry*, and he was able to open that, but there was no laundry inside, only an old-fashioned floor polisher and a standard lamp with a scorched cardboard shade.

At the end of the corridor, on the right-hand side, they found gray-painted double doors with wired-glass windows in them. The doors were locked, and the handles were chained and padlocked together. The room was in total darkness, so Nathan shone his flashlight through one of the windows. It had obviously been designed as a sanitarium, but there was only one bed in it, without any sheets or blankets, and the only hospital paraphernalia was a single drip stand and a tipped-over zimmer frame.

'Well, something must happen in here that Doctor Zauber doesn't want anybody to know about. Otherwise, why chain the doors like this? There's nothing to steal, is there? And look at the windows.'

Every window in the sanitarium had a black blind over it, like a photographer's darkroom, and every blind had been taped to the window frames with black gaffer tape.

Nathan said, 'Where would you keep a creature during the day if that creature couldn't tolerate daylight?'

Grace stood on tiptoe and peered into the sanitarium, too. 'My God,' she said. 'It could really be real, couldn't it? And look. I'll bet that's where it sleeps.'

Nathan angled his flashlight toward the corner of the room. There were two large mattresses lying side by side on the floor. They were sagging and frayed and heavily stained with something brown.

'You're right,' said Nathan. He turned around and looked back along the corridor. 'The problem is, where is it now?'

'You did bring the gun, didn't you?'

Nathan reached behind him and pulled the automatic out of his belt. 'Gun. And mirror.'

'I don't care about the mirror so long as you have the gun.'

'I don't want to *kill* it, Grace. That would defeat the whole object.'

'So what do we do now?'

'We go look for it, of course. It must be reasonably manageable, otherwise Zauber wouldn't be able to keep it locked up in the sanatarium, would he?' He paused. 'I was going to train my gryphon, if it had lived. I was even thinking of hiring a professional falconer.'

'Maybe we should call it a night,' said Grace. 'Now that we've found some evidence that your basilisk really exists – isn't that enough?'

'Grace, if it exists, I have to see it for myself.'

As they stood there, the corridor began rapidly to darken. A large cloud was moving across the moon, like a theater curtain, and within less than a minute, the whole extension was plunged into blackness.

Grace said, 'Come on, Nate. We can call the police. We can call the Department of Public Welfare. They'll take care of it.'

'Grace—'

'I'm frightened, Nate. I don't mind admitting it.'

'OK. Maybe you're right. Maybe this *was* a crazy idea.'

Nathan felt frustrated, but he had to admit to himself that he was relieved, too. It reminded him of the time that he had tried to jump off the Kidd's Mills bridge into the Shenango River to qualify for membership of a local gang. He had wanted to join that gang more than anything else in his whole life, but his uncle had come driving past before he could jump, and had ordered him down. He had protested loudly, and sulked, but secretly he had been deeply thankful. The Shenango was shallow, with a rocky bottom, and very cold.

He put his arm around Grace's shoulders and steered her back along the corridor. But before they could reach the corner where the extension corridor joined the main corridor, they heard the same scraping noise they had heard before. Then a pause. Then another scraping noise, and a sound like somebody dragging a very heavy sack along the ground.

Nathan took out his gun again, and cocked it. He took his shaving mirror out of his pocket, and held that up, too.

'Nate?' said Grace, and this time she sounded truly frightened.

'It's OK. It's OK. Let's just take this careful.'

He edged his way toward the corner, with the automatic in his right hand and the mirror in his left. Now the scraping and the scratching and the dragging noises grew louder still, and they could hear *breathing*, too: thick, clogged-up breathing. It sounded as if some huge locomotive were approaching them.

'Holy Mother of God,' said Grace.

Nathan took a deep breath. He felt terrified. He felt elated. Here, at last, he was going to come face to face with a living myth. A creature that hadn't existed since medieval days.

He stepped around the corner, and there it was, exactly as he had seen it in his nightmare. Huge and bulky and hunched, with a black bony coronet that scraped against the ceiling. It was all wrapped up in layer after layer of tattered black sacking, although he could see its claws and its scaly black feet, with a long sharp spur behind each heel. Its head was covered with sacking, too, so that its eyes appeared only dimly, as they had in his nightmare.

The creature saw him, or sensed him, or *smelled* him, because it uttered a furious and almost deafening hiss, like a bath full of scalded snakes. Its odor was overwhelming: an eye-watering mustiness as strong as cats' urine.

Grace screamed, '*Nate!*' and it was the first time that he had ever heard her scream in absolute terror. He pointed his automatic between the creature's eyes and thought to himself: *shoot it. Shoot it now, because it's going to tear you to pieces and then it's going to go after Grace.*

But a commanding voice called out, 'Doctor Underhill! Sir! You don't want to do that!'

ELEVEN

The Black Ultimatum

A figure stepped out in front of the creature and Grace immediately shone her flashlight across his face. It was a large-headed man, wearing a black silk shirt, buttoned up to the neck, and black pants. His steel-gray hair was slicked straight back from his forehead, and his eyes were concealed behind reflective spectacles with steel-gray lenses. He was carrying a riding crop.

'Doctor Zauber!' said Grace.

'Well, of course,' said Doctor Zauber, in his precise German accent. 'Who else would you expect?

He raised his hand toward Nathan and said, 'Please . . .

the gun. I promise you that the basilisk will not harm you so long as it is under my control.'

Close behind him, the basilisk shuffled and swayed, and its breathing sounded more and more labored.

'So you did it,' said Nathan. 'You actually bred one, and it survived.'

'Yes! But only thanks to you, Professor Underhill! I freely acknowledge my debt to you, and your research team. Without your admirable work, the basilisk could never have come back to life.'

He turned around, and looked at the basilisk. 'Mind you,' he said, 'it is far from a perfect creation. You can hear for yourself that it suffers from respiratory problems, and it has some serious malformation of its skeletal structure. It has survived, yes, but I don't know for how much longer. Which is why I have appealed to you for help.'

'What the hell are you talking about?' Nathan demanded. 'You had Richard Scryman steal all of my research, and now you want to pick my brains some more?'

'Please, the gun,' Doctor Zauber repeated. 'The basilisk is very sensitive to hostile intentions.'

'You said that you had it under control,' said Grace.

'Of course. But only in the same way perhaps that a dog handler has a pit bull terrier under control. If anybody should show aggression to its master, the pit bull will attack, *nicht wahr*? and there is nothing that anybody can do to hold it back.'

Reluctantly, Nathan pushed the SK back into his belt. Then he took out his flashlight and shone it on to the ragged black bulk of the basilisk, lighting up its huge misshapen head and its coronet of jagged horns. In response, the basilisk's eyes glowed a little brighter, as if it resented Nathan examining it so intently.

Doctor Zauber said, 'You and I have been working for nearly three years in co-operation with each other, Professor Underhill. I realize that it was a partnership of which you were totally unaware, but I did not think that you would willingly share your research with me.'

'Well, you got that right. How much did you pay him? Richard Scryman – for stealing my notes?'

'Not so much. Richard was not so interested in the money,

even though he told me that you paid him only a pittance. Just as I did, he wanted more than anything else to see a mythical creature come to life, and he realized very early on that neither of us could do it alone.'

Nathan was mystified, and incredulous, and angry, all at the same time. 'I bred a gryphon, goddammit, from embryonic cells and DNA, and it didn't take any help from you.'

'Of course you did,' said Doctor Zauber. 'And what you did was *unglaublich*. Unbelievable. But your gryphon died inside its shell, and every other gryphon you attempted to breed would have died inside its shell, too. You were missing the one vital ingredient for success that only I possess.'

'Oh, yes? And what is that, exactly?'

The basilisk suddenly lurched toward him, and its breathing changed to a high-pitched whine. Nathan reached for the butt of his automatic again, but Doctor Zauber clapped his hands together loudly and snapped, '*Halt Denk*! *An die Strafe*!'

The basilisk uttered an extraordinary noise in the back of its throat, as if it were being strangled. Doctor Zauber said, 'It is not a patient creature, the basilisk, as you can see for yourselves. Sometimes it has to be reminded where it came from – who made it, and who can help it to survive.'

'OK,' said Nathan, impatiently. 'But what is this magic ingredient that you have and I don't? And if you were so keen to co-operate with me, why didn't you approach me before? We could have worked together, couldn't we? Maybe my gryphon wouldn't have died and the Zoo wouldn't have axed my research program.'

Doctor Zauber shook his head. 'If I had approached you at any time, Professor Underhill, you would not have agreed to work with me. So there was no other way for me to recreate a mythical creature than to borrow your research and combine it with mine, without your knowledge.

'Now that your program has been curtailed, however, what could I do to carry on my own research except come to you direct, and ask if you would be prepared to assist me? Together, for instance, we could breed another basilisk, much healthier and stronger than this poor specimen. We could breed your gryphon, too, and wyverns, and salamanders, and maybe even a bennu bird.

'We could open our own clinic in Switzerland, and people would come from all over the world to be cured of incurable illnesses. Have you seen what Doctor Geeta Shroff is doing in India, with embryonic stem cells? She is even curing quadruple paraplegia, like that of Christopher Reeve, after serious sporting accidents.

'We would be living saints, Professor Underhill. We would change the face of medicine for ever, you and I. And of course we would be very, very rich.'

'So what is the magic ingredient?' Grace challenged him. 'And why don't you think that Nathan would have agreed to work with you before?'

Doctor Zauber said, with a humorless smile, 'Why did you come here yesterday night? And why did you come here tonight?'

'We came here because Grace told me about Doris Bellman dying,' Nathan retorted. 'And her cockatoo dying, too. And her plants. And she told me that one of your residents had seen a big black creature with horns. We came here because I had two nightmares, about the same kind of creature.'

'But you were not so sure, were you? You didn't call the police. Well, maybe you *were* sure, and you thought: there could be a basilisk, at the Murdstone Rest Home, there could really be a real living basilisk, and whatever the risk, I must see it for myself?'

'OK,' said Nathan defensively. 'But that first night I found a broken-off piece of horn in Doris Bellman's room, and took it back to the lab and analyzed it, and then I knew for sure. *Basilisk.* The only creature in millions of years to have all three varieties of DNA.'

Doctor Zauber nodded, as in approval. Then he said, 'You took quite a risk, *ja,* trespassing on my property? And to bring your wife, too, who is an MD, with a professional reputation to maintain? She could be struck off for such nefarious activities.'

'You *knew* that we were here last night?' Grace asked him.

'Of course. You think I run a residential home for thirty-eight seniors without knowing *everything* that happens here, twenty-four hours of every day?'

He paused. This was obviously a rhetorical question; but for some reason it sounded as if he was expecting Nathan to answer.

Nathan didn't respond; and after a while Doctor Zauber said, 'Last night, regrettably, you arrived too late to see the basilisk. It was almost daylight, and as you are aware the basilisk must hide in complete darkness during the day. But . . . everything was not lost. You found the piece of horn that I left for you, and that was obviously good enough to convince you that the basilisk was really here. Not all of my little plans work out, you know, but this one did.'

'So you *wanted* us to come here?'

'*Natürlich*. I wanted to meet you, and talk to you, and show you the basilisk. I wanted to ask you if you would consider working with me, now that your own project has been canceled.'

'Why the hell didn't you just phone me? Or send me a message through Richard? That would have been a damn sight easier, wouldn't it?'

'*Easier*, Professor, yes. But I am a careful man who protects his interests. There are certain aspects involved in the breeding of mythical creatures which cross over the boundaries of medical ethics. That is why I never believed that you would agree to work with me.'

'So what are you trying to tell me? That you're doing something illegal?'

'Not entirely. But I did take the precaution of making sure that you came to the Murdstone as a trespasser. Or – who knows? – maybe you are something more than a trespasser? Maybe you came here intent on theft? There are so many defenseless seniors here, with some very valuable items of jewelry, not to mention paintings, and books, and china figurines, as your wife would have told you. And you – you have just lost your job.'

'Oh . . . you really think that I'd break into a rest home to steal old ladies' necklaces? Give me a break.'

'Desperate people have done worse. And for me, the fact that you brought your wife with you is of course a bonus. What would they say at the Chestnut Hill medical practice, if she were to be arrested on suspicion of burglary? All I have to do now is call the police.'

Nathan said, 'You can't be serious. You can't threaten us like that.'

'Of course not. I am only making a joke, of sorts. But you

know that every joke has a tragic side to it; just as every dream can easily turn into a nightmare. Like *your* nightmares, Professor.'

'What?'

'Where do you think they came from, your nightmares? That basilisk, that reared up from the end of your bed? That face on your bedroom ceiling?'

'*What*? How do you know about that?'

Doctor Zauber stepped closer. He took hold of Nathan's wrist and twisted it upward so that his flashlight was shining directly into his face. Then he took off his reflective eyeglasses, and rolled up his eyes so that only the whites were showing.

Nathan tugged his hand away. It was Doctor Zauber's face that he had seen on the ceiling. And now he thought about it, it was Doctor Zauber's voice that he had heard, taunting him.

As I say, my friend, you are the expert in the difference between dreams and reality.

'How did you do that? I *saw* you! You were there, on the ceiling! You talked to me! And the basilisk, that was there, too! It almost froze me to death!'

Doctor Zauber made a soft clicking noise with his tongue, as if he were calling a horse, and the basilisk dragged itself a few feet nearer. Grace took three or four steps back. The musty smell was overwhelming.

'I have the ability,' said Doctor Zauber. 'I have always had the ability, all my life. It is something one is born with. Transvection, that is what they call it in English. Psychic transference. But, I had no intention of hurting you, Professor. I wanted to hook you, that was all. Like a fish! To arouse your curiosity and reel you in! And look! You're here!'

He laid his hand on the basilisk's hunched-up back. 'So many creatures used to exist in medieval times, in the days of magic. Dragons! Gargoyles! But I never thought that I would be able to bring any of them back to life. I dreamed about it, of course, but in spite of my natural abilities it needed much more than wishful thinking, or even the rituals of re-incarnation that were handed down from one great necromancer to another. The creatures were extinct. They were dead, they were gone. They had fallen from the skies and fossilized into stones. And who can get blood from a stone?'

He replaced his eyeglasses and looked at Nathan ruefully. 'It needed *science*, Professor. It needed a man like you.'

Nathan was growing increasingly edgy. The basilisk kept shuffling closer and its eyes began to shine brighter, even through three or four layers of blackened sacking.

'OK,' he said, 'it needed a man like me. But what kind of a man are *you*? Are you some kind of psychic or something? Some kind of conjuror?'

'You will find out, Professor, if you really want to. But if we are to work together, I expect from you equal respect for my abilities. Maybe I am not a scientist as you would recognize it, but what I am able to do is just as powerful. Without my contribution, your project will never come to anything. Ever.'

'Listen, Doctor, I don't even know what your abilities are, apart from giving me nightmares, and appearing on my bedroom ceiling like some goddamn Mardi Gras mask.'

Doctor Zauber shook his head. 'When I first came to Philadelphia, I knew nothing about you, or what you were doing. I found out about your cryptozoology project only three years ago, when your wife came to visit one of our residents and we started to chat together. I pretended to your wife that I was politely interested, but the truth was that I was thunderstruck. Suddenly I saw a way of making these mythical creatures come back to life. I felt that the clouds had parted and God Himself had appeared to me, in all His glory.'

Nathan and Grace looked quickly at each other but neither of them said anything. They both sensed that Doctor Zauber was right on the verge of telling them what Nathan had been missing, and why his gryphon had died. At the same time, however, Nathan could see that the basilisk's eyes were shining brighter and brighter, so that pencil-thin shafts of light began to play across the corridor.

'Listen,' said Nathan, 'I'm getting real uncomfortable with this. Maybe we should talk about this tomorrow, without the basilisk looming over us.'

'The basilisk senses that I need an answer,' said Doctor Zauber. 'It feels its own mortality, too.'

'So tell me. Where have I been going wrong? What can you and I do together than I can't do by myself?'

'Life-energy,' said Doctor Zauber. 'All mythical creatures feed on life-energy. They are *mythical*, that is what you have to understand. They are legends, existing halfway between the

real and the unreal. Stories made flesh. They find no nour-
ishment in dead meat, or carrion, or grain. They subsist on
the souls of the people who believe in them, and any other
kind of life that they can.'

'They feed on *souls*?' said Grace. 'What exactly does that
mean?'

'Exactly that. Take Doris Bellman. Physically, she was close
to the end of her natural life, but her soul was just as vibrant
as it was when she was a young girl.'

'So you let the basilisk take it from her? Is that it?'

'The basilisk needed sustenance, or else it would have died;
and if the basilisk had died, all of its resident stem cells would
have died with it. As misshapen as it is, this one creature can
save thousands of people who suffer from serious degenera-
tive illnesses. Multiple sclerosis, cerebral palsy. Don't you
think that the soul of one elderly woman is worth that?'

Grace said, 'For God's sake . . . you can't kill people for
the sake of medical research. That's what the Nazis did, and
the Japanese. Some people think you shouldn't even sacrifice
animals.'

'Anyhow,' said Nathan, 'how can you physically do it? How
is it possible to take someone's soul?'

The basilisk had started slavering and whining, and he
couldn't stop himself from glancing at it with increasing
unease. Its eyes were shining almost as brightly as car headlights, and if they hadn't been covered in layers of sacking,
they would have been dazzling. As a precaution, Nathan
reached for the mirror that was hanging around his neck, and
held it ready in his left hand.

Doctor Zauber said, 'If you agree to come here and work
with me, Professor, in a spirit of true co-operation, then I can
demonstrate it to you. It is not easy to explain it in words. It
involves procedures which date right back to the Middle Ages,
to the times of the great shamans – especially the *táltos* of
Hungary.'

'The *táltos*? Who the hell were they?'

'They were like guides to the spirit world. People who could
find the souls of the living when they inadvertently strayed
into the world of the dead, and the souls of the dead when
they inadvertently strayed into the world of the living.'

'This is insane,' said Nathan. 'Even if I believed you, I couldn't agree to take anybody's soul, no matter how many other people were going to be cured.'

'How can you possibly not believe me? Here in front of you is the basilisk – the living, breathing evidence that everything I am telling you is true. And you were equally instrumental in its creation. Without you, without your research, this basilisk could never have come to be.'

He briskly clapped his hands and shouted out, 'Bravo, Professor! Your gryphon died, but your basilisk still lives!'

Nathan dragged out his gun again. 'This is over, Doctor Zauber. If this is the only way that the Cee-Zee program can work, then I don't want to have anything more to do with it.'

Doctor Zauber warned, 'Please, Professor. Put the gun away. It really isn't necessary.'

Nathan stepped sideways, raising his gun so that it was pointing directly at the basilisk's head. He put his arm around Grace's shoulders, and pulled her in close to him.

'What we're doing now, Doctor Zauber, we're leaving.'

'Oh, yes? And after you have left, what are you going to do then?'

'You'll find out.'

Doctor Zauber took another step closer, so that the SK was leveled at his heart. 'You won't leave here, Professor. Not without agreeing to help me. You can't.'

'I can, and I will.'

'This creature behind me, it's your whole life's work, and mine. This is everything you studied for, worked for, argued for. This basilisk is *you*, Professor. How can you possibly leave? How can you possibly walk away? *Es ist total unmöglich.*'

'Oh, and what will you do, if we *do* walk away? Call for the cops, have us arrested?'

'Maybe. Maybe something much more simple than that, something more terrible. Maybe the creation could devour its creator.'

'Oh, yes? And where would that leave you? With one deformed basilisk, and no idea of what to do next?'

'*So können Sie nicht mit mir sprechen! Ohne mich würde es kein Geschöpf geben! Ohne mich würden Sie noch Jahre brauchen, um überhaupt anfangen zu können, geschweige denn Fertig zu werden!*'

Doctor Zauber was shaking with anger. 'Without me,' he

translated, 'you will be nothing at all. So the choice is yours. Fame, and wealth, and a place in biological history. Or obscurity.'

'Come on, Nate,' said Grace. 'We're going.'

'No!' shouted Doctor Zauber. He stalked forward, and pushed Grace to one side.

Nathan pushed him back, so hard that he collided with the wall, and almost fell over.

'Didn't you hear what she said? We're going!'

'You cannot! You cannot! You have to work with me!'

Nathan pushed him again, harder this time. 'Can't you get it through your head, Doctor Zauber? The answer is no, never!'

'You want never? You are asking for *never*?' Doctor Zauber raised his riding crop and jabbed it furiously into the layers of sacking that covered the basilisk's head. The basilisk hissed and snarled, and swung its head around and around, so that the sacking fell down to its hunched-up shoulders. Instantly, the light from its eyes flooded the corridor, so that Nathan could see nothing at all, but blinding whiteness, as if he were staring straight into an arc lamp.

His first thought was: *Grace, she mustn't look at it*. He held up the mirror in front of his face to protect his own eyes, and tilted himself sideways, grabbing hold of Grace with his left arm and pulling her into him, so that her face would be shielded by his chest.

Then he reached back behind him and fired three shots toward the light. The automatic kicked much more violently than he had thought it would: it was like somebody hitting his hand with a hammer. But he must have struck the basilisk at least once, because he heard a throaty cry and almost immediately the light from its eyes began to dim.

'What have you done?' he heard Doctor Zauber screaming at him. 'What have you done? Are you some kind of madman? *Sind Sie verrückt?*'

But he wasn't interested in Doctor Zauber. All he cared about was Grace. She had collapsed in his arms and was dangling like a puppet.

'Grace!' he shouted at her. 'Grace!'

'The creature is hurt! You have hurt it!' said Doctor Zauber. In the criss-crossing beams of their flashlights, Nathan saw him kneeling on the floor, rummaging wildly through the black sacking wrappings. On the wall behind the basilisk, there was a slanting spray of dark brown blood, which ended in a question mark.

'Grace,' he urged her. 'Grace, baby, come on, sweetheart.' He shone his flashlight in her face and saw that it was colorless. Her greeny-gray eyes were wide open but they were focused on nothing at all.

He turned to Doctor Zauber. 'You've killed her!' he screamed. 'You've killed her! You and your fucking monster! You've killed her!'

Doctor Zauber stood up. Both of his hands were smothered in blood. 'Whose monster?' he shouted back. 'Whose monster? *Our* monster, Professor – yours and mine!'

Nathan didn't have time to argue. He lifted up Grace in his arms and elbowed past Doctor Zauber and back along the corridor. Doctor Zauber called, 'You have to come back! You have to come back! The basilisk is badly hurt!' But Nathan continued to walk along the corridor as fast as he could, his knees slightly bent, Grace's arm swinging against his thigh.

'Come on, Grace, you're going to make it, sweetheart. You're not going to die. Nobody's going to take your soul, not tonight.'

As he tilted his way down the stairs he met the shaven-headed orderly and the Korean carer, both on their way up.

'Call nine-one-one!' he shouted at them.

'Hey, what's happened?' blinked the orderly. 'We heard shots! Who the hell are you, dude, and what are *you* doing here? And who's *that*?'

'Call nine-one-one!' Nathan repeated.

'But—'

'*Call nine-one-one*!'

The orderly dug into his overall, but came up empty. 'My cell – left it in the office.'

'Then use mine . . . it's in my left-hand pocket. Hurry, for Christ's sake!'

The orderly came up the stairs toward him, but as he did so, Doctor Zauber must have appeared on the landing behind Nathan, because the orderly stopped, and took one step down again.

'No, no,' said Doctor Zauber. 'By all means call nine-one-one. But ask for the police. These two people are trespassers. Thieves.'

Nathan turned around. Doctor Zauber was looking down at him in fury, his brow furrowed, his eyes glittering black – as if he wished that he, too, could take people's souls just by staring at them.

There was only one thing that Nathan could do. He pushed past the orderly and the Korean carer, and clattered down the rest of the stairs as fast as he could. He almost fell over, but he managed to balance himself against the banisters, and the wall at the bottom of the stairs, and then he hefted up Grace's lifeless body so that he was holding her higher, and more securely. Thank God she was so light.

He made his way along the corridor, panting. As he turned the corner, 'Michael Dukakis' suddenly appeared in one of the doorways, his hair sticking up wildly, like an apparition on a ghost-train ride.

'What's going on?' he demanded. 'Has the car arrived yet? We're going to be late.'

Nathan ignored him and kept on going. When he reached the back door, he managed to force the handle down with his knee, and open it. He carried Grace around the side of the building, although he was stumbling now, and his heart was thumping. Before he crossed the street, he turned his head around to see if anybody was following him, but nobody was.

He held Grace up against him while he reached into his pocket for his car keys.

'Grace?' he urged her. 'Grace? Can you hear me? I'm going to take you to the ER. Hang on, sweetheart, you're going to be OK.'

He opened up the SUV and lifted Grace on to the back seat. She was completely floppy, all arms and legs, as if she had been drugged, but her eyes were still wide open, and unblinking. He felt her carotid pulse. It was very weak, but there was no doubt that her heart was still beating. He leaned over her, and he could feel her breathing against his cheek, but even when he shook her he couldn't elicit any response.

'Just don't die on me, OK?' he told her. 'If you die on me, I swear to God I'll never forgive you.'

Or Zauber, either, he thought, as he climbed into the driver's seat and started the engine.

He pulled away from the curb with squealing tires, and as he did so he saw the shaven-headed orderly appear in the

Murdstone's gateway. The orderly watched him as he drove away, as if he wanted to be sure that he had gone, but it was clear that he had no intention of chasing after him.

Whatever Doctor Zauber was, he wasn't stupid. He would know that Nathan wouldn't call the police. What could Nathan possibly tell them? That Doctor Zauber had created a mythical creature, a creature that hadn't existed for hundreds of years, and that this mythical creature had put Grace into deep shock just by looking at her? Even if they believed him, Doctor Zauber could easily have hidden the basilisk by then: in the attic, or the cellar, or even in a sewer. And under the law, he had every right to protect himself and his elderly residents against intruders, using as much force as necessary.

Nathan turned toward the city center. He was headed for the Hahnemann University Hospital, at the intersection of North Broad Street and the Vine Expressway. At this time of night it was less than ten minutes away, and it had one of the best emergency rooms in Philadelphia.

Every now and then, he quickly turned his head to check on Grace, but she continued to loll on the back seat, staring up at nothing at all.

TWELVE

Coma

L ike a man in a dream, Nathan carried Grace in through the emergency room doors. Inside, it was brightly lit, with polished white floors, and utterly silent. Even when he thought about it later, Nathan couldn't remember if he had spoken out loud to the receptionist, or exactly what he had said to the two nurses in lavender-covered overalls who had taken Grace into triage. He knew that he had blurted out something about 'shock'.

'Electric shock?' one of the nurses asked him. A very calm black woman, with slanted eyes and a long nose, almost Egyptian-looking, like Nefertiti.

'No, no. Nothing like that.'

'Anaphylactic shock? Some kind of allergy? Peanuts?'

'No. More like neurological shock. More of a mental trauma.'

'What caused it? Do you have any idea?'

'Stress. I don't know. She just collapsed.'

'Try not to worry,' the other nurse told him. 'We need to run some tests, OK? Blood pressure, heart rate. We'll call you when you can see her.'

'Be honest with me. She's not going to die, is she?'

The Egyptian-looking nurse laid her hand on his arm. 'We'll take good care of her, sir. I promise you.'

He sat outside the triage room for a few minutes, but he was too distressed to stay still for long. He looked in through the porthole windows in the doors, but the nurses were still checking Grace's vital signs. One of them saw him looking in and raised her hand to reassure him that everything was under control. He went back and sat down. Then he stood up again.

More than twenty minutes passed. Eventually, a doctor came out of the triage room, her shoes squeaking on the polished floor. She was small, a Japanese-American, her hair fastened at the back with a large red enamel clasp.

'Mr Underhill? My name is Doctor Ishikawa. I need to ask you some questions about your wife.'

'Of course.'

'Can you tell me exactly what happened to her? Were you present when she went into shock?'

'We were on our way home. She just kind of gasped, and her head fell forward.'

'There was no obvious reason for this?'

Nathan shook his head. He hated lying, but even if he had told the truth it wouldn't have helped Grace in any way. There wasn't an ER doctor in the whole world who was trained to treat the trauma induced by a basilisk's stare.

Doctor Ishikawa said, 'Your wife has very low blood pressure and all the symptoms of cardiac arrhythmia. Does she have any history of heart trouble?'

'No. None at all. She's super-fit. She's an MD herself, at Chestnut Hill.'

'Any allergies?'

'Only to shellfish. And she hasn't eaten any shellfish.'

'Well, Mr Underhill, we will have to run further tests on her, including an ECG. If you want to stay here, there is a wait room just across the hallway. It has a coffee machine, and you can use your cell in there, too. We will call you as soon as we have any news.'

'Thank you. Please save her.'

He badly needed some fresh air, even if it was warmer outside than it was in the hospital. He needed night sky, and noise. He went outside on to North Broad Street and called Denver.

It had started to rain again, very softly, and the streetlights were reflected in the sidewalks like a dark, drowned city from which nobody could ever surface. The phone rang and rang for over three minutes, but Denver didn't answer. Sleeping with his mouth wide open, probably, after one too many beers. Nathan tried his cell number, in case Denver had woken up and discovered that he and Grace had gone out again, and decided to go out himself, but it was switched off.

He went back inside. The only other person in the ER wait room was a girl of about seventeen, her clothes spattered with blood, and a lint bandage over her right eye. She sat in one corner, shivering like a mistreated whippet.

It was dawn before Doctor Ishikawa came into the wait room, and the shivering girl had long gone. Nathan stood up. He felt bruised and disoriented, like the survivor of a traffic accident.

'How is she?' he asked. 'Is she awake yet?'

Doctor Ishikawa said, 'She is still unconscious. We are taking her upstairs now, for further observation. Her heart keeps going into spasms, quite prolonged, almost like a fist clenching. But so far we haven't been able to determine why.'

'Can I see her?'

'Of course. Come with me.'

She led him back through to the triage room. Grace was lying with her eyes closed, hooked up to a drip and a Casmed vital signs monitor. Nathan had never seen her look so white. She could have been dead, or an effigy of herself molded out of candlewax. He took hold of her hand and she was penetratingly cold.

Doctor Ishikawa said, 'I am very sorry, Mr Underhill, but

it is not yet possible for me to predict how long she is likely
to stay like this, in this comatose condition. She could regain
consciousness in a few hours. Equally, she could stay like this
for days. Whatever happens, though, we will ensure that she
has the very best of care.'

Nathan leaned forward and kissed her chilly lips. 'Grace,'
he whispered. He felt so guilty that it hurt. He had known
how dangerous a basilisk could be. Why had he insisted on
going to look for it, and taking Grace along with him? He
might just as well have led her into a pit full of black mambas,
and gambled that none of them would bite her.

'You're absolutely sure there's nothing more you can tell
us?' asked Doctor Ishikawa. 'The smallest piece of information could be very important. Your wife didn't say anything,
before she collapsed? Didn't complain of any chest pain?'

'No,' Nathan insisted, although Doctor Ishikawa looked at
him as if she suspected he was holding something back. She
was an ER doctor, after all. She must have had to deal with
hundreds of cases of violence and tragedy and sheer stupidity.

An orderly came in and they wheeled Grace off to the diagnostic unit upstairs. Nathan was about to follow them when
his cell rang.

'Pops? *Pops*? It's Denver. Where the hell are you?'

'Downtown, at the Hahnemann, in the emergency room.
Your mom's had an accident.'

'What? What kind of an accident? Is it serious?'

'The doctors aren't too sure yet. It was kind of a heart
attack. They're running some tests right now.'

'She's going to be OK, though?'

'I'm praying that she is. She's unconscious. I've been calling
you most of the night, but you didn't answer.'

'I was totally out of it. Bryce Evans gave me a bottle of
this cheap tequila. I only had a couple, I swear to God.'

'I don't care about that, Denver. I'm just worried about your
mom. Do you think you can get on down here? Take a taxi.'

'OK, pops.'

Next, Nathan called Richard Scryman, but Richard Scryman
wasn't answering. Maybe it was too early in the morning, or
maybe he had already spoken to Doctor Zauber, and knew
what had happened at the Murdstone last night. Maybe he
was hiding.

After that, he tried the Murdstone. The phone rang for nearly a minute before anybody answered it, and then a suspicious woman's voice said, 'Murdstone Rest Home. What do you want?'

'I need to speak to Doctor Zauber.'

'Doctor Zauber isn't here.'

'Oh, no? Do you know where he is?'

'No. But he isn't here.'

'OK . . . do you have a cell number for him?'

'No.'

'Do you have any idea when he's going to be back?'

'No.'

'Madam . . . this is very important. It could be a matter of life or death.'

'Doctor Zauber isn't here.'

He gave up, and closed his cell. But he still needed to speak to Doctor Zauber. He didn't care if Doctor Zauber was brought to justice for what had happened to Doris Bellman, or for stealing his research, or anything else. All he wanted to know was what he could do to save Grace. She was comatose, yes. But unlike Doris Bellman, and her cockatoo, and unlike Bishop Kadłubek's congregation, and the swallows that had dropped from the ceiling of St Andrzej's, she hadn't died. Not yet, anyhow.

The basilisk had turned its blinding gaze on her for only a fraction of a second, and she was still breathing, and still had a pulse. There had to be a way to bring her back, and maybe Doctor Zauber knew what it was.

For the first time since he had started his Cee-Zee program, Nathan felt ignorant, and inadequate. It occasionally happened at conventions, when he met eminent biologists and zoologists, and he realized how sweeping their intellect was. They spoke the language of pure science. They argued about genetic adaptation and nutrient limitation, and what these meant for the survival of the planet. His own work in recreating mythical creatures was right at the very edge of understandable biology, but he still felt excluded.

The Egyptian-looking nurse came out. 'Your wife is stable, Mr Underhill. No worse, but no better, not yet. But Doctor Ishikawa is very optimistic.'

'You gave her a CT scan?'

'Yes . . . and the result was perfectly normal. No brain tumor, no swelling, no cerebral bruising of any kind.'

'How's her heart?'

'Still seizing. But we're going to try to calm the spasms down with medication.'

'OK.' Nathan knew the dangers of the drugs that controlled tachycardia, but surgical ablation was even more risky, and its effectiveness could never be guaranteed. What upset him even more was the way in which he was thinking about Grace in terms of muscles, and nerves, and blood vessels, instead of the woman he loved beyond anything else.

Forty-five minutes later, Denver arrived. He was wearing a black hooded sweatshirt with sparkling raindrops on the shoulders and he looked puffy-eyed and tired.

He and Nathan held each other for a moment, in a way that they hadn't held each other since Nathan's father had died, more than five years ago.

'How is she?' asked Denver. 'Is she conscious yet?'

'Not yet, no. Her heartbeat's irregular, and her blood pressure's way down. But in every other test they've done, she's fine.'

'So what happened? I mean, like, where *were* you guys? And don't tell me that you were out looking at the moon again, because I won't believe you.'

Nathan said, 'No, we weren't. But if I promise to tell you the truth, I want you to promise me that you won't go crazy.'

Denver looked at him narrowly. 'In other words, what you're about to tell me is going to make me really, really freak.'

'If you're going to freak, I'm not going to tell you.'

'You *have* to tell me. It's too late now. You can't make me promise not to go crazy and then not tell me. That's going to make me freak even more.'

Nathan said, 'Forget it. I need some help now. I need some maturity. I don't need some arrogant self-absorbed kid who thinks that he knows everything about everything.'

Denver pointed to the door of the diagnostic ward. 'That's my mom in there, in case it kind of slipped your mind! That's my mom! You call me up and tell me that she's had some kind of a heart attack, and then you won't tell me what happened, in case I get angry! Well, I *am* angry!'

Nathan said, 'Angry is not going to solve this situation, Denver. If you want to be angry, then be my guest when your mom's recovered. Then, you can act as angry as you like. Get down on your hands and knees and chew the goddamned carpet for all I care. But right now I need stable, and calm, because nothing is going to undo what happened last night, except you and me being practical and sensible and working together like father and son. Like friends. You got it?'

Denver dragged down his hood and wiped his face with his hand. God, he looked so much like Grace.

'All right, Pops,' he said. 'You win. So tell me what it is that I'm not supposed to get crazy about.'

Carefully, quietly, Nathan told him everything. He told him about Doris Bellman dying, and his two nightmares about the basilisk, and the illicit visits that he and Grace had made to the Murdstone Rest Home. When he had finished, Denver sat back for a while with his hand covering his mouth.

'There,' said Nathan. 'That's all of it. That's what happened. Maybe I should have told you before, but you didn't seem to be very interested in my mythical creature project. In fact you were downright hostile.'

Denver said, 'Jesus. You knew how dangerous this creature was, and yet you still let Mom come with you?'

'She knows the Murdstone like the back of her hand, and she *wanted* to come. In fact she wouldn't have let me go without her. Sometimes people take risks for what they believe in, and your mom has always believed in what I'm doing, with a passion.'

'Oh, really. What choice did she ever have?'

'She's a doctor, Denver. She has to treat people every day of the week with Alzheimer's and MS and all kinds of diseases that nobody can cure, not at the moment. Sometimes she comes home from house calls and she's almost in tears. She knows how important my work is.'

'Jesus,' Denver repeated. 'If Mom dies, then I'm going to blame you, Pops. Like, for ever. No forgiveness. Ever.'

'Well, I'm going to do everything I can to make sure that she doesn't. But first I need to talk to Doctor Zauber again. I'm asking you to stay here at the hospital and keep me updated while I go look for him.'

'You really think there's some kind of magical cure?'

'I think that Doctor Zauber understands what's happened to your mom, and if he understands it, then maybe he knows how to reverse it. That's the best I can hope for.'

Denver said nothing for a few moments. Then he nodded. 'OK. For Mom's sake. But only if you call me, too, and let me know what you're doing.'

'I will. I promise.'

Nathan left the hospital and drove west on the Vine Street Expressway, toward the Schuylkill Expressway and the Zoo. Both expressways were busy now, but the rain had unexpectedly cleared and the sun had come out, and the Schuylkill River was sparkling like a river of broken mirrors.

When he entered the laboratory, he found Keira and Tim tidying up their work stations and packing their books and their notes and their pot plants into cardboard boxes.

Keira said, 'I've finished all of the stats now, Professor. I've copied them on to a DVD for you.'

'I'm real sorry about going AWOL yesterday,' Tim put in. 'They called me from the Wistar Institute and said they had an interview cancellation, so would I like to come to see them straight away.'

'Under the circumstances, you're forgiven,' Nathan told him. 'Any other time and I would have canned your ass. Either of you seen Richard this morning?'

They both shook their heads. Keira said, 'Are you *OK*, professor? You look kind of frazzled.'

'I need to speak to Richard, that's all.' He had tried three or four times to reach Richard on his cell that morning, but Richard hadn't picked up. He had tried the Murdstone, too, but he had been answered only by the rest home's recorded message, complete with soothing violin music.

'OK, then,' he said. 'I probably won't be coming back today. I'll try to catch up with you later in the week for a farewell drink.'

'Something's wrong, Professor, isn't it?' Keira persisted.

'Well, yes, as a matter of fact. It's Grace. She's had an accident, and she's in the hospital.'

'Oh, no! What kind of an accident? Is it serious?'

'She collapsed, and she's unconscious. They're running some tests.'

'She *is* going to be OK?'

'Yes, absolutely. I'm going to make sure of it.'

Keira came up to him and put her arms around him. 'If you need anything, Professor – anything at all – you only have to ask.'

'Thanks, Keira. I'll let you know how she gets on.' He looked around the laboratory, with most of his experiments dismantled now, and all of his charts taken down from the wall, and the blackboard wiped clean. 'Now this is all over, you can call me Nathan.'

He thought of driving home and taking a shower, but Millbourne was nearer. He drove to the Murdstone Rest Home and this time he stopped right outside. He tried calling the rest home's switchboard one more time, so that he could make sure that Doctor Zauber was actually there, but again he heard nothing but, *'This is the Murdstone Rest Home for dignified living . . . we deeply regret that we cannot personally answer your call at this moment in time, so please be kind enough to leave a message. Your call means so much to us.'*

'Zauber,' he said. 'This is Nathan Underhill. Phone me, you bastard.'

He walked in through the gates. He sniffed. He was sure he could smell smoke in the air. Maybe somebody was burning leaves. His neighbor was always doing it, especially when the wind was in the wrong direction.

As he came around the corner of the building, he saw Richard Scryman's red Saturn Sky parked in back of the building, close to the staffroom window – and there, sitting in the driver's seat, talking on his cell, nodding, repeatedly running his hand through his hair, was Richard.

Richard didn't see him at first so Nathan stalked over to him and knocked on his window, hard. Richard jumped, and dropped his cell. Nathan opened the Saturn's door and grabbed hold of Richard's coat and pulled him out.

'Do you know what's happened to my wife?' he demanded.

Richard tried feebly to twist himself free, but Nathan pulled him even closer, so that he was almost spitting in his face.

'Do you know what's happened to my wife? She's in the hospital, in a coma, because of you and Doctor Zauber and your goddamned basilisk!'

'I'm sorry,' said Richard. 'I'm really, truly sorry!'

'You sold me out, you little shit. I trusted you for all these years, and what were you doing? Selling me out behind my back.'

'I'm sorry! But you would never have agreed to collaborate with Doctor Zauber.'

'You're damned right I wouldn't! What kind of medical ethic is that, killing elderly people? It doesn't matter how many goddamned diseases you think you're going to cure.'

'But it's the only way! Every mythical creature needs to be fed on human life-energy, or it can't survive! And we never chose anybody who hadn't already lived out most of their useful lives.'

'Very considerate of you, not to pick anybody younger.'

'It's the only way! For Christ's sake! Don't you think we agonized over it?'

Nathan pushed him against the side of his car, denting the door. 'Agonized, did you? I'm sure that Doris Bellman would have been very reassured to know that.'

'Professor, listen—'

'I'm not listening to anything you have to say, Richard. You're a rat and you disgust me. You're worse than a rat, you're a slug. Do you really think that you and Doctor Zauber have some kind of divine right to decide who lives and who gets fed to the basilisk?'

Richard said, 'Maybe we don't. But maybe we're just trying to act like human beings. If *you* had a five-year-old kid with cerebral palsy, and there was this ninety-year-old woman who didn't know the difference between Tuesday and sliced bananas, whose life would *you* choose?'

'Lucky for me, I don't have a five-year-old kid with cerebral palsy. But what I do have is a wife who's in a coma because of your basilisk, and I want to know how to get her out of it.'

'I don't know. I'm sorry. I simply don't know. If I did, believe me, I'd tell you. Maybe Doctor Zauber knows.'

'So where is he?'

'I don't know that, either. He called me last night and told me what had happened, but that's the last I've heard from him. That's why I've come around here now.'

'Richard, I'm going to tell you this, straight to your face.

Nobody in my whole life has ever betrayed me as badly as you have.'

Richard waved his arms around like windmills. 'But don't you *dig* it? You never could have pulled it off! None of those creatures that you were trying to recreate could ever have lived! Don't you understand that?'

'Why the hell didn't you tell me earlier?'

'Because I couldn't. Because you wouldn't have listened to me. God knows, Professor, I wanted that gryphon to hatch out. I prayed for it. I did everything I could. You don't know how much I wanted to go back to Doctor Zauber and say, "forget it, man, Professor Underhill has cracked it and we don't need your old peoples' life-energy any more."'

Nathan turned away from him. He didn't know what else to say. All through history, scientists had been obliged to make decisions between life and death. Oppenheimer, and the A-bomb. How can you decide to kill two hundred thousand innocent people to save hypothetical numbers of other innocent people? Is one life worth more than another? If so, whose?

Richard said, 'I'm sorry. This all turned out wrong. I should have been straight with you, Professor, but I wasn't. Doctor Zauber gave me money in return for our Cee-Zee research, but you have to believe me. It wasn't just the money. More than anything else, I wanted to see one of those mythical creatures come to life. And it has. And I did.'

'Right,' said Nathan. 'We're going to find Doctor Zauber right now, wherever he's gone.'

'I don't think so,' Richard told him. 'I think I'm going to leave now, and forget that any of this ever happened.'

Nathan pulled his SK automatic out of his belt and pointed it directly under Richard's nose, so that Richard would have been able to smell the gun oil. 'No, Richard. You are coming with me. You and I are going inside, and if Doctor Zauber really isn't here, we're going to track him down, together, wherever he is.'

'Professor—' said Robert, lifting both hands.

'What?'

'You're scaring me. I'm scared.'

'That's wonderful, Richard. That's just what I was trying to do.'

He grabbed Richard's right arm and half-danced him toward the back door of the rest home. 'Open the door, Richard.'

It was then that Richard said, 'Smoke, Professor. Can you smell smoke?'

'Just open the goddamned door, will you?'

But Richard said, 'I can smell smoke, Professor. I swear it. And what's that noise?'

Nathan sniffed, and sniffed again. Richard was right. There was an acrid smell of burning in the air. Not just leaf smoke, or smoke from somebody's log fire, blown across the street by the mid-morning wind. It was much more poisonous than that, like burning plastic. And there was a soft whistling sound, too, like somebody sucking air in, between their teeth. Air, being drawn under the door, into the rest home. Air that was feeding a fire.

'Christ almighty,' said Richard. 'The whole place is going up.'

THIRTEEN

Inferno

He had hardly spoken when they heard a sharp fusil-lade of splintering cracks, just above their heads, and they were showered in fragments of glass. They stepped back, and looked up, and Nathan could see that all of the windows along the second-story corridor had burst open. Only a few seconds later, six or seven windows on the right-hand side of the rest home exploded, and pieces of white-painted sash scattered on to the driveway. Smoke began to pour out of the windows, filled with sparks and cinders and pieces of blazing drapes.

Nathan took out his cell and pressed 911. 'Fire department! There's a really serious fire at the Murdstone Rest Home, in Millbourne! And we're going to need the EMS, too. There are elderly people here, at least thirty of them!'

'Just *look* at this sucker,' said Richard. More windows exploded on the third floor, and then the fourth, and woolly gray smoke was already piling out of the building's seven chimneys and up into the morning-blue sky. The Murdstone Rest Home looked like the *Hindenburg* going down.

'Richard!' Nathan shouted, as yet another row of windows burst open, one after the other, and flames began to wave out of them, like orange banners. 'I'm going in there!'

'What?'

'I'm going in there! Doctor Zauber could still be inside!'

'You're crazy! The whole place is full of smoke!'

'But he's the only one who knows how to get Grace out of her coma!'

'I don't know that for sure! Jesus – *you* probably know more about basilisks than he does!'

'Well, that's a risk I'll have to take.'

He opened the back door. Inside, the corridor was hazy with smoke, but it wasn't too thick yet. He lifted one of the monk-like coats off its coat hook, and struggled into it. There was a plaid scarf tucked in the pocket, which he pulled out and tied around the lower part of his face.

Richard caught at his sleeve. 'You can't go in there, Professor! It's too dangerous!'

'I don't think I have any choice, do you?'

'But who's going to breed those Cee-Zees, if you don't?'

'Is *that* all you care about? Goddamn it, Richard, you're even more obsessed than I am!'

He tugged himself free, and set off along the corridor. Behind him, silhouetted against the smoky sunlight, Richard called out, 'I'm sorry! I'm really, truly sorry!'

He opened the staffroom door. There was nobody in there, although the TV was still on, playing a *Spongebob Squarepants* cartoon. He went further along the corridor, opening every door that he came to. A closet, filled with blankets and laundry. An empty bedroom with a bare bed in it, and no drapes at the windows. A staff toilet, with the seat up.

The smoke began to grow thicker and more eye-watering, and Nathan started to cough. All the same, he pulled down the scarf for a moment, and shouted out, 'Zauber! Doctor Zauber! Are you in here anyplace?'

There was no answer, only the crackling of the fire in the upper stories, and the *twang-snap*! of windows breaking in the heat.

He reached the room that Doris Bellman had occupied, and opened the door. A new resident had moved in, because there were china figurines on the table on which Harpo the cockatoo had once had his cage, and a large family photograph on the wall, all smiling at him through the smoke.

He drew back the drapes to let some light in. At first he thought the bed was empty, because all he could see was a huddle of pink loose-woven blankets. But then he saw curls of white hair, on the pillow, and he tugged back the blankets and shouted out, 'Ma'am? Ma'am! You have to wake up, ma'am! There's a fire!'

The elderly woman in the bed didn't stir. She must have been eighty-five to ninety years old, with high cheekbones and a hooked nose, and skin that was blemished with large coffee-colored moles. She was wearing a bottle-green hand-knitted bedjacket.

'Ma'am!' Nathan repeated. He took hold of her bony shoulder and shook her. She could have been drugged, or deaf, or both.

'Ma'am, you have to get out of here! The place is on fire!'

He leaned over her, with his cheek close to her open mouth. He couldn't feel her breathing.

'Ma'am, wake up!' He started a coughing fit, but at the same time he managed to place his fingertips against the woman's neck to feel her carotid pulse. He waited for twenty seconds, but he couldn't feel anything. He was pretty sure that she was dead.

He stood up. He didn't have any choice but to leave her where she was. He left the room, closing the door tightly behind him.

'Doctor Zauber!' he yelled out. 'If you're there, Doctor Zauber, if you're trapped, all you have to do is shout!'

Still there was no answer, and now the fire was raging even louder, as if it were a huge beast with a voracious appetite, devouring banisters and floorboards and doors and window frames. Smoke billowed down the staircase, thick with sooty sparks.

Nathan opened another door, and switched on the light. On the bed, lying on his back, was an emaciated old man in a blue striped nightshirt. Both of his hands were drawn up to his chest, like a praying mantis. His pale blue eyes were open

and his toothless mouth was gaping. On the nightstand beside
him stood a brass-framed sepia photograph of a young man
in naval uniform, with a battleship in the background.

Nathan left him, too, but he was seriously beginning to
question what had happened here. There had been very little
smoke in either of the rooms that he had entered – not enough
for anybody to die so quickly of smoke inhalation – even if
they were old, and their lungs were weak.

Coughing, he managed to climb the stairs to the second-
story landing, but here the smoke was so dense that he had
to crouch down low. He made his way crabwise to the first
door that he could find, and reached up to open it. The
aluminum handle was hot, but he decided to risk it anyhow.
He pulled it down, and gave the door a kick.

A huge blast of scorching air came out of the room, and
he had to shield his face with his hand. Inside, the drapes
were blazing, and so was the bed. It was like a funeral pyre.
A black-faced woman was lying on it, her hair and her skin
shriveling up in front of his eyes, her nightgown already in
flames. Nathan knew then that he was much too late. Even if
Doctor Zauber *were* here, he would have burned to death, and
so would the basilisk. But he didn't believe for a moment that
Doctor Zauber was the suicidal type; or even the type who
would want to go out in a Wagnerian blaze of glory.

He retreated down the stairs, and along the corridor. The
smoke was very much thicker now, and his eyes were
streaming. As he approached the back door, he heard Richard
shouting, '*Stay there! Stay there! The fire department is
coming!*'

He came out of the back of the rest home, wrenching the
plaid scarf away from his face and taking three deep gulps of
fresh air. Richard was standing about twenty yards away,
staring up at the roof.

'*Stay there!*' he repeated. '*I can hear the sirens already!
They won't be long!*'

Nathan looked up, too. Standing right on the edge of the
third-story parapet was 'Michael Dukakis', in yellow pajamas.
His arms were spread wide, as if he were giving a benedic-
tion to the whole world, and his wild white hair was flapping
in the wind.

'*I saw the beast!*' he screamed out.

'Hold on!' Nathan called up to him. 'We're going to get you down!'

'*I saw the beast! The great black beast! I saw it going from one bedroom to the next! I saw the lightning that flashed from its eyes! I know what it was doing! It was dealing out death!*'

'Michael!' Nathan shouted back at him. 'Michael, stay where you are! The fire department will bring you down with a ladder!'

He broke into uncontrollable coughing, and spat up smoke-blackened phlegm. Richard tried to clap him on the back, but Nathan twisted himself away.

Richard backed off, his hands held high. 'I'm sorry, Professor. I've told you I'm sorry.'

'You're *sorry*?' Nathan coughed. 'All this – this is all your fault! And you're *sorry*?'

'For Christ's sake! I didn't start this fire!'

At that moment, however, there was a high-pitched scream from the roof. They both looked up and saw that flames were leaping out of the center of the building. 'Michael Dukakis' was on fire. His white hair was alight, and two tall flames were rising out of his back, like angels' wings.

'Holy shit,' said Richard.

But there was nothing that either of them could do, except watch as 'Michael Dukakis' burned. He stood there for almost a minute, on the very edge of the parapet, while the fire consumed him. Anybody else would have jumped. Anybody else would have fallen, deliberately, rather than be burned alive. But whatever obsessions he had, whatever delusions had taken hold of his mind, they kept him there, on the edge of the building and the edge of sanity. Perhaps he thought that this was the final punishment which God had always had in store for him, and he deserved it.

At last, however, he pitched forward from the roof. The flames that engulfed him made a fluttering sound as he fell. He hit the asphalt with a flat, complicated thump, and lay there, burning furiously from head to foot, with his grinning teeth gradually appearing, and then his ribcage, and then his shinbones.

With a howling of sirens and a honking of air horns, the Philadelphia Fire Department arrived, three red-and-white

Kovatch pumpers, followed almost immediately by four red-and-white ambulances. Nathan and Richard both backed away as the fire officers rolled hoses round to the back of the buildings, and emergency medical teams brought out breathing equipment and gurneys.

Within minutes, water was being sprayed on to the Murdstone Rest Home from three sides, and teams of fire-fighters were entering the building with oxygen masks. The water drifted across the parking lot like a heavy shower of rain.

The emergency medical commander came up to Nathan, closely followed by the chief fire officer. The EMS commander was black, and very stocky. The chief fire officer was even more heavily built, but ginger, with a bristling gray moustache.

'Sir?' asked the EMS commander. 'Were you the individual who called nine-one-one?'

Nathan nodded, and coughed.

'Do you have any idea how many people are still inside?' the chief fire officer asked him.

'I'm not sure. I could only make it as far as the second-story landing. But Doctor Zauber told me that he had thirty-eight residents. All elderly. I don't know many staff were here. But there are five that I know of – Sister Bennett and two Korean carers and two male orderlies. There are probably more.'

The chief fire officer turned away and spoke into his radio transmitter. He listened to a distorted voice talking back to him, and then he turned to Nathan again. 'Anybody still alive, as far as you know? Did you hear anybody shouting out for help?'

Nathan shook his head, and pointed toward 'Michael Dukakis', who was now covered up with a silver fire-suppressant blanket. 'Only him, when he was up on the roof. I went into three rooms, two on the first floor and one on the second. I found a woman and a man on the first floor and they were both dead. The woman upstairs – well, she was just about cremated.'

The chief fire officer took a notebook out of his breast pocket, and a ballpen. 'If I could have your name please, sir.'

'Nathan Underhill. I'm Professor of Cryptozoology at Philadelphia Zoo.'

'Excuse me?'

'Crypto-zoology. We call it Cee-Zee. It's the breeding of hybrid embryos. Stem-cell research.'

'Can I ask what you were doing here?'

'I came to see Doctor Zauber, he's the owner. Well, maybe he's not the owner, but he runs the place. Or did. I wanted to ask him for some scientific data.'

'You think he's still in there?'

'I really don't know. Somehow I doubt it.'

'Oh, yeah? Why's that?'

'I don't have any proof, one way or another. He may be in there. He may be dead. But I don't think that Doctor Zauber is the kind of man who ever intended to end his life in a burning rest home.'

'Meaning?'

'Meaning I'm totally not sure if he's in there or not. But I think he's one of life's survivors.'

The chief fire officer asked Nathan over a dozen more questions, most of them related to what he had seen when he first entered the building. Where had the fire been blazing at its hottest? Which way had the smoke been blowing? Which doors had been open, and which had been closed? Had he smelled anything like gasoline or kerosene? Were the fire alarms sounding?

'No,' he said. 'I can tell you that for an absolute fact. I didn't hear any fire alarms.'

The chief fire officer moved on to talk to Richard. Meanwhile the EMS commander came up to him and said, 'How are you feeling now, sir?'

'I'm OK, fine. A little chesty.'

She touched her upper lip with two fingers, to indicate that Nathan had smoke smudges under his nostrils. 'All the same, we need to check you over. Smoke inhalation can seriously damage your throat and your lungs, and it can poison you.'

'I'm fine. I'll be fine.'

'You think so? I have never known anybody to be fine, after going through something like this, either physically, or psychologically. So come over to the ambulance with me, and we'll have you checked over.'

Nathan hesitated, and then he nodded. He was exhausted,

and he recognized that it was time to give in, and allow this woman to take care of him.

'I saw some TV documentary about stem-cell research,' she told him, as they walked around to the front of the building, where the ambulances were parked. 'Isn't that where you grow human babies inside of chickens' eggs? Or is it the other way around?'

'Something like that,' he replied, and attempted to smile. He sat down on the rear step of the ambulance, and two paramedics helped him to take off his borrowed coat. One of them shone a flashlight down his throat and up his nostrils.

'It's a little sooty up there,' the paramedic remarked. 'But lucky for you there's no thermal injury. No burning. Didn't even singe your nose-hairs.'

He wiped Nathan's face with a medicated paper towel and put an oxygen mask on him, while the other checked his pulse and his blood pressure.

'You seem like you're OK. But I just want you to sit here for a little while. You've had a shock, and shock can have a delayed effect on you, you know? Hit you when you least expect it.'

Nathan pictured Grace, lying waxy-faced in the Hahnemann IT unit, and thought: *you don't need to tell* me *what shock can do to people*. But the paramedic was friendly, and reassuring, and just at the moment Nathan badly needed people around him who cared about his welfare.

He was still sitting at the rear of the ambulance when a girl's voice said, 'Hey – looky here! It's the Dragon's Egg Egghead!'

He turned around and pulled down his oxygen mask. It was Patti Laquelle, in her puffy red squall and her sparkly red boots. A little way behind her came a listless gum-chewing young man with a ponytail, wearing a navy-blue Flyers fleece and toting a Sony video camera.

'Professor!' she said. 'What are *you* doing here? You haven't been hurt, have you? Jerry, would you believe it, this is Professor Underhill, who was trying to hatch all of those medieval dragons and stuff.'

Jerry shrugged as if he could care less, and carried on chewing, and looking around.

Nathan said, 'I was visiting somebody here, that's all, when the place went up. I went in to see if I could rescue anybody, but none of them stood a chance.'

'How many dead in total? Do you know?'

'I don't have any idea. You'll have to ask the fire department, or the police.'

'Is it OK if I interview you? It won't take long.'

'No . . .' Nathan stood up, and took off his oxygen mask. 'My wife isn't too well . . . she's in the hospital. I have to go see her.'

Patti said, 'I'm sorry. I hope it's nothing too serious. Maybe I can call you later.'

'Yes, maybe.'

The paramedics were busy in back of the building. Part of a wall had caved in and two firefighters had been hurt. There was a whole lot of shouting going on, as well as the constant roaring of the pumpers, and the clattering of water as it poured down the sides of the building.

Richard was standing on his own. He gave Nathan a quick, sheepish glance, and for a moment Nathan thought he was going to come over and try to apologize yet again. Nathan turned away. Right now, he didn't think that he would ever get over his anger at Richard's betrayal, and what he and Doctor Zauber had done. He walked back to his car, took out his cell and called Denver at the hospital.

'Denver? It's Dad. Any news about your mom?'

'I talked to the nurse about ten minutes ago. She's not getting any worse, but she's not getting any better, either. Listen – are you coming back down here?'

Nathan said, 'Please, Denver – hang in there for another half-hour, will you? I really need to take a shower and change my clothes.' He didn't tell him why. Denver had enough to worry about right now.

'OK, Pops. But don't be too long, will you?'

Nathan looked across at the smoking ruins of the Murdstone. Most of the front was burned out, except for the porch, where the gargoyle was still perched, grinning at him through the drifting smoke. Before he could do anything more, he needed to know if Doctor Zauber had survived the fire. Only Doctor Zauber knew how basilisks stole people's life-energy from them, and if there was any conceivable way of giving it back.

He pulled his automatic out of his belt, and stowed it in the glovebox. His shaving mirror was in there already – the one he had taken with him in the hope of deflecting the basilisk's lethal stare. He was just about to close the glovebox when he noticed that the back of the mirror had been discolored into rainbow patterns, like any metal when you heat it. He took it out, and turned it over, and the face of the mirror was shiny black.

Maybe it *had* worked – partially, anyhow. Maybe it had deflected some of the basilisk's stare, so that Grace had been shocked into unconsciousness, but not killed.

He sat looking into the blackened mirror for a long time. He could still see his face in it, like a ghost, but he had the feeling that he could see more than that. He had the feeling that he was being shown a clue.

All of the medieval books that he had read about basilisks had claimed that mirrors were essential to 'throwe back at the beast its essentiale evil, and thus destroie it,' but even the more detailed accounts made no mention of the mirrors turning black. He would have thought that this effect was so striking that at least one writer would have mentioned it.

He dropped the mirror back into the glovebox and started the engine. He had never felt so alone, and so completely lost. It was like finding himself in the suburb of some foreign city, without a streetmap. But at the same time he had never felt so determined. He was going to find Doctor Zauber, if Doctor Zauber was anywhere to be found, and he was going to reawaken Grace.

The morning wind blew a great black roll of smoke across the street, and for a second it looked to Nathan like a monstrous parody of the basilisk, with its hunched back and its branching horns. He pulled away from the curb, and headed toward home.

FOURTEEN

Night of the Hunters

He returned to the hospital at a quarter after two. Denver was waiting for him on the front steps outside, looking tired and jittery.

'Any change?' Nathan asked him, but Denver shook his head.

'The nurse said her brain was like a jammed-up computer. You know, when a program won't respond. Everything's in there, no brain damage. But it's all, like, *locked*.'

Nathan put his arm around his shoulders. 'We'll find a way to unlock it, I promise you.'

Denver frowned at him. 'You have a really bad bruise on your cheek, just there. How did that happen?'

'I went back to the Murdstone Rest Home. The whole goddamned place was on fire. It looked like somebody had tried to burn it down.'

'*What*? You're kidding me!'

'It's OK. I went in there, to see if anybody was still alive, but it was too goddamned hot for me to go too far. I called the fire department, and the EMS. That's why I had to go back home and clean up. I was stinking of smoke.'

'Jesus. Was anybody hurt?'

'There must have been some casualties, yes.'

'But what about what's-his-name? Doctor Zoober? Was *he* there?'

'I went in. I came right back out. That was all I could do. It was like an inferno.'

'But what if he was burned up in there? What are we going to do about Mom?'

'I don't believe he *was* in there, Denver. The guy's too wily.'

'Jesus.'

'Look,' said Nathan. 'Let me go see Mom. I'll tell you all about this later.'

'You're OK, though?'

Nathan looked at him; at his eyes that were just like Grace's. 'I'm all right,' he reassured him, squeezing his arm. 'I just don't think I'm going to be joining the fire department anytime soon.'

He left Denver in the wait room and went up to the IT unit to see Grace. She was lying there, still white-faced, and when he lifted her hand from the blanket her fingers were still deeply cold, as if she had just been rescued from the bottom of a lake. Doctor Ishikawa came in, with a clipboard under her arm.

'Ah, Professor Underhill!' she smiled. 'Yes – your son told me that you were a professor.'

'Not a professor of anything that can lift my wife out this coma.'

'All the same, you should try to be optimistic. I'm a little worried about her blood pressure, which is lower than it should be, but her vital signs are generally good.'

'So what do we do now?'

'We will just have to wait. It might do some good if you spend some time with her, talking to her.'

'I will. I'm just going to take my son out and buy him something to eat.'

'The hospital canteen is good. You should try their vegetarian lasagna.'

'Unh-hunh. He only eats Wendy's.'

He kissed Grace on her chilly, unresponsive lips, and stroked her hair. He wanted to say, '*Come on, Grace, stop pretending that you're unconscious. I've had enough of this game,*' but he knew that it would be futile. He left the room. Two men in gray raincoats were waiting for him outside, one of them with spiky white hair and a nose like a motor-horn bulb, the other nearly six-feet-five, with a long, lugubrious face and very sad eyes.

'Professor Underhill? I'm Detective Cremer and this is Detective Crane.'

'Oh, yes? How can I help you?'

'You witnessed the fire this morning at the Murdstone Rest Home. In fact a couple of other witnesses said you acted real courageous.'

'I only did what anybody else would have done.'

Detective Cremer sniffed, and tugged at his nose. 'The thing of it is, I've had a preliminary report from the medical examiners, and I need to ask you some questions about what you found when you went in there.'

'I found dead people.'

'Yes, sir. But I'd like to ask you what the precise circumstances were.'

Nathan said, 'I'm taking my son to Wendy's, why don't you come along?'

Detective Cremer looked at his wristwatch. 'OK, sure. I could use a cup of coffee.'

They all walked to Wendy's on North Broad Street. They found a table by the rain-spotted window, and ordered three coffees and a traditional cheeseburger for Denver. Nathan wasn't at all hungry. He could still smell burning bodies in his nostrils, although he knew that he was imagining it, most likely.

'So far we've located twenty-six victims,' said Detective Cremer. 'Obviously the MEs haven't had the time to examine all of them, but they've given five of them your cursory once-over, and the interesting thing is that none of them died from smoke inhalation.'

'What are you trying to tell me?' asked Nathan, as if he didn't know. If they hadn't succumbed to smoke inhalation, they hadn't been inhaling when the fire was set. They had all been dead already.

'Well, let's put it this way,' said Detective Cremer. 'It's much too soon to jump to any conclusions. We haven't even identified them formally. But we'd just like to know what you saw when you first went in there. Was the smoke pretty thick?'

'Not on the first floor, no. Not to begin with. I went into two rooms off the first floor corridor, and I found a woman and a man, both dead, as far as I could tell. But there was very little smoke in their rooms.'

'Any sign of physical injury?'

Nathan shook his head. 'Not as far as I could tell.'

'You went up to the second floor, too?'

'I tried to, but it was too smoky and too hot. I opened one door, and there was a woman inside, and she was actually burning. She was, like, chargrilled. That's the only word for it.'

Denver had just taken a large bite of cheeseburger, and he looked across at Nathan in slowly dawning disgust. He picked up his napkin and spat it out, and pushed his plate away, as well as his Oreo Twisted Frosty.

Nathan said, 'I'm sorry, Denver. I should have waited till you'd finished eating.'

'Oh, great. So that I could puke?'

'I'm sorry, really I am. But that's what I saw. I'm not an expert, but I would have guessed that the fire was started on the second floor someplace.'

'You think that somebody might have started it deliberately?' asked Detective Crane. Even his voice was sad.

'I don't know. It was very fierce, and it spread really quickly. But like I say, I'm not an expert.'

Detective Cremer drained his coffee. 'OK, Professor. We'll probably need to talk to you again later, if you don't mind. But thanks for that.'

He pointed toward Denver's half-eaten cheeseburger and said, 'Do you mind? I didn't have time for breakfast this morning.'

Denver said, 'Be my guest. It's like, you know, chargrilled. Cremated, even.'

He drove Denver back to West Mount Airy. Even though Grace was rarely home until six or seven, because of the home visits she had to make to her housebound patients, the house still seemed silent and empty, and dusty, too. Specks of dust were falling through the sunlight that shone through the living-room windows, as if they were settling on Grace's life.

'OK if I stay with Stu tonight?' asked Denver.

'I guess. I was thinking of going back to the hospital, in any case. Do you think that his parents will mind?'

'I asked him already. He said it's OK.'

Nathan sat on a stool in the kitchen, and opened up a can of Dale's Ale. 'Fine, then. I'll call you if anything happens.'

Denver hesitated by the door. 'Pops . . . I know that this wasn't your fault. Well, it was your fault, kind of. But it was Mom's fault, too. Both of you wanted to do this together.'

'No,' said Nathan. 'I should have said no. I shouldn't even have suggested it. It was much too dangerous, and I knew it.'

'Sure, but that's Mom, isn't it? Always taking risks.

You remember that time, when we were snowboarding, at
Aspen? She was crazy, the way she was always catching air.'

Nathan nodded. 'Don't you worry, Denver. We'll get her
back. I promise you.'

Early that evening, Nathan went back to the Hahnemann to
sit beside Grace's bed. He took with him her favorite book,
The Process, a dreamlike story about an American university
professor crossing the Sahara.

Doctor Ishikawa had gone home, but a young blonde
intern came in to tell him that Grace was stable, and that
an EEG had indicated that her brain activity was normal.
There was no reason to suppose that she wouldn't eventually
wake up.

Nathan sat down and took hold of Grace's hand. God, it
was cold – as cold as it had been when she had gone snowboarding and lost one of her gloves.

'I'm so sorry, Grace,' he told her. 'I don't know what else
to say. I just hope that you're having sweet dreams in there,
and not nightmares.'

Grace continued to breathe softly and steadily. It was
obvious that she was dreaming, because he could see her
eyeballs flicking rapidly from side to side under her eyelids.
But there was no way of telling if she was out in the yard,
cutting her roses, or whether she was running down the corridor
in the Murdstone Rest Home, pursued by the basilisk, its lungs
gasping like black leather bellows.

A nurse brought him a cup of coffee and he started to read.

'In Morocco, it is spring and the hills wash in torrents of
color. One mountain is blue, the next mountain is red and the
mountain behind it bright yellow with borders of purple. White
valleys below are great lacy aprons of waterwort meadow,
smelling even more hauntingly rotten-sweet than the orange
blossom odor of honey that sets my head spinning as it pours
through this train.'

He went on reading for nearly two hours, until his throat
was dry. Then he left her for a while, and went for a walk
along the corridor to the reception area. Two nurses were
sitting at their station, and both of them smiled at him in
sympathy.

'Anything you need, Mr Underhill?'

'A miracle would be good.'

'Believe me, Mr Underhill, we're all praying for that.'

He stayed at the hospital until the sky began to grow pale, and the street lights flickered off. One of the nurses came in and said, 'We're going to give your wife a wash now, Mr Underhill, and change her sheets. Why don't you take a break, get yourself some sleep? We don't want *you* to be sick.'

'Yes,' he said, wearily. 'Good idea.'

He drove home. He had only just stepped in through the front door when he heard the phone warbling. He picked it up and carried it across the living room, so that he could sit down and ease off his shoes while he answered it.

'Professor Underhill, this is Detective Cremer. How's your wife, Professor? Any improvement?'

'Still stable, but still comatose.'

'Sorry to hear that, sir. Hope she gets out of it real soon. Listen – the reason I'm calling you is that we now have a final count of the victims we recovered from the Murdstone Rest Home. Twenty-nine, all told. Twenty-six residents and three staff. Some of the bodies were very badly burned, but we managed to identify them all from the rest home's records.'

'How about Doctor Zauber? Did you find *his* body?'

'No, sir. No sign of Doctor Zauber in the building, alive or dead. He wasn't at his home, either. We went around there and found that he had left. A neighbor said that she saw him carrying a suitcase out to his car around six thirty in the morning. We searched the house and there was no sign of any personal papers or documentation, and no personal items of any value except for clothing and shoes in the bedroom closet.'

'So he's vamoosed?'

'It sure looks like it. We checked every conceivable form of transportation. Airlines, buses, trains, rental cars. Then about an hour ago we discovered that he chartered a Cessna Citation out of Brandywine Airport. He took off around twelve noon headed for Montréal. I'm waiting for the Mounties to get back to me, to see if they can find out where he went after that.'

Nathan felt a cold sliding sensation in his stomach: a sensation of utter hopelessness. If Doctor Zauber had managed to leave the country, God knows how he was ever going to track him down. Maybe he was being hopelessly optimistic in thinking that Doctor Zauber knew a way to rouse Grace out of her coma. But if anybody could, he could, and Nathan had to find out for sure.

'If you find out where he went, you'll be sure to call me, won't you?'

'Sure,' said Detective Cremer. 'No problem at all. Oh – and there's one more thing I meant to tell you. The fire at the Murdstone was started deliberately, as far as the fire guys can tell. But there was no trace of your usual accelerants. They said it looked more like somebody walked around the second floor with a giant blowtorch, playing it all over the walls and the carpets and the woodwork.'

'Strange way to set a fire.'

'Tell me something about this case that *ain't* strange. So far, the MEs haven't found a single victim that died of smoke inhalation. All twenty-nine of them must have cashed in their chips long before the fire was started, including the nurses and the orderly. They weren't shot and they weren't stabbed and nobody used a blunt instrument to whack them over the head. There's no trace of poison in their systems, either, so nobody laced their bedtime chocolate with strychnine. So how do you kill twenty-nine people without leaving a trace?'

Nathan could think of only one answer to that. *Basilisk.*

He showered, and then he made himself a pot of strong black coffee and a slice of wholemeal toast, with honey, although he could manage only one bite before he dropped it into the bin. His mouth was desert dry and his throat was constricted with tension, and he had no appetite at all. He chewed, and chewed, and then he spat.

He could only think of Grace, in her hospital bed, and Doctor Zauber, wherever he was. He wondered what Doctor Zauber had done with the basilisk. He could hardly have taken it with him, especially since he had left Philadelphia in daylight, when the basilisk would have been hiding in some darkened crevice – in an attic someplace, or a closet, or a crawlspace.

He called Denver. Denver's voice sounded as if his nose was stuffed up. He was subdued but no longer angry. He and Stu had decided to take the day off school so that they could chill together and listen to deathgrind music. He promised to come back later, in time for supper.

Nathan said, 'I'm not too sure I feel like cooking. I'm not too sure I feel like *eating*. But I think we should try to have regular meals. Maybe we'll go the Trolley Car Diner for *quesadilla*.'

'OK, Pops. Sounds cool to me.'

He sat down on the couch, eased his feet up, and tried to read through the final notes and graphs that Keira had prepared for the gryphon project. Nearly an hour later, the file dropped on to the floor and woke him up. At first he couldn't think where he was, or why. But then he sat up and looked around. The house was almost silent, except for the skittering of dry leaves across the yard. It had become very gloomy outside, as if a storm were brewing up.

He thought that he might as well get dressed and go back to the hospital. He couldn't concentrate on work; and there was nothing he could do to find Doctor Zauber, not until Detective Cremer got back to him.

He was just about to go upstairs when the doorbell chimed. He tightened the sash of his bathrobe and went to open it. It was Patti Laquelle, with a sympathetic smile on her face.

'I heard your wife is still sick. I'm so sorry.'

'Thanks. I was just about to go back and sit with her. What do you want?'

'I wanted to talk to you about the way you went into that burning rest home. I mean, that was an incredibly brave thing to do. But I'm really interested to know what you were doing there, and why you went inside. It has all the makings of a great *Web* story.'

'Oh, really? "Dragons' Egg Egghead Scrambles For Safety"?'

'You're a funny guy, Professor. In both senses of the word, if you don't mind my saying so.'

Nathan held the door open wider. 'You may as well come inside. You'll have to excuse the way I'm dressed.'

Patti stepped inside. 'I've seen worse. Councilman Pobjoy answered the door to me once wearing nothing but a kitchen apron. You should have seen him when he turned around. Well, as a matter of fact, you *shouldn't* have seen him when he turned around. What a GPA.'

Nathan led her into the living room. She perched herself on the arm of one of his armchairs, and took out her digital recorder.

'What I'm really interested in is whether you knew any of the people in the rest home. Is that why you were there, visiting somebody?'

'Do you want to keep this off the record?' Nathan asked her. 'Just for now, anyhow.'

Patti looked dubious, but she said, 'OK . . . so long as I don't go away with no story at all.'

'I was looking for Doctor Zauber, the owner.'

'Oh, yes? And did you find him?'

'Doctor Zauber had left, maybe only minutes before I got there. The night before, my wife and I had entered the rest home looking for something very special.'

He stood up, went across to the bookcase, and came back with a copy of *The Black Book*. He opened it, and showed her the woodcut of the basilisk.

'I don't get it,' said Patti. 'You were looking for this book?'

'Unh-hunh. We were looking for *that* thing. Part-lizard, part-cockerel, with some unidentifiable mammal DNA thrown in, for good measure. The basilisk, which actually means "little king" in Latin, on account of the horns that grow on top of its head, like antlers.'

'You're kidding me.'

'Not at all. I explained to you, didn't I, all about the mythological hybrids that I was trying to breed? The basilisk is one of them.'

'And you and your wife thought that there was a basilisk at the Murdstone Rest Home? Even if a thing like that really exists, what was it doing *there*?'

Nathan told her everything. He told her about Richard, stealing his research. He told her about Doris Bellman, her cockatoo and her ivy plants. And he told her what had happened to Grace, when Doctor Zauber and his basilisk had cornered them on the second floor of the rest home.

When he had finished, Patti sat with her mouth wide open, saying nothing.

'You don't believe me, do you?' Nathan asked her.

'I saw the gryphon you were trying to hatch out, and that was like nothing that I ever saw before, and I mean not *ever,* and I've seen a German shepherd that was born with two bodies, and a goose with no head that could walk around the barnyard and lay eggs.'

'So you *do* believe me?'

She came up close to him and spread her arms wide. 'I *want* to believe you. Like, what a story that would be! "If Looks Could Kill"! But let's face it, Professor. If I tried to file anything about a basilisk, my editor would definitely think that I had a hole in my screen door. Or else he'd fire me.'

Nathan looked her straight in the eye, trying to convey how serious he was. 'Patti . . . I'm telling you the truth. That was what actually happened. I know you can't file a story like that. But you *could* help me to locate Doctor Zauber, couldn't you? If you can ask your readers if they've seen him anyplace, or know where he might have disappeared to, that would be terrific.'

'What about my story? "Egghead's Hair-Raising Rescue Bid"?'

'How's this: I was driving past the Murdstone Rest Home when I saw smoke coming out of the upstairs windows. My wife treats some of the residents there, so I stopped and ran inside, to see if anybody needed to be rescued. Unfortunately the smoke and the heat were too much for me, so I had to come back out again, without being able to save anybody. That's all you have to say.'

'And Doctor Zauber?'

'The Philly police want to ask him some questions about how the fire might have gotten started.'

'Do they suspect him of torching the place himself?'

'You'll have to ask them that.'

'I already did,' said Patti. 'They wouldn't say yes and they wouldn't say no. They wouldn't even say maybe. What do *you* think?'

'I think that I'm very worried and I'm very tired, but if there's anything at all that you can do to help me, I'll appreciate it more than you can know.'

Patti stood up. She took hold of his hands, and squeezed them, and then she gave him an unexpected kiss on the forehead, as if he were her favorite uncle. 'I'll see what I can do. No promises. But the deal is, you have to let me know *everything* that happens. On the record, and off. Even if you think it sounds totally loony, like everything you've told me today.'

'OK, deal. I need to tell *somebody*, and apart from Denver, who else is going to believe me?'

Patti picked up her purse and walked to the front door.
Before he could open it for her, she looked up at him and
said, 'So what happened to the basilisk? I don't see how
Doctor Zauber could have taken something like that on a
charter jet, do you?'

'That's what I've been asking myself. I shot at it, and he
said that I'd hurt it, but I don't have any idea how badly.
Maybe I killed it, and he's buried it. Maybe he's put it down,
and disposed of its body somehow. But you're right. I don't
think he took it with him to Montréal.'

'OK,' said Patti. 'But if you have any brilliant ideas—'

'I'll call you. Don't worry about it.'

She opened the front door, and as she did so Denver was
walking up the driveway, wearing his big loose khaki jacket
and his Blue Jays cap on sideways.

'Hey, Denver!' said Nathan. 'Somebody here I'd like you
to meet!'

Denver came up to the porch. His face looked pasty, and
there were plum-colored circles under his eyes, as if he
hadn't slept. Inside the porch, above his head, there was a
dreamcatcher, which Grace had bought in Colorado. As
Denver came to stand underneath it, it slowly began to circle.
It was only being blown by the breeze, of course, but the
effect was strangely unsettling, as if he had brought last night's
nightmares with him.

'Patti, this is my son Denver. Denver, this is Patti Laquelle,
from *The Philadelphia Web*.'

'How's it going?' asked Denver. He was trying to act all
cool and offhand, but Nathan could tell that he liked her by
the way that he was shuffling his feet.

'Pretty good, thanks. I've been talking to your dad about
things that go bump in the night.'

'Oh, really? What did he tell you?'

Patti turned to Nathan as if to ask him how much she was
supposed to know. Nathan said, 'I told her everything. No
reason not to. She's going to post an article on the *Web*, asking
if anybody knows where Zauber's disappeared to.'

'Well, I'm going to *try*,' said Patti. 'Depends on my editor.
Pernickety schmuck that he is.'

'Good,' said Denver. 'Thanks.'

'Real scary, this basilisk,' said Patti.

'Sure is. I've really got my fingers crossed that I never get to meet it.'

'All the same, can you imagine it? What a story.'

Denver said, 'Pops – I just came to pick up my MP3, that's all. I left it in the kitchen. And I was wondering if you could advance me my next week's allowance?'

'Sure. Just hold on a minute.'

Denver looked at Patti as if he were amazed at Nathan's instant agreement. Like, normally, I have to pester him into the ground.

'So – what kind of music do you like?' asked Patti, as Nathan went back into the house.

'Deathgrind, mostly. Circle of Dead Children, Cattle Decapitation, Brujeria.'

'Hey!' said Patti. 'That's so extraordinary. Me too. I'll tell you my favorite band, Soilent Green. I love that southern sludge sound.'

The two of them stood together on the porch nodding at each other like dipping ducks, as they mentally agreed on the tracks that really got them going. They didn't have to say anything: they could hear the music in their heads.

Nathan came out and handed Denver his MP3 and fifty dollars. 'Don't spend it on anything sensible, OK? And I'll see you back here round about six thirty.'

He and Patti watched Denver lope back down the driveway, his Nikes slapping on the asphalt.

'Great kid,' said Patti. 'I can tell he's your son.'

Nathan said nothing. Denver reminded him too much of Grace. But he laid his hand on Patti's skinny little shoulder and said, 'Thanks. I'll catch up with you later. And – please – do whatever you can to get that appeal for Doctor Zauber online, won't you?'

Patti said, 'I lost my mother, you know, three years ago next Tuesday, breast cancer. She was in a coma at the end, so I know how you feel. You talk to them and hold their hand, but you know they're gone and they're never coming back.'

Nathan said, 'Grace is coming back, I swear to God. Grace is coming back because I'm not going to rest until I know where she's been, and what she's seen, and what that damned thing did to her.'

FIFTEEN

The Voice from the Wall

Once Patti had gone, he drove back down to the Hahnemann. The sky was squid-ink black and it was raining hard. He parked, and went up in the elevator to ITU. His hair was wet and spiky and he was shuddering with cold, emotionally as well as physically. Up until now, he hadn't allowed himself to think it, but supposing Grace *never* recovered consciousness? He could imagine Doctor Ishikawa asking him if he wanted to switch off her life support, so that she could die. But at the same time, he couldn't imagine life without her. Nate-and-Grace, that was what they were, that was what their friends and their family called them, and that it was they had expected to be for ever, until death did them part.

Grace was lying on her bed, as cold and as white as she had been before, her skin almost luminescent. The Egyptian-looking nurse was checking her blood pressure.

'She's fine,' she said, touching Nathan on the shoulder with a long-fingered hand that was strangely dry, like dark-brown finely creased leather.

'I guess I'll sit with her for a while. Read to her.'

'You can bring in music, too, if you think that will help.'

Music? He didn't really want to sit here listening to all of those songs they had danced to, on drunken summer nights. Van Morrison, Donna Summer, Coldplay. John Denver, too. Grace had always loved John Denver, 'Sunshine on my Shoulders', but neither of them had ever had the nerve to tell Denver where his name came from.

He read her some more from *The Process*. 'In the Sahara, there are plants with spined tendrils like elaborate steel traps and humanoid plants like silently screaming witches staked into the ground. I wouldn't trust the plants out here with as little as one drop of water.'

The day passed by, with the sun rotating through the room,

as it always does on hospital visits. Different shifts of nurses came and went. Grace continued to sleep, with her eyeballs flicking from side to side beneath her eyelids. Nathan closed the book and sat for a long while staring at her, at her pale white hand, until he began to fall asleep too.

I will allow you to find me, if you really want to, said a voice, and it was frighteningly close to his ear.

He opened his eyes. There was nobody else in the room, apart from Grace, and she hadn't moved, and certainly hadn't spoken.

I just dreamed that, he thought. I really need to get myself a decent night's sleep.

But you have a far more pressing priority, Nathan. Something much more urgent than catching some sleep.

He stood up. In the white plaster wall next to the door, about four feet from the floor, half of a human face had appeared, with only one visible eye, which was closed.

'I'm dreaming all this,' he announced, standing up and walking across the room. The white face didn't flinch, but turned itself away, as if he had offended it. Its eyes remained closed.

'What *is* all of this?' he demanded.

Transvection, the face replied. *Surprised you never heard of it, your father being such a talented medium.*

'My father was never a medium. He could predict things, that's all. Horse races, weather, nothing important.'

Who says that fortune-telling always has to be real? Fortune-telling is an inspired guess, based on all the known facts. But your father had the gift. That was why he was always so good at card games.

'I'm asleep. I'm sitting in the hospital, right next to Grace's bed. But where are you?'

I could tell you, Nathan. But that would depend.

'I don't know what you mean. Depend on what?'

It would depend on why you wanted to find me. I need you to work with me. I need your knowledge, and your skill.

'And I need you to tell me how to get my wife out of this coma.'

There is a way. But I'm not sure that I want to tell you what it is. In fact, I have every conceivable reason not to.

'If you don't tell me, then believe me I'm going to hunt

you down and find you and force you to tell me what it is, even if I have to cut your balls off.'

Well, I was afraid that was how you might feel. But if you agreed to work with me, and we produced the creatures that you and I were always destined to produce . . . then I might reconsider, and tell you how to bring her back.

'Where are you, you bastard?'

Right now, the way you're feeling, that's for me to know and you to find out.

'Where are you?'

Not here, Nathan. Not in reality. And not in your night-mare, either.

Nathan heard a wheezing, and a shuffling sound, close behind him. He turned around, and there was a huge black creature, almost filling the room. A massive basilisk, with branch-like horns, and a beaky face, with slitted eyes, and a huge distended body covered in shining blue-black scales, like hundreds of mussel-shells all joined together into some hideous, clattering cloak.

He knew that it wasn't real. He knew that he was dreaming it. But he could hear its breathing and he could smell its breath, like overheated metal and burned garlic.

This wasn't the hunched, deformed basilisk that he and Grace had encountered in the corridors of the Murdstone Rest Home. It wasn't covered in rotten sacking and rags, to protect it from the world around it. This was a new, fully developed basilisk, with shining claws and elaborate antlers, and eyes that shone as intensely as arc lamps.

See what we could do, between us. See the beasts that we could create.

The creature turned its head toward him, so that the lizard-like folds in its neck crinkled. Nathan immediately lowered his head and shielded his face with both hands, but even so the bright light lanced between his fingers and he had to shut his eyes tight, too.

'I wouldn't even think of working with you, you bastard, not unless you told me how to save my wife.'

So – if I were to promise to bring your wife back to you, you would consider it? I really need you, Professor. I need your scientific knowledge. I need your genius.

The light between Nathan's fingers gradually died. Very

cautiously, he lowered his hands and looked up. The basilisk was still there, but now it was leaning over Grace's bed, as dark as a thundercloud. There was no light shining from its eyes, but it was staring down at her with a look of reptilian curiosity, as if it couldn't decide what kind of creature she was, or if she were even alive. Was she prey, or was she carrion? Was she to be killed, or was she dead already?

It raised one curved black claw, and reached toward her face. Nathan immediately jumped up and threw himself toward it, shouting out, '*No! Don't touch her!*'

Somebody grabbed him, and pulled him sideways. He opened his eyes and it was one of the nurses, a stocky black girl with cornrow hair.

'Mr Underhill?' she said. 'Mr Underhill? What are you *doing*, Mr Underhill?'

Nathan twisted around. Grace was still lying on the bed, unharmed, and the basilisk had vanished.

'I was—' he began. The room suddenly seemed to tilt, and he gripped the end of the bed to steady himself. 'I must have been dreaming, I guess. Sorry. I thought I saw something that wasn't really there.'

'You need to take good care of yourself, Mr Underhill. I know that you're worried about your wife, but you won't be any good to her unless you sleep properly and eat properly.'

'I know. You're right.'

'There's a room on this floor where you can sleep if you want to. All you have to do is ask. If there's any change in your wife's condition, of course we will let you know right away.'

Nathan nodded, and whispered, 'Thanks.'

He maneuvered his chair closer to Grace's bed and sat down again. He was shaking, and motion-sick, as if he had just stepped off a roller-coaster ride. He knew that the appearance of the basilisk had only been an illusion, but he could still smell it, hot metal and garlic. He could almost *taste* it.

So Doctor Zauber still wanted Nathan to work with him. *See what we could do together*! *See what beasts we could create*! And he had definitely implied that he knew how to rouse Grace out of her coma. But at what price? How could Nathan possibly justify bringing Grace back to life, if it was going to cost the lives of countless elderly people? And even if he decided to do it, what would Grace say? Grace was a healer. How would she be able to live with herself, once she realized the commitment that he had made to Doctor Zauber, on her behalf? He could see her now, like Lady Macbeth, holding up hands that were smothered in blood. *And there was much weeping and gnashing of teeth.*

He stayed with Grace until six. He didn't read to her; but he talked to her, trying to remember all the good times they had spent together, ever since they had first met. Grace had always been funny, always ready to try anything and everything. As an MD, she had seen how short life could be, and how painful, and she had always been determined to live her life to the limit, no matter what. For no reason at all, he thought of the time that she had cajoled him into taking her to Denny's Beer Barrel Pub, in Clearfield, to try to eat Ye Olde 96er, America's largest hamburger – six pounds of beef in a specially baked bun, with pickles, lettuce, tomatoes, onions and mayo, dripping with cheese. They had made such a mess and laughed so much that Nathan had almost choked.

He knew that there was only one way out of this. He would have to hunt down Doctor Zauber and *force* him to bring Grace back to consciousness, no matter what it took.

Grace murmured, and stirred, and her right hand suddenly jerked. Nathan stood up and said, 'Grace? Grace, sweetheart? Can you hear me?'

But after that she stayed still and silent, although her eyes were still flickering wildly from side to side under her eyelids, as she walked through some surrealistic world that Nathan couldn't even begin to imagine.

Eventually, he kissed her cheek and said, 'Grace . . . I'll come back tomorrow, OK? Right now Denver needs feeding and I could really use some heavy-duty sleep.'

He was about to leave the room when he noticed that there was still a slight oval blemish on the wall where the face had appeared in his nightmare. He approached it, and examined it closely. It was a crater in the plaster where the door handle had constantly been striking the wall, every time somebody opened it. Nothing more than that. He reached out to touch it, but as he did so, it flicked open like an eyelid, with white eyelashes, and a chalky white eyeball inside it.

Nathan jerked back. The eye stared at him, unblinking.

I will be watching you, Professor. I always know where you are, and what you're doing.

'Listen – I'll give you anything you want, if you can make Grace better. But I can't *kill* people.'

You don't think so? The first two or three are always the hardest, but I can assure you that it very quickly becomes much easier. Sometimes, yes, they beg to be spared. But other times, when they are very old, and tired, and they are in constant pain, they look almost happy to be taken. Their pathetic little souvenirs! Their photographs, and their golf trophies! But I can tell you one thing with certainty, Professor. When we die, nobody really cares. Nobody misses us. The carousel of life keeps on going around and around, and up and down, with everybody screaming and laughing. The same thing will happen to you, and to me, so why are you so worried?

'Why am I worried? Are you kidding me? I'm not a serial killer, that's why. Everybody deserves to live as long as they possibly can, and it's not up to me or you or anybody else to decide when it's time for them to die.'

'Mr Underhill?' said a voice. Nathan turned. The nurse was waiting for him, in the open doorway. She must have heard him talking to the wall and thought that he had really lost it.

'I'm, ah – yes. I was just saying goodnight to Grace.'

He glanced back quickly behind the door, but the eyelike protuberance in the wallpaper had disappeared, and now there was nothing but the crater in the plaster, where the door handle had constantly been hitting it.

'You will take my advice, won't you, Mr Underhill? You will eat? You will sleep?'

'Yes,' said Nathan. *And go hunting for Doctor Zauber.*

Three days passed, and Nathan went down to the Hahnemann every morning at eight a.m., and sometimes earlier, and sat with Grace until five thirty in the afternoon. He came to the last page of *The Process.*

'The windows are streaming with gold. I look out to see we are spinning through the Sahara faster than the speed of light, escaping the clutch of the great hairy magnet of the Sun. From behind my back, this little old gink with one eye is asking me:

'"Why were you in such a hurry to get there, when the desert gets us all in the end?"'

He closed the book. It must have taken him nine hours to read it from cover to cover but Grace hadn't shown the slightest reaction. Not the hint of a smile when it was humorous and wry, not a single tear when it was sad. He looked up: Patti was standing in the doorway, watching him. She was wearing a fluffy white sweater and very tight blue jeans.

'Hi, Professor.'

'Come on in,' he told her, and stood up to bring a chair across from the corner of the room. 'What brings you here?'

'Did you get the link I sent you? "Paleontology Prof In Rest Home Rescue Drama"?'

'Yes, thanks, I did. I meant to get back to you, I'm sorry. That was great, that appeal to anybody who might have seen Doctor Zauber.'

'That's OK.' Patti nodded toward Grace. 'You have more important things to worry about.'

'Did you get any response?'

'No, not a single one. Well, two or three, but they were obviously hoaxes. Somebody said they saw Doctor Zauber eating a cheesesteak in Geno's, and somebody else saw him selling fake designer purses on Chestnut Street. But look what just came up.'

She handed him a computer printout. It was a news item from the international media site EINnews.com. The headline read, 'Sixteen Pensioners Die In Polish Bus Blaze'. It was accompanied by a color photograph of a burned-out bus, which had been reduced to a blackened skeleton on four charred wheels.

'Read it,' Patti urged him.

Nathan laid aside his book. According to the printout, sixteen elderly people from a residential home in Skawina had been heading to Oświęcim for a social evening and dance with the residents of another residential home. They had failed to arrive, and when police eventually went to look for them, they were found in their burned-out bus in a forest to the north of highway forty-four.

Nobody had yet been able to explain why they had turned off the main road into the woods, or how the bus had caught fire, or why none of the elderly people had made any attempt to escape.

Patti reached over and tapped the last paragraph with her pink sparkly fingernail. 'This is the clincher, right here.'

Nathan read it. 'Forensic investigators in Kraków have reported that although the bodies of the sixteen bus passengers were badly burned, none of them died as a result of smoke inhalation, which has led detectives to conclude that they were all dead before the bus was set alight.

'Police commissioner Grzegorz Schetnya said at a news conference yesterday that he believed that the elderly people could have been the victims of one or more assailants, who subsequently burned the bus in an attempt to conceal any evidence of their crime.

'He could not understand why anybody should have wanted to kill so many elderly people, none of whom were carrying money or any items of value. "I can only theorize that it was an act of wanton butchery," he said. "A thrill killing, for its own sake."'

'What do you think?' asked Patti. 'I mean – that sounds exactly like the Murdstone Rest Home fire to me. OK – it was a bus, and not a building. But all of those old folks were dead before they were burned, just like the old folks here.'

'You could be right,' said Nathan. He read the printout again. Then he said, 'Kraków . . . that's where the original basilisk was supposed to have come from. So that kind of fits. If there were any basilisk remains to be found . . . any bones or skin that could have yielded DNA . . . Kraków is the first place *I* would have started looking for them, before I looked anyplace else.'

'It's Doctor Zauber, isn't it?' said Patti, excitedly. 'The second I read that story, I *knew* it was Doctor Zauber.'

'Well, hold up a minute. There's no way of telling for sure. Maybe the bus had a leak in its muffler, and all those old folks died of carbon monoxide poisoning.'

'It's Doctor Zauber, you know it is! He's gone back to Poland to make himself another basilisk!'

Nathan couldn't help smiling. 'You know something, you're even crazier than me.'

'I'm not crazy, I'm unprejudiced, that's all. I'm prepared to believe that anybody is capable of absolutely anything, and that's how I find all my best stories. I put two and two together and make six-and-a-quarter. It was me who broke that story about the man who tried to kidnap Punxsutawney Phil – you know, the groundhog from *Groundhog Day* – and eat him.'

'What? I never heard about that.'

'It's true. He wanted to broil him and eat him so that he could forecast the weather, and get a job as a weatherman on NBC.'

'That *is* crazy.'

'Yes, but it happened, and it was true. Just like the basilisk is true.'

Nathan was silent for a moment. Then he said, 'I saw him again – Doctor Zauber. I heard him again, the same way I did before. I saw a new basilisk, too. Right in here.'

'When was this?'

'Three days ago.'

'Three days ago? Why didn't you tell me? You promised to keep me up to date.'

'I know. But it was only a nightmare. Or a daymare, rather. And I haven't had another one since.'

Patti tapped the printout again. 'Look at the date that happened. That was three days ago, too.' She paused, and then she said, 'Did you actually see Doctor Zauber's face, like you did on the ceiling? Did he say anything to you? What did he say?'

'Pretty much the same thing. He says he wants us to work together, to breed more mythological beasts. He says he needs me. He obviously knows how to bring these creatures to life, and how to *keep* them alive, but he doesn't know how to control their cell growth.'

'What does that mean?'

'They don't develop properly. You know, like kids who are born with only one eye, or spina bifida, something like that. The basilisk that Grace and I saw at the Murdstone was very badly deformed, but if we're going to use mythological beasts for stem-cell therapy, they'll have to be pretty well perfect. We don't want to cure somebody's multiple sclerosis but give them some other affliction that's even worse.'

Patti frowned at him. 'You sound like you're thinking of actually doing it.'

Nathan looked across at Grace. 'Doctor Zauber said that he could bring her out of her coma, if I did. And I have to admit that I was tempted, for a moment. But only for a moment.'

'So what are you going to do now?'

He held up the printout. 'I'm going to call my friend Rafał Jasłewicz, from the Museum of Zoology in Kraków, in Poland. Well, I say "friend". I only met him once, at a zoological seminar in Chicago, but he's like the world's leading expert on basilisks and chimeras and gargoyles, and he's a really great guy.'

'I thought *you* were the world's leading expert on all that stuff.'

'The biological side of it – yes, maybe. But Rafał knows all about the history, and the mythology. He was incredibly helpful when I was starting up my gryphon project. He agrees with me: he believes that most mythical beasts actually existed, but he doesn't believe that they were the result of natural evolution.'

'What do you mean?'

'Well, gryphons and basilisks didn't evolve naturally like apes and horses and elephants – or *us*, for that matter. They were bred deliberately by alchemists who had discovered how to cross one totally different species with another.'

He stood up, and took down his coat from the back of the door. 'Do you want to come along? I'm going home to make this call, and then Denver and I are going out to eat. You're welcome to join us.'

'Sure,' said Patti. She looked across at Grace and said, 'Any improvement?'

Nathan shook his head.

'Don't you worry,' said Patti. 'Wherever she is, God's taking care of her.'

'I wouldn't have thought you were religious.'

'Of course I am. When you've seen how evil people can be, you know that there must be a Devil. And if there's a Devil, there has to be a God. QED.'

It was nearly nine thirty in the evening in Poland when Nathan called Rafał Jasłewicz. He hadn't spoken to him for over three years, but Rafał greeted him as if they had gone out drinking together only the week before.

'Nathan! I hear about your disappointment with your gryphon! I am very sorry for this! Maybe you have better luck with the next try!'

'There isn't going to be a next try, Rafał. Not just yet. The Zoo canceled my funding.'

'This is ridiculous! Don't they understand how difficult it is, this work? This is not like rearing chickens! It takes many years!'

'That's for sure. But, listen, Rafał. I have something serious to ask you. Did you ever hear of a cryptozoologist called Doctor Zauber? He's German, but he's been living and working in the States for quite a few years.'

'You mean *Christian* Zauber? Yes, of course! He was once at the Jagiellonian University here in Kraków, maybe fifteen years ago. He wrote several papers on medieval magic. I remember one of them very well because it was all about mythical beasts, which of course is one of my specialties. And they were very notorious, these papers, at the time.'

'Notorious? Why was that?'

'Christian Zauber said that black magic was completely misunderstood, and that if we studied it scientifically, we would discover that it was not really magic at all, but a practical way to harness the existing powers of the world around us. *That* was not very popular with the university faculty, as you can imagine! And especially not the church! But it was his paper on the mythical beasts that caused such an outrage, and he was asked to leave the university before he brought it into further disrepute.'

'Really?' asked Nathan. 'What was so outrageous about it?'

'He called it *De Monstrorum*, which was the title of a very rare sixteenth-century treatise which was written by the monks of Leipzig University. As far as I know, only two copies exist, although I have never seen one. The monks had been trying to breed extraordinary creatures, but in secret they had been using local women to procreate with horses and birds and reptiles, and some of their experiments were monstrous.

'Zauber was convinced from what he had read in *De Monstrorum* that the monks had actually succeeded in re-creating several mythical beasts. They had also created some new ones of their own, such as a child with the tentacles of a squid instead of arms and a woman with a horse's legs, like a centaur. He said it was essential that we try to repeat their experiments, using modern technology, because there was no reason why different species should not intermingle, to make the best of all of our attributes. In the final analysis, he said, we are all God's creatures. Men should be able to swim like dolphins. Women should be able to give birth to dogs.

'Maybe Zauber was not completely serious about his ideas. Maybe he was simply trying to be provocative. But he was German, and his suggestions brought back too strongly the medical research at Belsen and Auschwitz. And, of course, he upset the Roman Catholic bishops.'

'Sure. I can understand that. I got enough flak from the church myself. What happened to Zauber after that?'

'He stayed in Kraków for a year or two. I know, because I used to see him almost every week sitting alone at the Nostalgia restaurant on Karmelicka Street, eating his lunch. Always the same, potato dumplings with mushrooms, and a glass of white wine.

'I saw one article about him, in the *Dziennik Polski* newspaper. He said that he had turned from medieval mythology to medieval archeology. He was exploring the cultural history of Kraków by digging down through the many layers of buildings which had been built on top of buildings, churches on top of churches, cellars on top of cellars.

'That must have been eight or ten years ago. After that, I never saw him again, and there was nothing about his archeology in the papers. Until you call me tonight, my friend, I never thought about Christian Zauber once.'

'Rafał, I really need to find him. I'll explain why when I get to Kraków.'

'You are coming to Kraków? For real? This would be excellent! I will take you to my favorite restaurant and fill you with *bigos*!'

'I look forward to it, whatever *bigos* is.'

He put down the phone. Patti said, 'Well?'

'I think I'm going to Poland,' he told her.

'So I was right?'

He nodded. 'I think so. I think he's gone back to Kraków and he's trying to breed another basilisk – and God knows what other monstrosities.'

'Well . . . if it was him who offed all of those old folks, it sounds like he might have done it already.'

'We can't jump to any conclusions. Like I say, we don't have any evidence that he had anything to do with it. But I think you're right. I think it is him. I just don't understand how this life-energy thing works. How do you take some-body's life-energy? Like, where is it, exactly? My cousin Jack is a neurosurgeon at the Temple University Hospital and he said that even after twenty years of poking around in people's brains, he still hasn't managed to locate anybody's soul.'

'Maybe Doctor Zauber does it by black magic,' Patti suggested.

Nathan said, 'I don't believe in that.'

'Doctor Zauber's face comes out of the wall and talks to you, and a seven-foot basilisk appears in front of you, and you don't believe in black magic?'

'It was a nightmare, like I said. Or if it *wasn't* a nightmare, there must be a perfectly good scientific explanation for it.'

'Oh, for sure! Except that you don't have the first idea what that perfectly good scientific explanation could possibly be. Like you don't have the first idea why your wife is in a coma, just because she was stared at by some shambling collection of old sacks.'

'Do *you* believe in black magic?'

'I believe in being totally open-minded.'

'OK. I'm prepared to accept that even if *I* don't believe in black magic, Doctor Zauber does, and he's going to be acting accordingly. So when I find him – *if* I find him – I'll watch out if he tries anything that looks like sorcery.'

'When *you* find him? What about me?'

'You don't want to come to Poland, do you?'

'Of course I want to come to Poland. This is my story and I'm sticking with it. Who found you that item from EIN?'

'I don't know, Patti. It could be genuinely dangerous. Especially if Zauber has actually managed to create another basilisk.'

'I like dangerous. Besides, you need me. My mother was Polish, and I know what *bigos* is.'

SIXTEEN

Night Flight

When Denver arrived home, they drove together to the Trolley Car Diner on Germantown Avenue. It had been raining again, and the lurid neon lights on the Trolley Car's façade were reflected in the black asphalt of the street outside. They found themselves a booth at the end of the diner and ordered fried chicken and soft-shelled crabs and strawberry shakes. The jukebox played doo-wop music.

Denver said, 'You're going to *Poland*? How long for?'

'I don't know. As long as it takes to find Doctor Zauber.'

'So what am I supposed to do?'

'I want you to stay here and keep an eye on Mom for me.'

'Yes, but if what you say is true, and you need to find this Zauber dude before Mom can wake up, what's the point of my staying here? If I come to Poland, too, I can help you to look for him. You can always call the doctor to check on Mom.'

Nathan looked at Patti and Patti shrugged.

'Come on, Pops,' Denver urged him.

'OK,' said Nathan. 'You can be my back-up. But I want you to stay well clear of Doctor Zauber, if we find him. I don't want you ending up in a coma like your mom. Or worse than that, dead.'

He wasn't sure if Denver would be more of a hindrance than a help, but on reflection he would rather have him close to him, where he could make sure that he wasn't getting into any trouble. And Denver was right: he could call the hospital at any time to check on Grace, and Poland was only half a day away. 'Let's finish up here and then we can go home and pack.'

They left the Trolley Car around nine. Patti promised to come around at seven thirty in the morning, well in time for their American Airlines flight from PHL. Nathan took Denver home, and logged on to his computer to book an extra ticket to Kraków. Then, while Denver packed his bag, he drove down to the Hahnemann to see Grace.

The room was dimly lit, and Grace lay there as pale and silent as if she were dead. It was only when he bent over her to kiss her that he could feel her breathing.

'Grace, sweetheart, I'm going away for a few days, but I'll come back as soon as I can. I promise you, I'm going to find that Doctor Zauber and I'm going to get you out of this coma, and I'm never going to mess with any of those Cee-Zee creatures, ever again. They say you shouldn't try to be smarter than God, don't they, because you never can be, and you'll get your comeuppance sooner or later.'

The Egyptian-looking nurse had silently entered the room, and had been standing in the corner watching him. When he realized that she was there, he turned around and said, 'Hi . . . I didn't hear you come in.'

'Where are you going?' she asked him.

'Poland. There's something I have to do there – somebody I have to find. I'm not sure how long I'll be away. You will take good care of her, won't you? You have my cell number, you can call me any time at all.'

'Of course we will take care of her, Mr Underhill. She appears to be quite stable, at the moment. Doctor Ishikawa does not anticipate any dramatic changes.'

She came up to him, and laid her hand on his arm.

'I know,' she said. 'You are feeling helpless, but there is nothing more that you can possibly do.'

We'll see about that, thought Nathan. He glanced across at the crater in the wall, where the door handle had dented the plaster. *Wherever you are, Doctor Zauber, I'm coming after you, and I'm going to find you, and you're going to give me my wife back.*

'What is it?' asked the nurse.

'What do you mean, "what is it"?'

'I don't know. Ever since your wife has been here, I have sensed something in this room. I don't know how to explain it.'

She looked around. 'You know – it is almost like somebody else is here, watching her. I have never felt like that with a patient before. Please – I don't mean to alarm you, or upset you. But I thought you ought to know.'

'There *is* somebody watching her,' said Nathan. 'I can't explain it, either, but that's the reason I have to go away.'

The nurse reached up with both hands and unfastened the catch of her necklace. She drew the pendant out from underneath her uniform and gave it to him. He held it in the palm of his hand and frowned at it. It was an ankh, an Egyptian cross, studded with black pearls. It was still warm from her skin.

'Take it with you,' she said. 'It will help to protect you from bad things.'

'No, I can't. Supposing I lose it?'

'You won't lose it. You will bring it back to me safe; and when you do that, your wife will wake up.'

Nathan looked at her narrowly. Was she aware of something that he wasn't? She was talking to him as if she knew exactly why Grace was in a coma, and why he was going to Poland. She was talking to him almost as if she had seen Doctor Zauber, too.

'Thank you,' he said, but he deliberately said it as if he was expecting an explanation.

'Just go,' she told him. 'Go and come back. Don't be worried. I'm a nurse, remember, and when you are a nurse you see things that nobody else sees. You see people very close to dying, with all of the color bleached out of their eyes. You see their spirits, like shadows standing in the corner. You see their souls.'

'Thank you,' Nathan repeated; but this time he meant nothing at all but *thank you*.

'I know where your wife is,' said the nurse. 'I know what kind of lands she is walking through. Once you discover how to do it, you will call her back, I promise you, and she will come to you.'

'How do you know this?'

'Because I was trained to watch people, and the way they behave. I was trained how to recognize fear, and worry; but I was also taught how to recognize bravery, and hope.'

'It's more than that, though, isn't it?'

'Mr Underhill, all of us have somebody who takes care of us, whether we know it or not.'

'If you say so, nurse.'

'You can call me Aisha. It means "alive".'

Nathan gave Grace two more kisses, once on the lips and once on the forehead. He couldn't bear to leave her but there was no other way.

'God keep you safe,' said Aisha.

Nathan walked out of the hospital and headed through the rain toward the parking structure. He didn't really understand how Aisha had any inkling of what he was intending to do; but he felt reassured and grateful that she was looking after Grace.

Outside the parking structure, a skinny young man was standing in a corner, trying to keep out of the rain. He wore a brown woolen hat pulled down over his ears, and a baggy parka.

'How about a little change, man?' he called out, in a thin, nasal voice.

Nathan dug into his pocket and came out with a handful of pennies and dimes and quarters. The young man looked down at it disdainfully. 'Is that all? I haven't eaten in three days.'

'It's enough for an egg McMuffin. Sorry if it isn't enough for you to score.'

'I put a curse on you, man.'

'Listen,' Nathan told him, 'if you don't want the change, I'll take it back.'

'Then take it!' the young man shouted at him, and showered the coins in his face.

Nathan stood there for a moment, half inclined to grab the young man and shove him up against the wall, but then he simply shook his head, and said, 'You don't know how lucky you are.'

'Lucky? You call this lucky?'

'You're alive, you're conscious. You have all of your faculties. What more do you want?'

'What the fuck you talking about, man? I've told you. I've put a curse on you. There's nothing going to go right in your life, ever again.'

Nathan walked away, and up the corrugated concrete ramp. As he reached the top, he turned around and saw the young man crouching down on the sidewalk, picking up the coins that he had scattered.

*   *   *

It took thirteen-and-a-half hours to fly to Kraków, changing planes in Chicago to the national Polish airline, Lot. Denver slept most of the way, with his MP3 player attached to his ears. Patti worked on her laptop for a while, moving her lips as she wrote, but then she folded it up and she fell asleep, too.

Nathan closed his eyes but he could think only of Doctor Zauber, and his white plaster face in the wall. Over the roaring of the engines and the hissing of the air conditioning, he could even hear Doctor Zauber's voice.

When we die, nobody really cares. Nobody misses us. The carousel of life keeps on going around and around, and up and down, with everybody screaming and laughing.

He had the terrible feeling that Doctor Zauber was here on the plane, leaning over him and staring into his face. He abruptly opened his eyes. He couldn't stop himself. But it was one of the flight attendants, leaning over him to tug Patti's blanket to cover her shoulder.

'I'm sorry,' she smiled. 'I did not mean to disturb you. Is there anything you would like? Coffee? Or a drink, maybe?'

'Thanks. Maybe a glass of red wine.'

After that, he didn't bother to try to sleep, but sat there nursing his glass of wine. Outside, it was already daylight, and the window shades were glowing with sunshine, although it was only four in the morning in Philadelphia. He still hadn't finished his wine before the flight attendants began to serve breakfast.

Denver opened his eyes, blinked and yawned. 'What's happening, Pops?'

'Breakfast.'

'What, already? I was having this really scary dream. All of these statues came to life and they were chasing me.'

'Just as well you woke up, then, before they caught you.'

They landed in Kraków at two thirty in the afternoon, leaving the sunshine five thousand feet above them and bumping downward through thick gray cloud. It was raining hard, and the raindrops crawled diagonally across the windows as they tilted and dipped toward the runway.

Rafał was waiting for them in the terminal of John Paul II International Airport. Nathan was surprised how much older he looked. He was a big, stocky man with short-cropped hair that had turned white since he had last seen him, and a heavy gray moustache like a yardbrush. He had bulbous cheeks and a bulbous nose and bulbous blue eyes, and he wore tiny steel-rimmed spectacles.

His droopy brown raincoat looked as if it belonged in a Cold War secret-agent movie, like *The Spy Who Came In From The Cold.*

'Well, well! Nathan! *Witają Polska*! Welcome to Poland!'

He gave Nathan a huge, bearlike hug and slapped him on the back. He smelled strongly of tobacco and wet raincoat.

'And this is your son! Welcome to Poland, young sir! And who is this charming young lady?'

Patti held out her hand. 'Patti Laquelle, *Philadelphia Web News*. Pleased to meet you, sir.'

Rafał took hold of her hand and kissed it. Patti blushed and said, 'First time anybody ever did *that* to me!'

'Old Polish courtesy,' grinned Rafał, showing tobacco-stained teeth, 'Now, you must be very tired. I will drive you to your hotel, and you can maybe rest for a while. Then we can meet for a drink and some food and talk about what you need to do here.'

He had a silver Renault Espace waiting for them outside. He helped them to load their suitcases and then he drove them eastward toward the city.

'I have booked you rooms at the Amadeus, near the Grand Square, which is very convenient for the Old Town and the Jewish Quarter. It is old-fashioned hotel but I think you prefer it. Maybe you do not have much time for seeing sights, I don't know.'

Nathan said, 'I don't think we will, I'm afraid. You heard about all of those old people who were burned alive in a bus?'

'You mean here, near Kraków? Yes, of course. But what does that have to do with Doctor Zauber?'

'I suspect it has everything to do with Doctor Zauber,' said Nathan, and he told Rafał about his encounter with Doctor Zauber and his basilisk at the Murdstone Rest Home, and what had happened to Grace, and how so many of the Murdstone's residents had been killed by fire.

Rafał shook his head. 'All for this "life-energy"? This is very hard to believe. If anybody else but you had told me this—'

'Rafał, I saw it with my own eyes. Otherwise I wouldn't believe it, either.'

Although it was raining, the streets of Kraków were teeming with tourists wearing plastic capes and carrying umbrellas. Rafał drove them past the old stone walls which had once surrounded the city, and pointed out the baroque turrets and elaborate spires of Wawel Castle, on a hill overlooking the River Vistula.

'In medieval legend, you know, a terrible dragon lived in a cave there on Wawel Hill. The story goes that some stupid boys did not believe it existed, even though the village elders told them to stay well away. The dragon had been hibernating for hundreds of years but the boys went into the cave and woke it up. After that it came out every day, killing and eating cattle and sheep and even some people when it caught them unaware.

'The dragon was killed in the end by a wise alchemist called Krakus. He mixed up a paste of nitrate, tar and sulfur, and coated six dead sheep with it. He left the sheep outside the dragon's cave and the dragon came out and ate every one of them with a single bite. Inside its stomach the paste started to burn like fire, and so the dragon flew down to the Vistula and drank and drank as much water as it could.

'But the river water made the paste burn even hotter, and in the end the dragon drank so much water that it burst apart, and died.'

'Great story,' said Nathan.

'And it has a moral, too,' said Rafał. He stopped at a traffic light and a blue-and-white tram went moaning past, with faces staring out of every window, like a moving gallery of sad, pale portraits. 'The moral is that just because we cannot see something, that does not mean that it does not exist. Like the dragon of Wawel Hill.'

He drove them to the Rynek Główny, the huge market square in the center of the city, which covered almost ten acres. On the far side of the square stood the Cloth Hall, with a Gothic façade that had been built over seven hundred years ago; and the thirteenth-century Town Hall Tower. There were cafés and restaurants all around the square, with umbrellas and awnings that flapped in the rain.

'What an amazing place,' said Patti, and Nathan would have agreed with her, if it hadn't been raining so hard, and they hadn't come here to Kraków on such a dangerous and miserable mission.

Rafał drove them to Mikołajska Street and parked outside their hotel. The Amadeus was a flat-fronted eighteenth-century building, painted white, with a decorative porch. A porter came out to take their luggage, while Rafał gave Nathan another bear hug, and kissed Patti's hand again.

'I will see you six o'clock, yes? I have made some research for you which may help you. And I have been asking many people about Christian Zauber, if they have seen him or heard where he might be. If he is here in Kraków, I promise you that we will find him. I have many friends in many different walks of life. Students, tram conductors, shopkeepers, waiters. People who notice what is going on.'

They were checked in by a pretty, bosomy girl with blonde pigtails and intensely blue eyes. Patti nudged Denver and said, 'Hey, Denver, she's too old for you. And you don't speak the lingo.'

'Who needs to speak the lingo?' Denver retorted.

'I guess you're right. A slack, goofy grin speaks a thousand words, even in Polish.'

Nathan eased off his shoes and rested on his bed until five forty-five p.m. His room had a high cciling, but it was very gloomy, with a huge mahogany bed and a massive antique wardrobe that could have accommodated an entire family, as well as their pets. On the wall hung a dark picture of a peasant woman with a brown headscarf, walking through a field under a thundery sky. It suited his mood.

He closed his eyes but found it impossible to sleep. There were too many unfamiliar noises, like the elevator whining, and the wobbling sound of car tires on the cobbled street outside.

Eventually he picked up the phone and called the Hahnemann, and spoke to one of Grace's nurses.

'No change, Professor, I'm afraid. I wish I could tell you different.'

'Well, if you could just tell her that Nathan loves her, even if she can't hear you.'

'Of course.'

He showered, and changed into black corduroy pants and a gray denim shirt. As he combed his hair in the bathroom mirror he thought how haggard he was. *And I thought that Rafał looked as if the years had beaten him down.*

He went downstairs in the cramped little elevator, surrounded on all sides by countless reflections of his haggard self. He walked through to the dimly lit restaurant and found Patti and Denver already sitting in one of the brown-leather booths together. He didn't know what they were talking about but they were sitting with their heads very close together, and nodding to each other in unison, as if they were listening to the same inaudible song.

'You want a beer?' he asked Denver, as he sat down next to them.

'A beer? Sure. Thanks. But I ordered myself a Coke already.'

'Cancel the Coke and have a beer. If you're old enough and ugly enough to help me track down Doctor Zauber, you're old enough to have a beer.'

A few minutes later, Rafał arrived, smelling of carbolic soap and tobacco. They went through their now-familiar ritual of hugging and back-slapping and kissing Patti's hand. Rafał sat down and ordered a glass of vodka and some dark chocolate cookies, which tasted of spice.

He knocked back his vodka and held out his glass to the waitress for another. 'A half-hour ago,' he announced, 'I had a phone call from a friend of mine, a real estate agent who rents out property in the Kazimierz district.'

'Oh, yes?'

'He told me that more than five years ago Doctor Zauber took out a lease on an old house near the intersection of Kupa and Izaaka Streets. It is very fashionable to live there now, but in those days not so much. It used to be very run-down. But Doctor Zauber did not live there himself. He sub-let the house to two couples, and also an artist. About a month ago, though, he gave his tenants notice to quit, and now he has moved back into the house himself.'

'So he *is* here,' said Nathan.

'What did I tell you?' Patti put in. 'We should schlep round there, pay him a visit?'

'I don't know. I don't want to scare him off. If he disappears again, he may disappear for good.'

Patti said, 'You think? He doesn't sound like the kind of guy who scares easy.'

'What do you think we should do, Rafał?' Nathan asked him.

'It is difficult for me to say. Doctor Zauber was always a very unpredictable man. One minute all smiles, the next minute angry like a volcano. He may welcome your arrival here in Kraków, on the one hand, because he wants so desperately to pick your brains. On the other hand, you have told him that you will have no part in killing old people, for this so-called "life-energy" that he needs to keep his creatures alive. In final analysis, I don't think he will trust you.'

'Maybe he will, maybe he won't. That's a chance I'll have to take. But I do have some leverage over him. The Philadelphia police are very anxious to talk to him, and if he had anything to do with that bus fire—'

'Yes, the Polish Policja would probably be very interested in talking to him, too.'

'I think we just have to play it by ear,' said Nathan. 'I'm not going to do anything until I find out how to bring Grace out of her coma.'

'I think to be cautious is right,' Rafał agreed. 'Particularly since you suspect that Doctor Zauber may be breeding another basilisk, and maybe other creatures. It is not wise to go hunting for basilisks at night. Or gryphons, for that matter, or any of those beasts. Much safer in the daytime, when most of them are sleeping.'

Rafał took them to the Wierzynek Restaurant on the Grand Square, only a short walk away, because it served food in the traditional Polish style. It had stopped raining and when they reached the restaurant it was warm and noisy and very crowded, with candles burning everywhere.

They sat at a circular table in the corner, and Rafał ordered beetroot soup and cheese *pierogi* and crayfish, as well as roast duck and saddle of venison and river pike.

Then he raised his glass and said, '*Jedzcie, pijcie i popuszczajcie pasa*! Eat, drink, and loosen your belts!' Nathan raised his glass, too, but his mouth felt dry and he had very little appetite. He couldn't help feeling guilty because he was sitting here in this lively restaurant, eating good food and drinking wine, while Grace was still lying unconscious in hospital. At least he hoped that she was unconscious, and that she wasn't trapped inside some terrifying nightmare.

Rafał carefully wiped his moustache with his napkin. 'I have left until last the most important evidence that I have discovered,' he said. 'You remember that I told you that when Doctor Zauber was obliged to leave the Jagiellonian University he gave up mythology and said that he was turning instead to archeology. I found at the university one of the students he paid to help him – although this student is now a lecturer. Doctor Zauber and his students excavated many different historical sites all around the city, but the most important was the vault underneath Saint Casimir's Basilica, a small church which overlooks Zygmunt Square.

'According to this gentleman, Saint Casimir's Basilica was constructed in the late fifteenth century on top of a much older church. But the builders used the existing vaults and the ruins of the older church as their foundations. This was common in Kraków, and some churches even have glass panes set into the sidewalk next to their walls, so that you can look down and see the more ancient layers underneath.'

Nathan was beginning to see where this was going. 'So what was Zauber looking for, exactly?'

'He told his assistants that he was looking for holy relics. After all, there is a story that all of the nails that were taken from the true cross were sealed in a casket and eventually found their way to Kraków, brought here by pilgrims from the Holy Land. It is also rumored that the gold medallion worn by Pontius Pilate is secreted somewhere in the walls of the Basilica of the Virgin Mary. There are supposed to be many more artifacts, such as hair from the beard of John the Baptist.

'Doctor Zauber and his assistants dug down through three vaults, each of which had collapsed on top of the other. In the very lowest vault they discovered the skeletal remains of three monks, still in the rotted remnants of their habits. They also found a parcel of leather tied up with cord, and sealed with black wax.

'My informant at the university tells me that he remembers this parcel well, because Doctor Zauber opened it immediately, which of course is not the usual practice with valuable historical relics. Usually, they are wrapped up and taken carefully to a laboratory to be examined under controlled conditions.

'Doctor Zauber also refused to allow any of his assistants to take photographs of this parcel. He told them whatever it was, it was undoubtedly a fake, and he did not want to be made a fool of in the academic journals.'

'So what was inside this parcel?' asked Patti. 'Did your friend manage to get a look?'

Rafał nodded. 'He said that it was a collection of large bones which looked as if they had come from a large animal like a horse, perhaps, and also some smaller bones, like black branches. But there was also a fragment of skin, scaly and thick, like that of a large snake. It was dark gray or black, he thinks, but Doctor Zauber wrapped it up again very quickly, and the light was poor.'

'Did he have any idea what it was?'

'No – none whatsoever, although one of his fellow students thought that it looked like the bones of a demon. He said maybe it had been exorcized and killed by priests, and its remains sealed with black wax to prevent it from ever escaping and reconstituting itself. But he was just trying to give everybody the heebie-jeebies. That is right, yes? "*Heebie-jeebies*"?'

Nathan said, 'That student was nearer the mark than he realized. It wasn't a demon, but it was something pretty close to a demon. And if there was any DNA left in those bones or that skin, then it *was* capable of being brought back to life.'

'Then you think the same as I think,' said Rafał. 'Doctor Zauber was searching for the remains of a basilisk, and he found them.'

Denver said, 'OK, so he found them. But he didn't have any kind of laboratory, did he, like Pops?'

'No . . . but that is why he went to the United States. He had obviously read about your father's work in cryptozoology, and he wanted to take advantage of his expertise. But he must have realized that your father would not condone the killing of elderly people to take their life-energy, or their soul, or whatever you want to call it. That is why he bribed your father's assistant to steal his research.'

Nathan said, 'All I want now is to find out how to bring Grace out of that coma. I'm not interested in what happens to Zauber, so long as he tells me that.'

'That is very gratifying to know,' said a thickly accented voice, very close to his ear.

He turned around in his chair, knocking over his glass of red wine, as if blood had suddenly splashed across the table-cloth. Standing close behind him – unnervingly close – was Doctor Zauber, grinning at him so that his eyes sparkled and his teeth glistened in the candlelight. He was wearing his usual black suit and a black silk shirt, with a black bow tie.

'Please . . .' he said, lifting one well-manicured hand. 'Please – you don't have to get up.'

Nathan stood up all the same, and Rafał did, too, dropping his napkin on to the table, and aggressively bunching his fists.

'Well, well,' said Nathan, even though he felt breathless. 'The good Doctor Zauber. How did you find us?'

'The same way that you found me, I expect. Intuition. Putting two and two together. I have an exceptional talent for it.'

Doctor Zauber smiled at Denver and Patti, and said, 'So invigorating to see young people getting involved in scientific exploration, don't you think? I sense that this young man is your only son, Professor. And this young lady is a *very* wayward spirit.'

'*Hey*,' Patti protested.

'No offense meant,' said Doctor Zauber, soothingly. But then he turned back to Nathan and said, 'I knew you would come, sooner or later. If you hadn't, I would have had to visit you again, and give you more encouragement.'

'Why don't you cut out the crap,' Nathan retorted. 'You need to tell me how to get my wife back, and I need you to tell me right now.'

'I understand your anxiety,' said Doctor Zauber. 'But *you* need to understand that everything in this world has a price. You have eaten this fine meal, you will be billed for it. Your wife, sad to say, was billed for her intervention in my affairs. This account now needs to be settled.'

'She did nothing to you. Nothing at all.'

'Of course she did, Professor. Maybe it was you who shot and mortally wounded my creation, and not your wife, but she aided and abetted you, did she not? It was only by sheer chance that both of you weren't killed where you stood. You deserved it, God knows. Even a basilisk is a living creature, with a right to life.'

'I want her back, Zauber. And I won't give you a moment's peace until you tell me how.'

'What will you do? Beat me? Torture me? Put me on the rack until I squeal? You know what I want from you, Professor. If you give me your co-operation, and your assistance, I will tell you exactly what you need to do to restore your wife to consciousness. I swear on the Bible.'

Nathan lost his temper. He had sworn to himself that he wouldn't, when he eventually confronted Doctor Zauber, but all the stress and the anger that had been building up inside him suddenly exploded, and he went for Doctor Zauber with all the pent-up fury of an attack-dog.

Except that Doctor Zauber was no longer there. He was standing on the opposite side of the restaurant, behind another table crowded with diners, still smiling, his eyes glittering in the candlelight.

Denver stared at him with his mouth hanging open. 'How'd he *do* that? I never even saw him move.'

Rafał crossed himself, twice, and promptly sat down, his face as purple as if he were suffering from a heart attack. But Patti said, 'Holy moly. What a story *this* is going to make.' She dug down into her bottle-green handwoven bag and brought out a camera.

'Patti,' Nathan warned her, 'be careful.' He realized now that they were dealing with somebody far more complex and powerful than he had first imagined. He had tried to explain away Doctor Zauber's appearances on his bedroom ceiling and the wall of Grace's hospital room by ascribing them to some kind of extra-sensory perception, or delayed hypnotic suggestion, or by dismissing them simply as nightmares. But he couldn't explain how a man could instantly move from one side of a crowded restaurant to the other, so fast that nobody saw him do it.

'You should really consider your options, Professor,' said Doctor Zauber, and now he was standing so close behind Nathan that he could have reached out and put his hand on his shoulder.

Denver shook his head slowly from side to side and said, 'Wow, dude. That is *awesome*.'

Patti focused her camera but Doctor Zauber raised one hand and said, 'No photographs, please. It is a waste of time. They will show nothing at all. And I do not care for the flash.'

Nathan turned around to face him. 'So what are you proposing?' he said, although he was still trembling with anger. 'Come on, what exactly do you want me to do, in exchange for this precious information?'

Doctor Zauber raised his right eyebrow. It looked like a crow rising from a barren field. 'I am doing exactly the same thing that *you* have been doing, except that I have been working on the project from the other side, as it were. You and I, we have been like two engineers trying separately to build a car. You have successfully designed the engine. I have successfully designed the body. Now we need to get together so that we can finally assemble our wonderful vehicle, and drive off into the future.'

'But to do this, people have to die. Was it you who killed all of those old people on that bus at – where was it?'

'Brzeźnica, just off highway forty-four,' Rafał put in. 'Sixteen of them, all together. Most of them were burned beyond any recognition.'

Doctor Zauber's expression darkened. 'I am not admitting to anything, Professor. You think I am a fool?'

Patti lifted her camera and took a flash photograph. Doctor Zauber whipped up his hand to shield his eyes, and everybody in the restaurant turned around to look. Now the head waiter was weaving his way between the tables toward them, his bald head shining like a bright pink lightbulb, to see what all this disturbance was about.

Doctor Zauber snapped, 'I told you, did I not? No flashes!' Then he faced Nathan and said, 'You need to think about this very deeply, Professor Underhill. The only lives which will be taken will be lives which in any case are almost at their very end. The loss will be infinitesimal but the benefits will be infinite. If you consider that wars are worth fighting, in which thousands of young men are killed, then surely this is worth striving for. Extinction for a few, yes. But health and happiness for so many more.'

'All right,' said Nathan. 'I'll think about it.'

Doctor Zauber nodded in appreciation. 'I will give you one night and one day. Tomorrow evening at the same time meet me at Dekafencja, it's a café on Slawkowska Street. Then we can talk about this and make the best decision.'

The head waiter came up to them. 'There is some kind of trouble here?'

Rafał shook his head. 'No. No trouble. Lively argument.'

'How about you, sir?' asked the head waiter, turning toward Doctor Zauber. But Doctor Zauber was no longer there. He had been talking to Nathan, only inches away from him, but even Nathan hadn't seen him disappear.

Nathan sat down again, unsteadily. 'What are we dealing with here, Rafał?'

'He's so *cool*, man,' Denver put in. 'The magic disappearing dude.'

'Well, you use the word "magic" so easily,' said Rafał. 'But I believe that this is exactly the correct description. However, this is not magic like stage magic, like walking into one closet and appearing out of another, or sawing some pretty girl into two pieces. This is serious control of elemental forces. Doctor Zauber can use light, space, and above all time. This is how he creates his mythological beasts.'

Nathan said, 'I think I could use a drink.'

But Patti was looking at Rafał intently. 'You're trying to tell us that Doctor Zauber is a *magician*? But a *real* magician, not like Doug Henning or David Copperfield?'

'I think it is obvious that he has learned the knowledge of the ancient alchemists and sorcerers – those people who first discovered how to bring mythological beasts to life. Of course I have read about such processes but I have never known for certain if they really worked. In a similar way that Professor Underhill uses DNA and embryonic stem cells, Doctor Zauber must use his alchemical ability to turn bones and skin back into the creature which they used to be.

'Once he has brought them back, however, it seems that he doesn't know how to control their growth, so they end up deformed in some way.'

'So what the hell am I going to do?' asked Nathan.

Rafał put his knife and fork together, even though he had only half finished his venison. 'He said you have a night and a day. Well, we must find out more about how Doctor Zauber re-creates his creatures, and most of all we must find out the one thing that you have come here to Kraków to discover: how to save your wife.

'You cannot be party to killing people and taking their life-energy, no matter what the justification. And I know just the woman who can help us.'

SEVENTEEN

Mistress of the Dark Arts

'So who's this woman we're going to see?' asked Patti, as they stepped out of the restaurant.

'I regret only Professor Underhill and myself,' Rafał told her. 'She is not an easy person.'

'Oh, come on, Pops,' said Denver. 'This is just getting really interesting. Real black magic and stuff. I can't wait to tell Stu.'

Rafał laid a hand on his shoulder. 'Why don't you take Patti maybe to a club for a while, relax, have some fun? I recommend Frantic Club, on Szewska Street. Good drink, good food, also house and techno.'

'House and techno?' said Denver, in amazement. 'You know about that?'

'I have daughters,' said Rafał. 'You may even meet them there.'

He hailed a taxi for Denver and Patti, and then he linked arms with Nathan and said, 'Let us walk there. It is on Szeptem Street, not so far. And I need some fresh air, I think, after our little confrontation with Doctor Zauber. You know something, he does not look a single day older than he did when he was lecturing at the university.'

Nathan said, 'What would you do, in my position?'

'I don't know.' The street lights were reflected in Rafał's spectacles and made him look blind. 'I think it is very hard choice for you to make. But if there is one thing I have learned in my life, it is to make my own choice, and not the choice that somebody else expects of me. If anybody offers you *this*, or *that*, like Doctor Zauber, you should decide on something else altogether. Your own way. That is why we go to see Zofia Czarwonica.'

They crossed the main road together and then Rafał led Nathan along a dead-end street, lined on both sides with tall brown-painted houses, most of them with peeling stucco and darkened windows and soiled net curtains. Their façades were streaked with damp and some of them had weeds and wildflowers growing high up in their guttering. Nathan and Rafał had been walking arm-in-arm but now they had to make their way along Indian-file because there were so many cars parked halfway up on the sidewalk. Nathan could smell the sweet mustiness of old buildings.

'Not so long ago, most of the old Jewish Quarter was like this,' said Rafał. 'Now they have renovated so many buildings, a single-bedroom studio can cost you quarter of a million euro.'

They reached a narrow, maroon-painted building with a gray stone porch which was overhung with ivy, its leaves dry and white with disease. The paint on the door was blistered and the brass doorknocker was black. It was a wolf's head, snarling. Rafał banged on the door three times, hard.

They waited for over a minute. Rafał banged again, but there was still no answer. 'Seems like nobody's home,' said Nathan.

'Zofia is *always* at home. But I should have called her, maybe, to let her know that we were coming. Sometimes she is involved in ritual, or cooking her magic herbs.'

He stepped back and shouted, 'Zofia! Zofia Czarwonica! This is Rafał! Open the door!'

He was still looking up when the front door suddenly opened and a woman appeared. She was white-faced, with smudgy black eyes and wild black hair that was brushed up into an alarming shock. She was wearing a clinging black cotton dress that revealed a thin, almost emaciated body, but disproportionately large breasts. On both wrists she wore at least half a dozen silver bangles, decorated with Polish amber and turquoise and multi-colored enamels.

'Rafał Jasłewicz!' she said, in a high, dry voice as if she had been smoking too much. 'What are you doing here? Such a long time since I see you! I think you forget me!'

Nathan was surprised that she was speaking to Rafał in English, but she immediately turned to him and said, 'You are American. It is only polite.'

'Do I *look* that American?' said Nathan.

Zofia tapped her forehead with one very long black-polished fingernail. 'Zofia Czarwonica sees everything, sir. Besides, I heard you talking outside my door. I listen. I am always suspicious who comes to my house.'

Rafał gave Zofia one of his bear hugs and kissed her on both cheeks, twice. Then he stepped back and said, 'You look even more beautiful than ever, Zofia.'

'You want something,' Zofia retorted.

'Of course. I would not normally come to visit you so late. This is my friend Nathan Underhill, he is professor of zoology from Philadelphia.'

Zofia looked at Nathan directly. 'He has very bad problem,' she said.

Nathan nodded. 'You guessed it. I'm sorry if we're disturbing you.'

'Come in. You must tell me everything about it. I am one of the *znakharka*, and it is my duty to protect people from bad things.'

Rafał looked at Nathan and pulled a face which meant: *Why not? Let's go for it. What do we have to lose?*

Zofia disappeared back into the darkness, and Nathan and Rafał followed her. Inside the house, they found themselves in a gloomy hallway, with a highly polished floor of green and black linoleum. It smelled of lavender wax and boiling cabbage. On the right-hand side stood a dark mahogany hall-stand, with umbrellas in it, and assorted hats hanging from pegs. It had a mottled mirror in the middle of it, and Nathan caught sight of his reflection as he walked past. He looked like a man drowning in an algae-covered lake.

They climbed a very steep, creaking staircase. At the top, a door led off to the left-hand side, and Zofia opened it and beckoned them in.

This was her living room, with a window overlooking Szeptem Street, although it was dark now, and all Nathan could see was the window of the house opposite, with sagging orange curtains. The room was warm and stuffy, and smelled of dried herbs and old books. There were books everywhere: in bookcases, and stacked on the table, and built into teetering stacks of their own.

Two brindled cats were sleeping on a worn-out brocade couch. Zofia shooed them off and invited Nathan and Rafał to make themselves comfortable.

'You would like tea?' she asked them. 'I can make you

saxifrage tea which will protect you against evil magic. Or coffee, if you prefer. I have decaf.'

'We just came from Wierzynek Restaurant,' said Rafał. 'Maybe a glass of water.'

Zofia's kitchen was divided from her living room by a black-beaded curtain. She disappeared through it, and then returned with a red tumbler filled with water, like a conjuring trick.

'So, you have a serious problem,' she said. 'Nathan is very worried about somebody he loves. She is sick, maybe. He wants to find a way to cure her sickness, but something is preventing him. Some knot. Some dilemma.'

Nathan glanced at Rafał. 'I'm impressed,' he said.

Zofia raised one hand, with silver rings on every finger. 'No, no. It is not magic. It is sensitivity. Observation. Like Sherlock Holmes. You come to a *znakharka* because you are looking for some kind of cure. You do not yourself look sick, so I say to myself that you have come here on behalf of some-body close to you. You are American, and United States has most advanced medical treatment in whole world, so why has Rafał brought you here to see *me*?'

She made a twisting motion with her hands. 'Because of a knot that United States medical treatment cannot untie. Because of a dilemma.'

Nathan said, 'I'm still impressed.'

Zofia turned to Rafał. She had a wide, feline face with very high cheekbones. She was strikingly pale, as if she never left her apartment, but her skin was so flawless that her face could have been carved out of ivory. Now that he could see her in the lamplight, Nathan realized that she was also much younger than he had first supposed: no more than twenty-seven or twenty-eight, he would have guessed.

'You know of Christian Zauber?' Rafał asked her.

'Of course. What of him?'

'Nathan will explain to you.'

Nathan told Zofia all about his Cee-Zee project, and how his gryphon had died, and how Richard Scryman had stolen his research. He told her everything that he had told Rafał – all about the Murdstone Rest Home, and the fire, and the basilisk – both the real basilisk and the basilisk that he had seen in his nightmares.

'*Basilisk*,' Zofia whispered, when he had finished. 'Such a

terrible creature. Why should Doctor Zauber wish to bring
such a thing back to life?'

'I'm guessing that he plans to use a basilisk to cure cancer
patients, or anybody else who suffers some kind of invasive
disease.'

'How could he do that?'

'Think about it. When the basilisk looks at *anything* –
human, animal or vegetable – that organism instantly dies.
If a surgeon could direct and concentrate that look, he could
kill metastasizing cancer cells, or staphylococcus, or virtu-
ally any kind of bacteria. He wouldn't need a knife, or a
laser, or any kind of chemical therapy.'

'Well, you are right,' said Zofia. 'It is the eye of the basilisk
that holds the secret. The water inside, what do you call it?'

'Optic fluid.'

'That is correct, the optic fluid. In a basilisk, this can
sometimes shine like a very bright light, as you have seen for
yourself, and dazzle you. It has the same effect as what the
Greek people call *matiasma* and the Italian people *malocchio*,
the evil eye. It can make babies sick, or cattle to stop from giving
milk, or crops to wither up. If it is powerful enough, it can stop
a man's heart where he stands. Or – as you know – a woman's.'

Nathan reached into his coat pocket and produced the mirror
that he had taken to the Murdstone, with its blackened silver
and its mottled back.

'I think this mirror stopped Grace from being killed outright.
Do you have any idea why, or how? I've read all kinds of
folk legends about basilisks, and almost all of them say that
the only way to destroy them is to use a mirror to reflect their
own stare right back to them.'

Zofia turned the mirror this way and that, and then handed
it back. 'You are probably right, Nathan. But from what I
have read about basilisks, one mirror alone is not enough to
kill them. It always takes at least five.'

'*Five*? How so?'

Zofia stood up. 'Suppose that you are the basilisk and I am
the basilisk hunter. I make sure that when I approach you, I
hold one mirror up in front of my face, so that I cannot see
your eyes. But I hold a second mirror in my other hand, and
when you look at me, I shine the light from the mirror in
front of my face on to my second mirror.

'Now I have a friend with me, Rafał, and he is holding a third mirror. He uses this to reflect the light to another friend, who in turn reflects it to one more friend. The third friend reflects it back to the second friend, who now reflects it into the basilisk's eyes.

'The reflected light, from one mirror to another, makes a pentacle, which gives the light five times more magical brightness. This is supposed to blind the basilisk, and kill it with its own evil.'

'But what can I do about Grace? Do you know of any way that I could get her out of her coma?'

Zofia went across to the fireplace. The hearth itself was cast iron, and heaped with white wood ash, although it was still giving out warmth. The mantelpiece was made of elaborately carved oak, with bunches of grapes and leaves all the way around it, although it had been deeply stained by centuries of smoke and cracked by the heat of the fire.

She took a brown ceramic pot from the mantelshelf and set it down on top of a pile of books. It was filled with dried green herbs, and she picked up a box of matches and lit them, so that they smoldered.

'Meliot,' she explained. 'Sometimes they call it lemon sweet clover. It is used to protect those people who have been given the evil eye.'

'OK. But does it cure them?'

Zofia shook her head. 'It is impossible for me to tell you. I have never personally known anybody who has been put into coma by a basilisk. Kraków is famous for its basilisks, yes, as well as its dragons, and many other creatures. But none of these have been seen here for four hundred years.'

'There is a way. There *must* be a way, otherwise Doctor Zauber wouldn't have offered it to me, in exchange for helping him out.'

Zofia sat down on the couch close to him, and took hold of his hand, as naturally as if they had known each other for years. 'Has it occurred to you that he is trying to trick you, and that there *is* no cure? What if you help him, and then he says, "Sorry, my friend, I was lying"?'

'No. He may be unscrupulous, no doubt about that, and he may be totally unfeeling. But I think he knows what I would do to him if I found out that he was trying to con me.'

Rafał said, 'We know where he lives. I say we should go around there and beat it out of him.'

'Oh, sure. And what if he refused to tell us, even then? And what if he called the cops? What good would *that* do us? Or Grace?'

But Zofia said, 'He has something that you want, which is a cure for your wife, if such a thing exists. You have something that *he* wants – your knowledge, and your skill, and your experience. But what if you had a better hand than him? What if you had something that would make it impossible for him to carry on his experiments?'

'What do you mean?'

'I know from books that if anybody wants to bring back to life a basilisk or any other creature like that, they will need skin and bones. You cannot breed a basilisk out of thin air. So instead of going to Doctor Zauber's house to beat him, why don't you go to his house and take away the skin and bones that he dug up from Saint Casimir's Basilica?

'*Then* you can say to him: "if you don't tell me how to bring my wife out of her coma, I will destroy these things and you will never see them again." And where else is he going to find the remains of a basilisk?'

Nathan looked at Rafał. 'It's a plan, isn't it? The trouble is, how do we break in and burglarize the place? How do we know if he's home or not? Or even if he *isn't* home, how do we know he's not suddenly going to reappear, the same way he kept shooting around that restaurant?'

'I can help you with that,' said Zofia. She went across to an old roll-top bureau, and opened one of the drawers. She rummaged inside, and eventually produced a small decorative bag, thickly embroidered with blue glass beads. She held it out to Nathan and said, 'There. One of my favorite *ladanki*.'

Nathan dubiously took it from her. Although it was small, it was quite heavy.

'Open it up,' Zofia encouraged him. 'Take a look inside.'

'*Ladanki*,' put in Rafał. 'That means "charm bags".'

Nathan loosened the leather drawstring and peered inside. He took out a small brass cylinder with a stopper at one end. When he pulled open the stopper, he found a neat roll of yellowish paper inside, covered with dense black handwriting.

'That is a spell,' Zofia explained. 'Whoever wears this charm bag, it protects them from bad surprises. Nobody can creep up close behind them and attack them, they will always be able to sense that they are there. And they will always know if an enemy is hiding and lying in wait for them.'

Next, Nathan took out a collection of smooth stones – amber, and marble, and turquoise, and some pale purple stone that he didn't recognize. 'These make it possible for you to see more further, and hear much more better, and also to keep open your eyes even when you are very tired.'

There were all kinds of bits and pieces in the bag: a hank of coarse brown hair, tied up with wire; a medallion with a likeness of a gorgon on it, with waving snakes on top of her head; a tiny dagger, with a ruby set in the end of the handle; a small *bouquet garni* of dried herbs.

'White bryony, which protects your happiness; mint, which protects your health; birch leaf, which brings good fortune, and also protects you from the evil eye.'

Lastly, Nathan lifted out an egg, which had been richly decorated with red-and-white pictures of birds and snakes.

'A *pysanka*,' said Zofia. 'A symbolic egg. They are given in Poland as gifts of life. Each egg has a different pattern and a different meaning. You would give a dark one with rich colors to an old person, because their life is almost filled, but an egg with lots of white spaces on it to young children, because their life is still a blank page.

'You would place one in the coffin of somebody you loved; or on the graves of your family.'

'And this one?' Nathan asked her.

'It is decorated with birds, because they mean sun and heaven and hope, and to push away darkness and evil; and also this, snakes, the *had*, which protects from all kinds of catastrophe.'

'So what do I do with this charm bag?'

'You can wear it around your neck.'

Nathan unbuttoned his shirt and drew out the black pearl cross that the Egyptian-looking nurse at the Hahnemann had given him. 'I have a good-luck charm already.'

Zofia reached out and held the cross between finger and thumb. She closed her eyes for a moment, and then she said, 'This is good. A *znak*, we call it. It is very protective. It carries the warmth of somebody who wants you to return home safe.

'But you will find this charm bag is very special. It will not only protect you from danger, it will tell you if somebody who wishes you harm is coming close. If you wish to break into Doctor Zauber's house, it will let you know if he is inside the house or not. It will also warn you if he is returning.'

'Oh, really? And how will it do that?'

'You will know, if and when it happens, believe me.'

Nathan weighed the bag in the palm of his hand. 'You're serious, aren't you?'

'I have used it myself,' smiled Zofia. 'Once I had to enter the apartment of a very jealous lover, to find some jewelry which he had refused to give back to me. The charm bag told me that he was not at home; but it also alerted me when he was coming up the stairs on his way back. I was able to hide in a closet, and when he took a shower, I escaped without him even knowing that I had been there.'

Nathan didn't know if he ought to believe her or not. But here, in her apartment, with its antique books, and its strange herbal aromas, and its magical paraphernalia like crystal balls and eggs decorated with flying witches, it was easy to think that such things might be possible. On the wall behind her, there was a painting of a green-faced hobgoblin, and it was winking at him in a conspiratorial way, as if it were saying, *Go on, Nathan, you can do it. You can do anything, if you put your mind to it. You could even jump from one side of the room to the other, like Doctor Zauber.*

'All right,' he said. 'Let's go for it. I'll bring you this back, when I'm finished with it.'

'You can keep it,' said Zofia. 'You never know when you may need it again. And I can always make another. I am *znakharka*, after all.'

It was almost midnight when Nathan and Rafał got back to the Amadeus Hotel. They went into the bar and ordered a glass of red Bohemian wine and a vodka. The wine was strong and rough, compared to Californian or Chilean wines, but Nathan knew what would happen if he started to drink vodka.

'What do you think?' asked Rafał. 'You think we should really break into Doctor Zauber's house?'

'I don't think he's given me much of an alternative.'

'He is a very dangerous man, Nathan. If he can kill all of those elderly people with no conscience at all . . .'

'Hey . . . you were the one who wanted to beat up on him.'

'I know. But then I saw myself in the mirror when I came back to the hotel, and I remembered how old I was, and not so healthy and strong. It is many years since I used to do rowing, and weightlifting. And how can you hit a man who never stays in the same place from one second to the next?'

Nathan took a mouthful of wine, and grimaced. 'I think we should try. Even if Zofia is right, and he doesn't really have a cure, at least we will have stopped him from killing any more old people. If he doesn't have the wherewithal to breed himself another basilisk, he won't need any more life-energy, will he?'

'But what about Grace?'

'Maybe Patti's right about Grace. Maybe she's in God's hands, not mine.'

They were still debating whether they should have another drink or not when Denver and Patti appeared. They came giggling and weaving their way across the bar and threw themselves down next to them.

'Have a good time?' Nathan asked them.

'Totally wicked,' said Denver. His hair was sticking up because he had been sweating so much, and his eyes were pink. 'That Frantic is absolutely the best club I've ever been to, bar noplace at all.'

Patti was flushed, too. She reached across the table and squeezed Denver's hand and said, 'I have to tell you something, Professor. Your son can dance the legs off of anybody.'

'I assume you had a couple of drinks?'

Denver shook his head so emphatically that his lips flapped. 'Only blackberry juice. Nothing else.'

'Blackberry juice? Is that all?'

Denver tried hard to focus on him. He held up his finger and thumb to indicate a very small measure of spirits. 'With a little vodka in it, but only to sterilize the glass. Well, wodka, as a matter of fact, with a wubble-you. Except that, in Poland, "wubble-you" is pronounced "vuh", like in Volkswagen.'

Nathan said, 'OK. Glad you had a good time. But you should

hit the sack now. We're going to be doing something real serious tomorrow morning, and I want you both in good shape.'

'Patti is already in good shape,' Denver blurted out. 'She has the goodest shape ever, bar no shape at all.'

Patti looked across at Nathan and smiled. He saw a lot in that smile: amusement, affection, and almost a feeling of family. But he also saw her determination not to be left out of whatever was going on. She was young, and she didn't take herself too seriously, but she wanted to go back to Philadelphia with the story to top all stories.

'I think I might actually need to barf,' Denver announced.

'Here,' said Rafał. 'I guide you to toilet.'

He helped Denver to stagger back across the bar. When they had gone, Patti said to Nathan, 'So what's this real serious something that we're supposed to be doing tomorrow?'

'A little larceny, that's all. But if you don't want to get yourself involved, that's fine.'

He told her about Zofia Czarwonica, and showed her the charm bag. 'Take a look inside,' he said. 'There's some real weird stuff in there. But this Zofia swore that it worked.'

Patti picked out the scroll, and the tiny dagger, and the egg, and the colored stones. 'This is magic, isn't it? Like, the real genuine thing. I'm finding it hard to get my head around this.'

'You believe in God.'

'Sure I do. But that's different. God may be invisible, but His world has rules, right? Like people don't appear and disappear, *snap*! like Doctor Zauber did. And people don't walk around with bags full of eggs, and hair, and all this other junk, thinking that they're going to protect them.'

Nathan put his elbows on the table and leaned forward. 'I sense a "but" coming.'

'Yes. You do. I don't understand any of this stuff, but that doesn't mean I'm not prepared to believe in it. I'll come with you tomorrow. Somebody has to record what happened, even if it all goes wrong. *Especially* if it all goes wrong.'

Nathan ordered another glass of wine and another vodka for Rafał. Patti asked for a peach juice.

Rafał came back after five minutes or so, shaking his head. 'Denver is OK. He was very sick, but he has gone to bed now. He will be fine tomorrow.'

He sat down, picked up his glass of vodka and said, '*Na zdrowie*! Good health to all of us, and long lifes!'

'I'll drink to that,' said Patti. She lifted her glass of pale orange peach juice and said, 'Long lifes!'

EIGHTEEN

The House of Empty People

The next morning, Nathan and Denver and Patti had breakfast together in the hotel dining room. The sun was shining through the stained-glass windows, and the air was swarming with sparkling motes of dust.

Patti wore a tight white rollneck sweater and a very short blue denim skirt, while Denver was wearing a purple T-shirt with *Like, Duh* emblazoned on the front. Denver had completely recovered from his blackberry-juice binge, and ate two hard-cooked eggs, as well as salami and Gruyère cheese and half a basket of rye bread.

Nathan settled for a glass of sweet, synthetic-tasting pomegranate juice and two cups of strong black coffee.

He explained to Denver what they were planning to do, trying to sound as matter-of-fact as possible. 'Without those remains, Doctor Zauber is totally stymied.'

He had been seriously worried that Denver would think that the whole idea of breaking into Doctor Zauber's house was too flaky, or too risky. But Denver shook his head admiringly from side to side and said, 'Wicked, man. Totally wicked,' with his mouth full.

'Just remember,' said Nathan. 'If you decide to come along, you'll have to do exactly as I tell you and don't try to be a hero. I wouldn't have asked you to come along at all, but we need to search through that entire house, top to bottom, as quickly as possible. God alone knows where Zauber keeps those remains, if he keeps them there at all.'

'So we're looking for, like, bones and skin, all wrapped up in an old leather parcel?'

'Bones and skin, yes, like a snake's skin. Zauber may have

taken them out of the leather parcel by now. But it's the bones
and skin that we're after. They contain the DNA which he
needs to re-create a basilisk. He doesn't do it the same way
I do it, with embryonic stem cells. He uses some kind of
medieval hocus-pocus, as far as I know. But however he does
it, he still has to start with the same genetic ingredients.'

At ten twenty-five, Rafał appeared, in a green tweed shooting
coat with brown suede shoulder patches. He was carrying a
red string shopping bag. He bear-hugged Nathan and Denver,
kissed Patti twice on each cheek, and then sat down.

'We are all ready for this adventure?' he asked. 'We have
not lost our courage?'

'I think it's going to be *ur*-mazing,' said Denver.

Patti said, 'Raring to go, Raffo.'

'I drove past Doctor Zauber's house on my way here,'
Rafał told them. 'From the outside it looked as if there was
nobody home.'

'You brought the mirrors?' Nathan asked him.

'Of course.' He lifted up the shopping bag. 'Five altogether.'

'And we're all clear on exactly how we're going to use
these mirrors, if we need to?'

Patti said, 'Me on your right, Raffo on your left, and
Denver in between the basilisk and me. We got it, Professor.'
She pointed her finger to each of them in turn, as if she
were shining an intense light. '*Bing – bing – bing – bing
– whamm*!'

Rafał handed out circular shaving mirrors, with magnifying lenses. Denver peered into his, and pulled a face.

'Pops?' he asked. 'Do you really think that what's-his-name
has bred himself another what-do-you-call-it?'

'To be honest – no, I don't. I think it's more likely that
he's been holding off in the hope that he can persuade me to
help him with the cell development. He doesn't want another
deformed monster on his hands. But even if he *has* gone ahead,
I wouldn't have thought that he's had enough time to breed
a full-sized basilisk. Not that I have any idea how fast a basilisk
can grow.'

'Let us just pray that he has not,' said Rafał.

Nathan pocketed his two mirrors and stood up. 'OK,' he
said. 'Let's do it.'

*   *   *

They walked through the bright cobbled streets to the inter-section of Kupa and Izaaka. Nathan felt as if they ought to have theme music playing as the four of them made their way along the crowded sidewalks, like *The Magnificent Seven* or *Gunfight at the OK Corral.*

The buildings on either side of them were four and five stories, gray and flat-fronted, like the buildings he had seen in wartime newsreels about the invasion of Poland. Most of them were being remodeled now, but a few of them still had empty, shattered window frames, and were pockmarked with shrapnel scars.

Up above them, the sky was a piercing pale blue, with frag-mented white clouds that had drifted here all the way across southern Germany and the Czech Republic.

They turned into Kupa Street. Thirty yards to the left there was a narrow alley, and on the corner of this alley stood a tall angular house, four stories high, rendered in gritty gray concrete, with peeling brown shutters and empty window boxes. A rusty yellow plaque with the number seventy-seven was attached to the wall beside the front door. The door was painted a dull maroon color, with a brass knocker in the shape of a hammer. There were two bell pushes, one labeled *R. Cichowlas* and the other labeled *Walach.*

'Robert Cichowlas was the artist who rented the top-floor studio,' said Rafał. 'The Walachs . . . I don't know. I think they worked for some tourism company.'

Nathan said to Denver, 'Want to try the bells? Just to see if anybody answers.'

Denver pressed both buttons. They waited and waited, while tourists and shoppers elbowed past them on the sidewalk, but nobody came to the door.

'Try again,' said Nathan. 'And knock this time, too, just in case the bells don't work.'

Denver pressed the buttons again, holding each of them down for almost half a minute, and then he banged on the door with the hammer-shaped knocker. They could hear it echoing inside the house.

Patti came up to Nathan and peered down the front of his leather jacket. 'How about your charm bag? What's that telling you?'

'Not a peep,' said Nathan. 'Although I don't know what it's supposed to do if there *is* somebody home.'

'Cough? Scream? Rattle? Didn't your witch lady tell you?'

'No. But she said that I'd know if it happened.'

'Maybe it whistles Dixie.'

Rafał said, 'I think we can assume there is nobody here. There is a side window which overlooks the alley.' He opened his tweed coat, just enough for them to be able to see the handle of the screwdriver that he was carrying in his inside pocket. 'Denver, please to come with me. You will find it easier to climb inside than me.'

There was nobody in the alley except for an old woman in a black shawl sitting on a wooden chair more than fifty yards away. She was leaning back with her eyes closed, with a ball of red wool and a half-knitted sleeve in her lap, basking in a foot-wide slice of sunlight that was falling between the tenement buildings opposite. A mangy Pomeranian lay asleep at her feet.

Nathan and Patti stood in the entrance to the alley, pretending to have an animated conversation together, to distract the attention of passers-by along Kupa Street.

'So where do you want to go next?' Nathan demanded.

'I don't know!' snapped Patti. 'Where do you want to go?'

'I don't know! *You* choose!'

'Jesus,' said Patti. 'We sound like those crows in *Dumbo*.'

Meanwhile, resting his shoulder against the wall, so that he kept his back to the old woman in the wooden chair, Rafał took out his long, wide-bladed screwdriver. He forced it into the side of the window frame, an inch below the catch. He looked around, just to make sure that nobody was watching, and then took hold of the screwdriver in both hands and wrenched it sideways. The wood was so rotten that he cracked the frame apart, which loosened the screws that fastened the catch.

Denver clawed the window open, while Rafał got down on one knee and clasped his hands together to give him a boost. Denver took one step back, and then jumped up on Rafał's hands and dived over the window sill like an acrobat. Nathan heard a clattering sound, and then a crash, like a vase breaking, and Denver saying, '*Shit*.'

'Denver?' called Rafał, trying to keep his voice down.

Denver's face appeared at the window. 'It's OK, Raffo. I'm fine. Broke some jug, that's all.'

He hesitated for a moment, looking around, and listening.

Then he said, 'Doesn't seem like there's anybody here. I'll let you guys in, OK?'

Rafał carefully closed the window and wedged it shut with a triangular splinter of wood. He came back to join Nathan and Patti and the three of them returned to the front door. Denver opened it almost at once, and said, triumphantly, 'Tah-*dah*!'

'You should be a burglar when you grow up,' Patti told him, as they stepped inside.

'You think so? So what are *you* going to be, when *you* grow up?'

'Come on, you two,' Nathan interrupted them, 'we have some serious searching to do.' But he knew that they were only bantering like that because they liked each other.

Doctor Zauber's house was gloomy and cold inside, because it was so deeply overshadowed by the buildings that surrounded it. The interior looked as if it hadn't been redecorated since the war. The wallpaper was covered in tiny red-and-yellow flowers, but on one side of the staircase they had been erased completely by years of shoulders rubbing past, and up on the landing they had faded to a pale sepia color, as if they were real flowers that had dried up and died. The doors and the skirting boards and the banisters were all painted dark brown, and the paint was scabby and cracked.

'Rafał and I will start looking up in the attic,' said Nathan. 'Why don't you guys start searching down here?' He opened the door on the right-hand side of the hall, and peered inside. 'Living room,' he said. It was stuffy and dark, with thick net curtains that were heavy with dust, and overcrowded with 1930s-style furniture. A large mirror hung over the fireplace, so that they could see themselves standing in the doorway, looking in.

'Looks like a dining room next door, and a kitchen in back. You'll need to search through every closet and every drawer. If you think you've found what we're looking for, don't touch it. Just yell out.'

Denver and Patti went into the living room and started to tug open the drawers of an elaborate walnut cabinet. 'Take a look under the chairs, too,' Nathan told them.

He and Rafał climbed the stairs to the second-floor landing. A chandelier with two of its five bulbs missing hung from the ceiling like a giant spider. The ceiling itself was cracked all the way across and stained with brown blotches of damp.

'If you fix up this house, you make yourself fortune,' said Rafał. On the wall beside him hung a reproduction of a sour-looking monk, with a sinister-looking monastery in the background, and a sky that was peppered with rooks. The picture was rippled with damp, which made the monk look as if he had leprosy.

They climbed up the next flight of stairs, and then the next. Rafał was wheezing by the time they reached the door to the attic, and he punched his chest with his fist. 'I need to take more exercise,' he said. 'Not so much beer, not so much potatoes, not so much *kiełbasa*!'

Nathan cautiously opened the attic door. It was brighter in here than it was downstairs, because there were six large skylights in the ceiling, although the three south-facing skylights had dark gray roller blinds drawn down over them. This was Robert Cichowlas' studio. It smelled strongly of oil paint and turpentine and stale cigarettes, and there was a long wooden table crowded with half-squeezed tubes of paint, like wriggling metal worms, as well as jars filled with brushes and paint-dotted palettes and multi-colored rags. At the far end, up against the brick chimney breast, there was a single bed with a grubby green quilt dragged over it.

Twenty or thirty oil paintings were stacked against the attic wall, as well as charcoal studies and pencil drawings and sketchbooks. On an easel in the center of the room stood a half-finished painting of a thin naked woman standing in a forest. Her head, however, was not the head of a woman, but of a wildly staring cat, with yellow eyes.

The painting of the head was highly detailed and so realistic that Nathan could almost imagine the cat-woman leaping out of the canvas. There was something both frightening and pathetic about her, as if she knew how grotesque she looked, and wished that she were a normal woman again, even if she had never been strikingly beautiful.

Rafał looked around the studio, sliding open the drawers in the artist's plan chest, and rummaging through the sweaters and jeans that were heaped untidily in one of the triangular closets underneath the eaves.

Nathan knelt down and looked under the bed, and under

the mattress. Then he turned to Rafał and said, 'I thought your realtor friend told you that Doctor Zauber had ended this guy's lease.'

'He did. But maybe he could find no place to store all of his things, and Zauber allowed him to keep them here.'

'But there are so many clothes here. And – look – next to the washbasin. A razor, and a toothbrush. He must still be living here.'

They searched the attic thoroughly, looking through cardboard boxes filled with letters and photographs torn out of magazines, as well as books and diaries and bundles of pencils and a plaster hand taken from a store-window dummy. Nathan even took a steel ruler from Robert Cichowlas' table and pried up two ill-fitting floorboards, but found nothing underneath except plaster dust and a mummified rat and a crumpled pack of *Extra Mocne* cigarettes.

'There's something not right here,' said Nathan. 'I can feel it.'

'Well, maybe,' said Rafał. 'But maybe not. Maybe Zauber kept him on here simply because he wanted his rent. Even monsters like Zauber need money.'

They took a last look around the attic and then went downstairs to the third floor, where the three main bedrooms were. When they opened the first bedroom door, it was immediately obvious that the Walach family were still here, too. There was a high, old-fashioned double bed, covered with a rose-colored satin eiderdown. On one pillow lay a neatly folded pair of blue-and-white striped pajamas. On the other pillow lay a brushed-cotton nightgown, with a frilly collar.

Rafał turned the key in the closet and opened it. It was full of clothes – mostly dresses, but a brown fur coat, too, and two men's suits. It smelled strongly of moth repellent. On top of the closet there were two hatboxes and a small leather suitcase.

'Looks like your friend was misinformed,' said Nathan. 'Maybe he was wrong about Doctor Zauber, too. Maybe he *hasn't* moved back in here.'

Rafał shook his head in bewilderment. 'He was sure. He said that Doctor Zauber had even come into his office to sign all the necessary papers.'

'Yes, but if he hasn't moved back in here, we're wasting

our time. The question is: if he's not here, where the hell is he?'

They checked the other two bedrooms. One was clearly a teenager's room, with posters for Coldplay and Oddział Zamknięty, one of the biggest Polish rock bands. In one corner there was a small white desk with a laptop on it, and a black canvas chair with six or seven T-shirts and two pairs of jeans thrown over the back.

The third bedroom was a young girl's room, with three shelves that were crowded with Barbies and Bratz and stuffed pandas and teddy bears.

'That's it, then,' said Nathan, closing the door behind him. 'This whole thing is a total bust.'

He turned to go back downstairs. As he did so, however, he felt an extraordinary *shriveling* sensation in his chest and his upper arms, as if he had been electrocuted, and he almost lost his balance. He swayed, and held on to the banisters for support.

'Nathan?' asked Rafał. 'Are you feeling all right?'

Nathan felt another convulsion, even more painful than the first, and this time his heart seemed to stop in mid-beat, and hesitate before it started up again. He pressed his hand against the front of his coat and realized that the pebbles in Zofia Czarwonica's charm bag were shaking and clattering and jumping around as if they were alive.

He dragged the bag out from under his coat and held it up. It was rattling so wildly that it looked as if it were filled with struggling scorpions, as well as stones.

'He's here,' he told Rafał. 'Zauber's here. Zofia said that I'd know it, as soon as he came close.'

As soon as he said it, he heard a girl screaming. She was so high-pitched and she sounded so terrified that it took him two or three seconds before he recognized that it was Patti. At the same time, Denver shouted out, '*Pops! Pops! Help us! Pops!*'

Nathan launched himself down the staircase, four or five stairs at a time. Patti's screams grew shriller and more panicky, and Denver was so frightened that he was almost roaring.

'*Pops! Help us! It's got her! Pops!*'

Nathan reached the hallway with Rafał clambering down the staircase close behind him. He almost tripped on a loose-weave mat at the bottom of the stairs, but he managed to grab the newel post to steady himself, and to swing around and hurry toward the back of the house, where the screaming and the shouting was coming from.

He burst into the kitchen. It was cold and gloomy, with a yellow blind drawn down over the window. The walls were tiled in white and green, and there was a large pine table in the center of the room, with a streaky marble top. Copper saucepans hung from the ceiling, like church bells.

Denver was crouching in the corner, next to the old-fashioned sink. As Nathan and Rafał came in, he shouted hoarsely, '*There*! *She's in there*! *I tried to get her free but I couldn't*!'

On the far side of the room there was another door, half open. Inside, it was even gloomier than the kitchen, but Nathan could make out the corner of a white-enameled washing machine, and white towels hanging from a wooden frame.

Patti was in there, with whatever it was that caught her, and she was still screaming, although her screams were becoming more like sobs.

Nathan shouted, 'Patti! It's OK! We're coming! *Patti*!'

He crossed the kitchen floor and kicked the door wide open. At first he couldn't understand what he was looking at, because Patti and her assailant must have fallen against a clothes horse, and they were all tangled up in sheets and pillowcases, so that they looked like two struggling ghosts.

But then Patti twisted herself sideways, and desperately reached out her hand to him, and he understood what was holding her.

It was a huge gray creature, as large as a man, but much bulkier than a man. It had a dome-shaped head, with bulbous black eyes, and glistening pale-yellow eyelids around them that kept on rolling and unrolling, like a snail's. Yet underneath its eyes it appeared to have a man's face, with a man's nose and a man's mouth, although its lips were dragged downward, as if it were disgusted by its own existence.

It was clinging to Patti with six gray tentacles, rope-like and slimy and constantly waving. The main part of its body was a big shapeless sack, covered with thick corrugated skin.

It had a nauseating smell, like strong human body odor mixed with rotten shellfish.

'*Patti*!' Nathan shouted at her, trying to make himself heard

above her screaming. '*Patti, you have to calm down! Patti!*
Take hold of my hand, and try to calm down! Patti!'

He gripped Patti's hand and it was cold and slippery with
the creature's slime. He tried to tug her free, but the harder
he pulled, the tighter the creature wound its tentacles around
her. It was holding her around her hips and around her waist
and around her breasts, too. One tentacle kept waving and
flapping in her face.

Rafał came up right behind Nathan. 'Holy Mother of God,'
he said. 'Is that what I think it is?'

'*Get me free get me free get me free!*' screamed Patti. '*I
can't stand it! Get me free!*'

She kept kicking and struggling, and Nathan tried to grab
one of her ankles, but the instant he took hold of her, one of
the creature's tentacles wound itself even more tightly around
her leg, and made it impossible for him to pull her away.

Patti kept on begging and screaming, but then the creature
wound a tentacle around her mouth, and all she could manage
was a muffled bleating.

'No question,' said Nathan. 'It's a living, breathing
Schleimgeist.'

Rafał took off his glasses, because they had been smeared
with foul-smelling mucus, and tried to wipe them on his sleeve.
'One third squid, one third slug, and one third man. Why
would Zauber want to breed anything like this?'

'Let's just get Patti free.'

Rafał went back to the kitchen table. He noisily pulled out
the drawers underneath the marble top, and found a whole
selection of knives and forks.

'Here!' he said, holding up a ten-inch boning knife.

He pushed his way back into the laundry room. The slug-
creature had dragged Patti into the corner now, and it was
winding its tentacles tighter and tighter around her chest,
until she was gargling for breath. Rafał dodged to the left,
and then to the right, with the carving knife held low. Then
he stabbed the slug-creature in the side, twice, as hard as he
could.

The slug-creature let out a harsh, angry screech, but the
point of the knife hadn't even pierced its skin. Rafał stabbed
it again, and then again, and then again, but he couldn't make
any impression at all.

'It is too solid!' he panted. 'It is like rubber! Like – medicine ball!'

Nathan was tugging at the slippery gray tentacle that was wound around Patti's mouth. It had slipped between her lips and was pressing up against her tightly clenched teeth. She was staring at him, her eyes wide with fear. But the tentacle was far too muscular for Nathan to pull it away.

Rafał was holding the knife in both hands now, and furiously stabbing at the slug-creature's sides, grunting loudly with every stab. But he couldn't even make it bleed.

'It's no good,' Nathan panted. 'Slugs don't have exterior shells, but they can contract their bodies so hard that almost nothing can hurt them.'

'So what can we do? We cannot just stand here and let this monster crush her alive!'

Nathan turned back toward the kitchen. Denver was standing up now, both hands raised, biting at his knuckles in helplessness. His eyes were bursting with tears. 'Pops, it's going to kill her, Pops! Don't let it kill her, please!'

It was then that Nathan thought: *slugs*. And he remembered his mother, after it had been raining, and those huge gray *limax maximus* came crawling across the path, intent on eating her geraniums.

He crossed the kitchen to the pinewood hutch which stood beside the door. Behind him, in the laundry room, Patti must have managed to twist her face away from the tentacle that was wound around her mouth, because she let out three more hysterical screams.

'*Nathan!*' called Rafał. '*What are you doing? Come back! Help me! Please!*'

'Hold on!' Nathan shouted back. 'I'm coming!'

On the second shelf of the hutch there was a line of large white ceramic jars, with green italic lettering on them. *Cukier, pieprz* and *sól*. Nathan picked up the jar marked *sól* and opened it. It was almost full.

'*Nathan!*' Rafał bellowed. '*It is breaking her ribs!*'

Nathan pushed his way back into the laundry room. Rafał was still frantically chopping at the slug-creature's back. He had managed to puncture its skin two or three times, because it was oozing glossy black blood, but he obviously hadn't succeeded in piercing the bony internal keel which protected its lungs.

Patti was in a bad way now. The slug-creature had managed to wrap two of its tentacles around her face, and the other four were tightly entwined together around her chest. Nathan knew that it would be almost impossible to cut through them, or pull them free. Slugs themselves often became entangled with each other when they were mating, and the only way in which they could get free was for one slug to eat the other's penis.

Holding the ceramic jar up high, Nathan circled around behind Rafał until he was almost standing on the gray frill that surrounded the slug-creature's foot. Then he leaned forward as far as he could, placing one hand on the slug-creature's side to steady himself. The slug-creature felt disgusting: chilly and slimy and hard, like an inflatable boat smothered in jelly. Nathan tipped the jar so that cooking salt poured steadily out of it, all across the slug-creature's back. He kept on pouring, shaking the jar from side to side as he did so, until it was empty.

He stepped back, dropping the jar and wiping his hand on his coat. For a few dreadful moments, he thought that he might have made a fatal mistake, because the slug-creature seemed to react to the cooking salt only by contracting its muscles even tighter, and he heard Patti gasp as even more breath was squeezed out of her.

Then, however, Rafał said, '*Look*!'

Where the point of his kitchen knife had managed to nick the slug-creature's skin, milky white slime-bubbles were beginning to froth up. The slug-creature suddenly shuddered, and started to writhe, and ripple. Its skin started to melt, turning from black to liquid gray. Fumes poured off it – choking, acrid fumes that smelled like charred fish-skin.

'Salt!' Rafał exclaimed. 'Yes! I should have thought of salt!'

The slug-creature let out a throaty gargle of pain, like the voices of twenty different demons all moaning at once. As soon as the salt had dissolved its tough outer epidermis, it ate into its flesh faster and faster, and the pale gray juice that had once been its muscles began to pour across the laundry room floor.

But still it wouldn't release its grip on Patti. Even though it must have known that it was going to die, it seemed to be determined to squeeze the life out of her before it did so.

Nathan went around and confronted its eerie half-human face. The fumes from its liquefying body were so thick now that they were filling up the laundry room, and Nathan had to cough, and cough again, before he could speak.

'Let her go!' he demanded. 'You can't survive this! You're dying! You're dead already! Let her go!'

The slug-creature's eyelids rolled and unrolled. Then – to Nathan's horror – it spoke to him. Its voice was blurred with pain, and came from a mouth which had rows of tiny razor-sharp spines instead of teeth. But he could understand most of what it said.

'*You don't understand. You should have joined him. What you and Doctor Zauber could have done together. What we* all *could have done together.*'

Nathan stared at the slug-creature in disbelief. Gradually, with a rising sense of pity and disgust, he began to understand what it was; or, rather, who it had once been. Its protuberant eyes were grotesque, and the expression on its face was like that of some suffering medieval saint. But he suddenly saw the distinctive nose and narrow-faced features of Richard Scryman.

'Richard,' he said. 'Christ almighty, Richard. Is that you?'

'*It was our chance to make history, Professor,*' said the slug-creature. '*It was our chance for immortality.*'

'For Christ's sake, Richard, what did you let him do to you?'

'*Should have joined him,*' the slug-creature repeated. It gave a hideous convulsion as the salt melted through its muscle all the way down to its keel, its carina, and it let out a strangled cry in the back of its throat. '*God, this hurts, Professor. You can't imagine pain like this.*'

'Let Patti go, Richard. You have to let her go.'

The slug-creature's eyelids rolled. '*Sorry, Professor. I'm taking this one with me.*'

'Let her go! What good is it going to do you, if you kill her?'

But the slug-creature closed its eyelids, and didn't answer.

Nathan tried again to wrench away its tentacles, but they were like greasy ropes, and they were wound around Patti's chest so tightly that he couldn't even force his fingertips underneath them, to get a grip.

'*Goddammit, Richard*!' he yelled, but the slug-creature's eyes remained closed, and its expression remained calm, almost beatific, even though it must have been suffering agony beyond all imagination.

'Rafał!' said Nathan. 'Go into the kitchen! Over by the stove, there's some copper saucepans hanging up!'

'*What*?'

'Please, just hurry. Bring me two of them, big ones!'

Rafał lumbered across the kitchen. Denver had already heard what Nathan had asked for, and he had unhooked two of the larger saucepans and was holding them out ready for him. Rafał brought them back, banging and jangling, and handed them over.

'I do not understand,' he said. 'What can you do with saucepan?'

'Watch,' Nathan told him. 'Watch, and pray.'

With that, he held both saucepans by their handles, and pressed their bases against the slug-creature's sides, like a paramedic shocking a heart-attack patient with electric paddles. Instantly, the slug-creature's eyes bulged open, and it let out a terrible *hurrrrrrrrrrrhhh*!

Its tentacles splayed open as stiff as human fingers, and they stuck out rigidly, quivering, so that Patti toppled forward on to the floor.

Grunting with effort, Rafał stooped down and picked her up, and carried her into the kitchen.

The slug-creature was trying to rear up, but too much of its body had now been eaten away by salt. It was shaking like a wildly speeded-up film, so that Nathan could barely focus on it, and sticky strings of mucus were swinging out of the sides of its mouth.

'*You never understood*,' it whispered, and then it collapsed, fuming, with a heavy, wet, rubbery sound. A clothes horse draped with sheets tipped sideways and covered it up. Underneath this makeshift shroud, it continued to crackle and fizz, as it dissolved.

Nathan came out of the laundry room into the kitchen, wiping his hands on one of the towels. Patti was sitting on one of the kitchen chairs, coughing and gasping for breath. Denver was standing next to her, holding a cup of water, his arm around her shoulders.

'Patti? How are you feeling?'

She had to take several gasping breaths before she could answer him. 'Winded,' she said. 'I think it broke one of my ribs.'

'Is it dead?' asked Denver.

Nathan nodded, and set the two saucepans down on the table. 'That was another thing my mother taught me about slugs, apart from pouring salt on to them.'

'They can't stand saucepans?'

'In a way. They need slime to slide around, but if their slime comes into contact with copper, it causes a chemical reaction that gives them a severe electric shock. That's why some gardeners surround their plants with copper strips.'

'You don't know how delighted I am that you knew that,' Patti told him. She reached out and took hold of his hand, and held on to it.

'What do we do now, Pops?' asked Denver.

'I don't know. We still haven't found the basilisk bones, have we? But if you've all had enough of this, maybe we should go back to the hotel and try to work on Plan B.'

'Plan B?'

'Maybe I should tell Doctor Zauber that I *will* work with him . . . but only if he tells me how to wake up your Mom.'

'And you seriously think that I will believe you?' said a loud, Germanic voice.

NINETEEN

Hybrid

Standing in the doorway, his face concealed by shadow, was Doctor Zauber, in his black suit, and shiny black leather gloves.

He stepped forward into the kitchen, and stood there for a while, saying nothing, but looking at them with the tightly controlled impatience of a father who has found his children misbehaving.

He nodded toward the laundry-room door. Fumes were still

drifting out of it, and they smelled strongly of dissolving slug, squid and human being.

'So . . . you have murdered your erstwhile colleague, and destroyed my latest creation.'

'Self-defense, actually,' Patti interrupted him. 'That disgusting thing was trying to squeeze the life out of me.'

'He was doing nothing more than protecting himself.'

'Protecting himself?' Denver protested. 'Against a hundred-pound girl? Come on, man, she almost got killed!'

Doctor Zauber raised one hand. 'You cannot blame him. If you want to blame anybody, look no further than me. Like many of my creations, he had serious physical and psychological imperfections, one of which was intense paranoia. He perceived you as a threat to his existence, which you clearly were.'

'It was Richard Scryman,' said Nathan. 'Well, some of it was Richard Scryman. What the hell did you do to him?'

'I used a process devised by Albertus Magnus when he was Bishop of Ratisbon in the year 1261. He called it "*Verwirrung*", which means "tangling". Albertus Magnus was one of the greatest of all alchemists . . . and, as you have just discovered, his alchemy worked.'

'He found out how to make slug-people?'

'Not only slug-people. He discovered how to combine many different species with each other. Not just two species, but three, or four, and once he succeeded in combining *five*, with a creation that was woman, fish, insect, bird and dog.'

'You combined Richard Scryman with a squid and a slug! For Christ's sake, Zauber! How sick is that?'

'Not sick at all, Professor. And if you had allowed him to live, he could have been of great benefit to people who *are* sick – with muscular dystrophy, for instance, or myasthenia, in which sufferers lack the necessary neurotransmitters for muscular contraction.'

'It was still an unholy thing to do.'

'Richard volunteered, my friend. He *wanted* to do it. He wanted to make medical history. He always complained that for all of your genius, Professor, you lack the one quality that brings a scientist the chance to be immortal. You were never prepared to make that one great leap of imagination, and entertain the idea that these mythical creatures needed not only mitochondrial DNA, but a high degree of *magic*, too.'

Suddenly, Doctor Zauber had vanished. But almost as suddenly, he was standing beside Nathan's right shoulder. 'You will never work with me, will you?' he said. 'You will never have the vision, or the necessary courage. A pity that your beloved Grace will have to spend the rest of her days in a coma. The sleeping beauty of Philadelphia, with no knight prepared to cut through the thorns and rescue her.'

'How the hell can you expect me to work with you when you've murdered all of those elderly people? And you're going to be murdering a whole lot more.'

Doctor Zauber shook his head. 'No. No more old people.'

'You're not? I thought you needed their life-energy.'

'Even if he has decided not to kill any more, he is still responsible for those he has killed already,' Rafał put in, with unexpected vehemence.

Nathan turned and looked at Rafał. He could see by the intense expression on his face that Rafał was urging him not to weaken and agree to help Doctor Zauber simply for the sake of saving Grace.

Doctor Zauber licked his black-gloved fingertip and smoothed his right eyebrow. 'Yes, my friend. You are absolutely right. I cannot restore the lives that I have taken. Regrettably, it transpired that they were not as useful to my project as I had first hoped. They were too old, too worn-out. They were like batteries which are nearly at the end of their life, with very little charge left in them.

'That is why I asked if Richard would volunteer for the *Verwirrung* procedure with the slug and the squid. Richard was young, and full of vigor. It needed youth and strength for such an operation to succeed, and for the creature to survive.'

'So what exactly are you saying?' Nathan demanded. 'You're going to need *young* life-energies, instead of old ones? You're going to start murdering *kids*?'

Doctor Zauber disappeared again, and reappeared in the hallway outside the kitchen door.

'Doesn't this dude *ever* stay still?' Denver complained.

'You thought it was cool, the first time he did it,' Patti reminded him.

'Sure . . . but that was before he tried to have you squished.'

Doctor Zauber said, 'Before you finally say no to me, Professor Underhill, let me show you what I have created, using only the life-energy of the elderly. Then I will show you what you and I could do together, with all of your scientific brilliance and my magical skills and the power of vigorous young folk.'

Opposite the kitchen door, there was another door marked *Piwnica*, which clearly led down to the cellar. Doctor Zauber opened it, and switched on the light. 'Please, follow me.'

Nathan said, 'Whatever you're trying to show me, Doctor Zauber, I'm not really interested. I came here for one thing and one thing only.'

'You broke into my house. Why did you do such a thing? I could have you arrested, all of you. Were you looking to steal something from me, perhaps?'

Nathan didn't answer him. But Doctor Zauber came up close to him and looked him directly in the eye and said, 'I am not a fool, Professor Underhill. I know what you wanted, and I also know why. But you are much too late. Those remains have been put to use now, and when you find them, you will discover nothing less than your nemesis.'

With that, he went through the cellar door and started to go down the plain wooden staircase, his shiny black shoes clattering on the treads.

Nathan looked at Rafał. Rafał shrugged and said, 'What do we have to lose?'

'Oh, like, only our lives,' said Denver. 'Supposing there's another one of those sluggy dudes down there?'

Doctor Zauber had paused, halfway down. 'There is nothing down here that will hurt you, I give you my word.'

Nathan approached the cellar door. He could smell damp, and mold, and mustiness, the usual cellar smells. But he could smell something else, too, like cats' urine.

'Please,' said Doctor Zauber. 'You will find this very interesting, Professor Underhill, I promise you.'

'OK . . .' said Nathan. 'Rafał, are you coming?'

'We're coming, too,' said Patti, taking hold of Denver's hand. 'There's no way I'm going to let you guys leave us again.'

The four of them followed Doctor Zauber down the stairs. The cellar had a very low vaulted ceiling, and its rough brickwork was painted dark brown, which made it feel even more claustrophobic. It was lit by only two naked bulbs, so that its corners were engulfed in deep shadow.

Up against the left-hand wall stood a large oak table, with dozens of glass storage jars and tripods and test tubes and pipettes, as well as stacks of books, some of them antique, in cracked leather bindings, with rough-cut pages. Underneath the table there were wicker baskets with dried twigs and more glass storage jars and some tarnished brass devices that looked like sextants and astrolabes.

'My laboratory,' said Doctor Zauber. 'Perhaps not as high-tech as yours, Professor, but this is where my creations come to life.'

As he reached the bottom of the stairs, Nathan heard a fluttering, scratching noise. He peered into the darkness and saw that the far end of the cellar had been caged off from floor to ceiling with heavy-duty wire mesh.

Doctor Zauber beckoned him to follow him, and as he did so a cry came from the cage like a cockerel, but very much louder than a cockerel, and ending in what was almost a growl.

Patti squealed and said, 'Oh, *shit*! What is *that*?'

Nathan felt a sliding sensation all the way down his back, and the charm bag around his neck began to shift and twitch. There was another cockerel cry, and then another, and now he knew exactly what Doctor Zauber was going to show him.

Doctor Zauber went right up to the wire mesh and beckoned him again. His eyes glittered in the gloom. 'Come closer, Professor. You have no need to be frightened. Even if it escaped, it is too deformed to hurt any of us.'

As he said that, something half crawled, half flopped out of the shadows, a grotesque tangle of feathers and fur. It had a head like an eagle or a hawk, with a downcurved beak, and staring red eyes. It had wings, too, although they looked stunted and underdeveloped, and trailed at its sides. But its body was the body of a young lion cub, with a tawny pelt and legs with a lion's claws.

Nathan guessed that it was only two or three weeks since it had hatched, but it had already grown to the size of a large dog, and it would grow much larger, if it survived.

'Oh my *God*!' Patti exclaimed. 'Oh my God, I don't believe it!'

'Jesus, Pops,' said Denver. 'What the hell is it?'

Nathan was silent for a moment, but then he said, 'It's the same creature that I was trying to breed. A gryphon. Half bird, half lion.' He paused. 'This one's an *opinicus* gryphon, which means it has a lion's front legs.'

He turned to Doctor Zauber. He could feel himself shaking. 'How did you do it?' he asked him.

Doctor Zauber looked down at his creation with a mixture of pride and pity. 'Our late friend Richard brought me all of *your* research, of course. But I also used a formula that was described by Doctor John Dee, the famous English mystic from the days of Queen Elizabeth the First. He visited Poland in the late sixteenth century with a nobleman called Albert Laski, and learned from alchemists in Kraków how gryphons were reared.'

'This is unbelievable,' said Nathan. He leaned forward and peered at the gryphon more closely, feeling angry and jealous, but ragingly curious, too. He had worked so many years to breed a creature like this, and here was one, right in front of him. It stared back at him with its unblinking red eyes, and uttered a high, creaky sound in the back of its throat.

'I almost succeeded, as you can see,' said Doctor Zauber. 'But this poor creature suffers from serious skeletal malformation, especially its hindquarters. If it had turned out to be perfect, it would be a very fearsome beast indeed, and we would not be standing here talking about it so blithely. But now you see why I need your talents so much.'

The gryphon continued to drag its way toward them, letting out another cockerel cry. It reached the wire mesh and tried to peck at it with its beak. Rafał stepped back and crossed himself.

'So, you've managed to breed a gryphon,' said Nathan. 'What are you going to do with it?'

'Well, I will have to destroy it, sad to say. I cannot use its stem cells because of its deformity. But at least I have learned that, with Doctor Dee's formula, it is possible to create such a creature, and that it can survive.'

Nathan hunkered down in front of the wire mesh. Denver came up to him and laid a hand on his shoulder, almost as if Denver were the father and he were the son.

'Pops, it's a no-brainer.'

'I know.'

'The doctors at the Hahnemann, they can find a way to get Mom out of her coma. They *must* be able to.'

'Let's hope so.'

Nathan stood up. He turned to Doctor Zauber and said, 'If there was any other way of doing this, without killing anybody, believe me, I'd do it.'

'Nobody will actually suffer,' Doctor Zauber assured him. 'I use ketamine. They are never aware of what happened to them. It is just like putting down cattle, in the *Schlachthaus*.'

Nathan shook his head. 'There's no way. I can't be any part of this.'

'So that is your final decision?' said Doctor Zauber. His voice was steady, but Nathan could tell that he was furious.

'That's right.'

'You are going to abandon your wife, and your entire life's work, for the sake of some high-minded moral principle?'

'I don't think that declining to murder people is exactly a high-minded moral principle.'

'In spite of the fact that you will be saving thousands and thousands more people than you will ever eliminate? Maybe even *millions*.'

'Doctor Zauber, for the last time, I'm not going to help you.'

'So what are you going to do? Report me to the police?'

'I should. Whether I do or not – well, I haven't decided yet.'

Doctor Zauber said, 'This is the gravest mistake you will ever make in your life. You know that, don't you?'

Nathan put his arms around Denver and Patti and said, 'Come on, guys. We're leaving. Rafał?'

Rafał nodded and the four of them walked back to the staircase.

Doctor Zauber turned his back on them. Inside its cage, the gryphon let out another screaming cry, followed by a growl, and jumped up against the wire mesh.

Rafał laid his hand on Nathan's shoulder. 'Maybe it was better that you did not succeed in breeding one of those creatures. It is worse than something that you meet in your bad dreams, yes?'

They climbed the stairs and came out into the hallway.

'Come on,' said Nathan. 'Let's get the hell out of here and then we can decide what to do next.'

As they walked toward the front of the house, however, they heard a banging noise from upstairs, like somebody slamming doors, one after the other. Nathan looked up, and saw that the first-story landing was in total darkness.

Before he could work out what was happening, however, there was another loud bang, and the shutters that covered the hallway window flew shut. Immediately, there was a double bang from the living room, and another bang from the kitchen.

Within less than ten seconds, they found themselves standing in absolute blackness, as if they had all suddenly gone blind.

'He's closed all the shutters,' said Nathan.

'How did he *do* that?' asked Denver.

'Don't ask me. Telekinesis. Magic. Some kind of remote control. Can anybody find the goddamned light switch?'

Rafał slid his hands along the wall. 'It is not on this side. Maybe it's next to the door.'

'Hold on,' said Nathan. 'I'll just find my flashlight.'

'Nathan – I have found the front door,' said Rafał. Nathan took his flashlight out of his pocket and switched it on. Rafał was trying to twist open the catch, but it was locked solid. He tried rattling the handle, but the door still wouldn't open.

'Come on, we'll have to try the back of the house.'

They were making their way to the kitchen when Doctor Zauber stepped out of the cellar door, right in front of them, like a stage magician appearing from nowhere. Nathan shone his flashlight directly into his eyes but he didn't even blink.

'I don't know what you're trying to pull here, Doctor Zauber, but we're going to be getting out of here whether you want us to or not.'

Doctor Zauber said, 'Yes, you will be getting out of here. Of course! Although not perhaps in the same form in which you entered.'

'What are you talking about?'

'I am talking about *you*, my friends. All of you. I am talking about your life-energy.'

Rafał stepped up to him, his fists bunched and his moustache bristling pugnaciously. 'You will move out of our way, please, Doctor. You cannot stop us.'

'My dear friend, I am not even going to try.'

With that, he took a step to one side, and vanished. Nathan said, 'Let's go, quick!' But immediately there was a muffled roar, almost as if the whole house were collapsing. Patti screamed, and even Rafał shouted out in fright.

Out of the open cellar door a monstrous black figure emerged, with branching horns and a hunched back and a narrow skull like some terrible horse.

'*Basilisk*!' Nathan shouted. 'Don't look at it! Whatever you do, don't look at it!'

He pushed Denver and Patti back along the hallway, and into the living room, and Rafał was right behind him. He tried to close the door, but he was too late. The basilisk burst into the room and stood in the doorway, breathing deeply and harshly. Its eyes were not yet fully lit. They shone like two dim lamps, but they were gradually growing brighter and brighter.

'Don't look at it,' Nathan repeated. 'It can kill you. It can instantly stop your heart. However much you're tempted, just don't look at it.'

Patti was sobbing. 'I can't do this! I can't take any more!'

'Do you have your mirror?' Nathan demanded. 'Do you all have your mirrors? Get them out! This is the time! We can beat this, if you all remember what we were going to do!'

'I can't do it! *I can't do it*!'

'Patti – yes, you can! Take out your mirror! Get yourself ready! Remember what we were going to do! Reflect the light from one to the other, remember?'

'*I'm too scared*!' Patti wailed, and sank to the floor on her knees.

Denver put his arm around her and tried to lift her up again. 'Patti, you *can* do it! We have to do it!'

The basilisk stayed in the doorway, its head swaying, its horns scraping against the ceiling. It looked first at Rafał, and then at Nathan, and then at Denver and Patti, and as it did so its eyes began to shine so brightly that the whole living room was illuminated.

'Mirrors!' Nathan shouted, keeping one hand lifted to protect his eyes. 'Take out your mirrors!'

Rafał took out his mirror and cupped it in his hands; as did Denver. He tried to take out Patti's mirror, too, but Patti was sobbing now, the way a small child sobs, and she was almost hysterical. The *Schleimgeist* had been too much for her, and she simply couldn't face another creature.

Nathan stood in front of the basilisk, his head lowered. He knew what would happen if he looked directly into its eyes. All around him, the room was so bright that all the colors were bleached out of it, and there wasn't a shadow anywhere.

He was just about to give the order for all of them to raise their mirrors, and deflect the basilisk's stare, when he saw Doctor Zauber's shiny black shoes standing on the carpet right in front of him.

'You think you can destroy me, Professor?' Doctor Zauber asked him. His voice sounded detached, and whispery, as if he were hearing it inside his head.

'You need to call your basilisk off and let us go,' said Nathan.

'*My* basilisk? Well, that's very true. It is *my* basilisk. And the basilisk is me.'

'What? What are you talking about? You need to let us go!'

'I needed a young life-energy to make the *Schleimgeist*, Professor, and Richard Scryman volunteered for that. But I needed so much more life-energy to breed another basilisk. I needed the life-energy of Robert Cichowlas, the painter; and the life-energy of the Walach family. But even *they* were not enough. Not for a creature as powerful as a basilisk.'

'Doctor Zauber, no good is going to come of this. You know that as well as I do. For Christ's sake, just let us go.'

Doctor Zauber said, 'I cannot do that, Professor. I need you. And I promise you that I will give you back your wife, if you agree to help me.'

The basilisk's eyes swept the living room from one side to the other, and they were as blinding as a lighthouse.

'This manifestation you see of "Doctor Zauber", this is merely transvection, in the same way that I appeared in your bedroom. Psychic transference.'

'Call this damned thing off, will you? You want to be guilty of *our* murders, too?'

Doctor Zauber came closer. 'I cannot call it off, Professor. As I told you, I am the basilisk and the basilisk is me. It would not have survived without my life-energy. That is why I need you more than ever. I need you to be the human face of our joint enterprises, while I am the source of all of our power.'

The basilisk was looking at him directly now, and the light from its eyes was so intense that Nathan had to clamp his hand over his face to prevent himself from being dazzled. But all the same he said, 'What part of "no" don't you understand, Doctor Zauber?'

'You cannot refuse me!' Doctor Zauber screamed at him. 'Not now! *Sie können nicht ablehnen!*'

Nathan said, 'Rafał! Denver! Patti! Mirrors – now!'

He lifted the mirror in his right hand, shielding his face with it. Rafał was standing on his right, and he held up his right hand, too, so that the light was reflected to Patti, who was standing on his left.

But before Patti could catch the light in her mirror, the basilisk swung its horselike head around and concentrated its glare on Rafał.

'Rafał!' Nathan shouted. 'Turn your face away!'

But Rafał had fumbled a second too long trying to aim his reflected light into Patti's mirror. He glanced toward the basilisk – only for in instant – but he instantly stiffened, and shouted out '*nie!*' and dropped his mirror.

'*Rafał!*'

Rafał was caught in the glare of the basilisk's eyes as if he had been caught in the headlights of an oncoming truck. He pitched over backward, hitting his head against the tiled surround of the fireplace, and lay awkwardly jammed between the fireplace and one of the old-fashioned armchairs, shaking and juddering. The lenses of his spectacles were completely blacked out, and his face was reddened.

Denver and Patti both stepped away from the basilisk, unsure of what to do next, now that they had lost Rafał and his mirror. But Nathan said, 'Denver! Patti! The mirror over the fireplace! Use that instead!'

The basilisk swiveled its head back toward him, and Nathan

held up his mirrors again. He deflected the light from the
basilisk's eyes to Patti's mirror, and she shone it toward
the mirror over the fireplace. The shaft of light came back to
her, at an angle, and this time she shone it to Denver, and
Denver shone it back to Nathan.

Nathan had to guess where to aim his second mirror, because
he didn't dare to look straight into the basilisk's eyes. He
jiggled it slightly from side to side, hoping that it would flash
the basilisk's glare directly back to it, even if only for a split
second.

The basilisk let out a deafening screech, and lurched toward
him. He heard a splintering, crackling sound, and he was
showered by dozens of sharp black bone fragments. The
blinding light from the basilisk's eyes swiveled all around
the room, from one wall to the other, from the ceiling to the
carpet, and it felt as if the floor were tilting.

Still shielding his eyes, Nathan looked quickly to each side
of his mirror. Denver was crouching down in the corner, behind
one of the armchairs, and Patti was backing away from the
basilisk with both hands held over her face.

The basilisk screeched again, in rage and pain. Nathan
lowered his mirror and saw that it was swaying and stag-
gering. Its horns shattered, and its entire body seemed to be
collapsing, like a huge black tent.

We've done it, he thought. *We've destroyed it, and Doctor
Zauber with it.* But at the same time he thought: *how am I
going to save Grace now?*

At that moment, however, the basilisk turned toward him.
Its glare was nothing like as dazzling as it had been before,
but it was still intense enough to make Nathan lift his hand
up in front of his face. There was no mistaking the creature's
fury. Its teeth were bared – three rows of sharp, barbed spines,
with a thin, snakelike tongue lashing between them, and it was
groping at the air with both of its front claws, as if it wanted
to rake him open from head to foot.

He backed away until he could back away no further,
because the couch was right behind him. But the basilisk's
breathing was becoming increasingly labored, whining and
whistling through slowly collapsing lungs, and its eyes were
growing dimmer and dimmer. As it did so the room grew

darker, too, and after a while Nathan thought it was probably safe for him to lower his hand.

'Patti,' he said. 'How about switching on the lights?'

Patti went across and found the light switch by the door. A wrought-iron chandelier with five branches was hanging from the ceiling, like a large dead spider. Only three of its light bulbs were working, but that was enough to illuminate the living room with a harsh, unflattering light.

Nathan watched the basilisk struggling for breath. He realized that he was probably witnessing the end of his dreams. It was clear to him now that it took much more than genetics to breed mythological creatures successfully. It took a high degree of sophisticated sorcery, too; and as Doctor Zauber and his basilisk came closer to death, the knowledge of that sorcery was dying with them. Nathan didn't feel at all triumphant that they had managed to defeat this creature. He felt only frustration, and sadness, and regret.

'Pops?' said Denver. He was kneeling on the floor next to Rafał. 'He just said something. I don't know what it was, but he's still alive.'

Nathan was about to turn around when the basilisk's eyes suddenly flared up again, blindingly bright, and it let out one last hate-filled scream. It was a shrill, throaty scream, like a turkey-vulture, but it had a sharp hiss to it, too, like a deadly poisonous snake. It also had a human resonance: the angry shout of a man who knows that his life is nearly over, without having achieved his life's ambition.

Nathan closed his eyes tight shut, but he still felt as if he had been slammed into a solid concrete wall. He fell backward, just as Rafał had done, and toppled over the corner of the couch. He lay on the carpet – blinded, deafened and breathless, unable to move.

'*Pops!*' Denver shouted.

TWENTY

Eye for an Eye

Nathan blinked, and blinked again. Gradually his vision began to return, and he could see Denver's face leaning over him, although at first he looked like a photographic negative, with white eyes and gray skin.

'Pops, are you OK?'

'*Can't – move –*' Nathan whispered. He couldn't feel his arms or his legs, and he still had a high-pitched singing noise in his ears.

Denver stood up. The basilisk's eyes had dimmed again now, and it was standing in the middle of the room, swaying, as if it had used up almost all of its remaining life-energy. Underneath its scaly skin, its skeletal structure was gradually collapsing, joint by joint. It made an intricate pattern of snapping noises, like somebody breaking branches. But it was still huge, and its shattered horns still scraped the ceiling as it swayed.

'*You goddamned monster!*' Denver screamed at it. '*You goddamned murdering piece of lizard shit!*'

He picked up the long brass poker that was hanging beside the fireplace, and approached the basilisk with it, prodding and feinting at it as if he were a swordsman.

'You want a fight? You want to try and murder me, too? Come on, then, you ratty black bag of mythological crap!'

The basilisk snarled and spat, and tried feebly to claw at him. Its eyes began to light up again, too.

Patti said, 'Denver – its eyes!' But Denver said, 'Oh, no! There's no way you're doing *that* to me, dude!'

He grasped the poker in both hands, and stabbed it into the basilisk's left eye. There was a bursting sound, and a large glob of optic fluid rolled down the basilisk's cheek, clear and transparent, but lambent, too, with its own pale-yellowish light.

The basilisk screeched, and wildly threw its head from side to side, but Denver stabbed it again, in its other eye.

There was a moment of terrifying fury, when the basilisk screamed and thrashed and beat its black umbrella-like wings. It hurled itself around the room, colliding with the chairs and the side tables, and smashing into the glass-fronted bookcase. Denver pulled Patti behind the door and held her tight. The basilisk crashed into the other side of the door, and Patti squealed, but then it spun around and dropped down on to the couch, quivering and twitching.

Nathan, still lying on the carpet beside the couch, looked up. The basilisk's horse-like face was staring down at him, but both of its eyes were blinded, and if it wasn't dead yet, it was very close to it.

As he lay there, a long glistening string of the basilisk's optic fluid dripped down on to his cheek. It had lost most of its glow, and it felt like cold, runny jelly. He felt it slide into his ear, but he couldn't move his arm to wipe it away.

'Denver?' he whispered. 'Denver, Patti, are you OK?'

He listened, but he still had a high-pitched singing in his ears. 'Rafał?' he said. 'Rafał, are you still hanging in there?'

He listened again, and as he did so, a large gobbet of optic fluid dropped down on to his lips. He tried to spit it away, but he couldn't even shake his head to get rid of it. It tasted faintly of oysters, and its consistency was disgusting – not only gelatinous, but stringy, too. He tried to keep his lips tight shut, but after nearly a minute he couldn't breathe, and he had to open his mouth and swallow the fluid that ran down his throat.

'*Blecchh*,' he said, and almost retched. It was then that Denver and Patti appeared, staring down at him like two anxious ghosts.

'Pops? How are you feeling?'

'Just get me out of here,' Nathan whispered. 'This damn thing's dripping glop all over my face.'

Together, Denver and Patti dragged him out into the middle of the floor.

'How's Rafał?' he asked.

Patti went across and said, 'Raffo? Can you hear me? Are you OK?' She knelt down and put her ear close to Rafał's face. 'I can't feel him breathing.'

'Try his carotid pulse,' said Nathan. 'Two fingertips, on the left side of his neck, next to his windpipe.'

Patti waited for a moment, and then she shook her head and said, 'No. I think he's dead.'

'Shit. We should call an ambulance.'

'You need an ambulance more than he does. Poor Raffo. I can't believe it.'

Nathan suddenly realized that the tinnitus in his ears had faded, and that he could hear Patti quite clearly. He reached up to touch his left ear and that was when he also realized that he could move his arm.

'Hey,' said Denver.

He looked at his left hand and flexed his fingers. Then he lifted his right hand, and flexed the fingers of that hand, too.

'Denver,' he said, 'help me to sit up.'

Denver took hold of both of his hands and pulled him up into a sitting position. He found that he was breathing more easily now, and that his vision had brightened. He looked around at the basilisk, hunched up over the couch. One of its wings was still shivering, but he guessed that was nothing more than the last unraveling of its central nervous system.

He reached out for the arm of the nearest chair, and heaved. He dropped back the first time, but when he heaved again, he was able to stand. At first, the living room swam around him as if he had been taking Ecstasy, but after a few moments he regained his balance. He could see himself reflected in the mirror over the fireplace and he looked surprisingly normal, even if his hair was sticking up.

'How are you feeling, Professor?' Patti asked him. 'You look so much better already. Like, you have your color back.'

'I'm not too bad,' said Nathan. 'Not quite a hundred per cent. But let me check Rafał out.'

Rafał's face was gray and his lips were pale blue. Nathan checked his breathing and his heart rate. 'I'm not sure,' he said. 'He could have a very faint pulse. The basilisk only looked at him for a split second, didn't it? Same with Grace.'

'But how come *you're* OK?' asked Denver.

Nathan looked across at the dead or dying basilisk. Two shining strings of optic jelly were dangling from its eye sockets.

'I swallowed some of its optic fluid,' he said.

'What?'

'The stuff that came out of its eyes. I swallowed some. I couldn't help it.'

'You're kidding me. Do you really think that might have cured you?'

'I don't know. But it could be like snakebite antidote, which has snake venom in it. Maybe it produces antibodies, which overcome the effects of shock.'

He took off Rafał's blackened spectacles and gently lifted one of his eyelids with his thumb. 'His pupils are dilated and fixed, but that doesn't necessarily mean he's dead. The same thing happens when you get concussed, or you're in a coma. Denver – why don't you bring me that mug from the kitchen? And maybe a spoon, too, if you can find one. Quick as you can.'

Denver returned with the mug and a large metal spoon. Nathan held the mug underneath the basilisk's eye sockets, and carefully scooped out as much of its optic fluid as he could. As he pushed the spoon deep into the second socket, the basilisk shuddered, and made a clicking noise in the back of its throat, and he froze. But it was nothing more than rigor beginning to set in, and the last exhalation of a creature that was already dead.

Denver blew out his cheeks and said, '*Phewf*', in relief.

Nathan managed to save almost a third of a mug of jelly-like optical fluid. It was wobbly and clear but it no longer shone with any inner light. He carried it across to Rafał, lifted his head, and spooned a little of it down his throat.

'You really think this is going to work?' asked Patti. 'Like, what a story this could make, if it does.'

Nathan looked across at her. 'You can't fool me, Patti Laquelle. You're not just in it for the story any more.'

Patti gave a little shrug. 'Sometimes, when you go through really scary situations with somebody, you get close, don't you? I love Raffo. And I love you guys, too.'

Nathan checked his watch. 'I'm going to give this five minutes. If Rafał doesn't show any sign of life by then, I'm going to call for an ambulance.'

'Oh, yes?' said Denver. 'And how do we explain to the paramedics what happened to him? I mean, *think* about it, Pops. And how do we explain this dead monster-thing lying on the couch? Not to mention that *live* monster-thing down in the cellar?'

'Denver—'

'Yes, but we're totally in shitsville, aren't we? What about the people who lived here? That artist, and that family? Doctor Zauber said he took their life-energy, didn't he? I mean, that's like killing them, right? And I bet the bodies are hidden in the house someplace. Suppose they accuse *us* of killing them?'

'Denver, let's worry about all that if and when we have to. Let's just see if we can wake Rafał up first.'

With a sudden rustle, one of the basilisk's wings dropped sideways on to the floor, and they all turned around to look at it.

'Don't worry,' said Nathan. 'It's absolutely dead, I promise you.'

'You're sure of that?' croaked a feeble voice.

They turned back. Rafał had opened his eyes, and was trying to focus on them. He reached up with one hand and felt his nose. '*Gdzie są moje okulary?*'

Patti held up his blackened spectacles. 'Sorry, Raffo. They got kind of incinerated.'

Between them, Nathan and Denver helped Rafał to sit up. 'What happened to me? I felt as if I fell off a tall building and hit the ground very hard.'

'It was the basilisk. It put you into total shock. But I think we've found the cure for it, thanks to Denver here.'

He held up the mug of optic fluid. 'You know what it says in the Bible, about an eye for an eye.'

They gave Rafał a few minutes to recover. Then Nathan said, 'We'd better get out of here and think of the best way we can explain all this to the police.'

'I don't see why we have to explain it at all,' said Patti. 'Let's just go back to our hotel, pack our bags, and fly out of here before anybody finds out what's happened.'

'Oh, you don't think our fingerprints are all over the house?' Denver retorted. 'I promise you, they're going to arrest us for mass murder and monstercide and we're going to spend the rest of our natural lives in some Polish slammer, eating cabbage.'

Nathan said, 'I want to go back down to the cellar first. I don't really know what we're going to do about that gryphon. Besides that, I want to take a look at Doctor

Zauber's books. If he has a copy of *De Monstrorum*, I might be able to use it to re-create some more mythical beasts.'

'You'd really try making *more* of them, after everything that's happened?'

'It's probably not possible. But the work is still so important. I wouldn't breed anything as dangerous as a basilisk, but there again – if its optic fluid can bring people out of comas . . .'

'OK,' said Rafał, climbing to his feet, and gripping Nathan's forearm for support. 'I will come down to the cellar with you. I know which books will be useful to you. Especially *De Monstrorum*, if Doctor Zauber had a copy. The legend is that it contains all of the alchemical formulae, as well as the rituals and procedures for bringing such creatures back to life.'

'We'll all go together,' said Patti. 'Then I think we should hotfoot it out of here, don't you?'

Nathan led the way back down to the cellar. The gryphon squawked when it saw them, and scrabbled furiously at the mesh of its cage. Nathan stood and looked at it for a while, partly in admiration at what Doctor Zauber had managed to breed, and partly in pity. He couldn't possibly try to take the gryphon with him. He would either have to put it down, or leave it here to starve.

Rafał was sorting through Doctor Zauber's papers and books. 'Look at this, Nathan!' he exclaimed, holding up a small volume bound in faded red leather. '*Die Verwirrung der Sorte*, by Albertus Magnus. *The Tangling of the Species*. This book alone is worth thousands of złotys!'

Nathan had found a clean test tube on Doctor Zauber's table and was using a glass funnel to pour the basilisk's optic fluid into it. He stoppered it with a plastic cork and put it carefully into his pocket. He just hoped that it wouldn't start to decompose too quickly on his way back to Philadelphia, and Grace's bedside.

'How about *De Monstrorum*?' he asked Rafał. 'Can you see that anywhere?'

Rafał picked up another book, and then another. 'All of these are amazing. I cannot begin to think where Doctor Zauber managed to find them. Look at this one, *Kitab Al-Ahjar – The Book of Stones* by the great Arab alchemist Abu Musa Jābir ibn Hayyān. He was said to have created living lizards and scorpions in his laboratory, and this book contains all of his instructions, written in code.'

Denver had been rooting around underneath the table, examining all the strange brass instruments in Doctor Zauber's baskets. He suddenly said, 'Pops? There's kind of a clock down here. And it's, like, ticking.'

Nathan said, 'Ticking?' and hunkered down beside him to take a look. In a large basket half hidden by two other baskets, he saw a red plastic kitchen timer, and Denver was right: it *was* ticking. Behind it, there was a folded brown cloth, like a tablecloth, which Nathan cautiously lifted up. He had never seen a bomb before, except in the movies, but here was a large bottle of clear liquid, with two batteries fastened to one side of it with duct tape, and several wires.

And there were less than ten seconds left on the timer.

He thought he shouted out, '*Bomb! Run! Get out of here!*' although he could never remember hearing his own voice. He pulled Denver out from under the table and grabbed Rafał's sleeve. Patti was over by the gryphon's cage, taking footage of it with her video camera, and he grabbed her, too.

They scrambled up the staircase, but they had only climbed up a few steps when there was a deep, shuddering bang, and they were blown against the wall by a blast of superheated air and flying debris.

The gryphon screamed, and Nathan saw it flung across its cage, with its feathers blazing.

'Come on!' he urged, and the four of them struggled up the stairs and into the hallway, deafened and shocked. Nathan slammed the cellar door behind them, and they stood there looking at each other, panting. A shard of glass had cut Nathan's forehead, and Patti had a pattern of five or six cuts on her chin; but apart from half-blackened faces they were otherwise unhurt.

'That was not a very big bomb,' said Rafał, pronouncing it 'bom-buh'. 'An incendiary device, yes? Doctor Zauber must have planted it there to destroy all of his work, in case events did not work out the way that he had planned them.'

'Which, of course, they didn't,' said Nathan.

'What about the gryphon?' asked Patti. 'The poor thing's going to be barbecued.'

Nathan opened the cellar door, but only by two or three inches.

It was already an inferno down there, and the draft moaned like a banshee as it was sucked past them by the heat. They heard glass shattering – Doctor Zauber's retorts and test tubes and pipettes – and a single desperate cry that sounded more like a baby than a mythical beast. Then there was only the deep roaring of a fire that was already out of control.

'*Now* it's time to get the hell out of here,' said Nathan. Denver led the way back to the kitchen, but when he tried to open it, he found that the kitchen door was locked, too, and that Doctor Zauber had removed the key.

'Shit, man!'

'We'll be OK,' Nathan told him. 'We'll just have to go out the same way that you broke in. And don't say "shit".'

He went to the window in the hallway and opened it up. It was covered by brown-painted wooden shutters, which were fastened together with a rusted hook, but he gave them three hard jabs with his elbow, and they juddered apart. Nathan lifted Patti out first, then he and Denver laced their fingers together to make a step for Rafał, who by now was wheezing like an asthmatic.

'I am too old for adventures like this,' he gasped, as he rolled over the window sill, and dropped down into the alley. 'Next time I stay in my library!'

'Go on, Pops,' said Denver; but Nathan said, 'No – you go first.'

Denver climbed out of the window, while Nathan went back to the cellar door. He carefully placed his hand against it, and the woodwork was almost too hot for him to touch. He tugged down the sleeve of his coat so that it covered his right hand, and then he took hold of the door handle, and pushed the door inward.

There was a loud thump – almost as loud as Doctor Zauber's original bomb – and a huge ball of orange flame rolled out of the door and up to the ceiling. Inside, the cellar was a crawling mass of fire, and the staircase was already burning like the staircase down to Hades.

Nathan hurried back to the window, and awkwardly climbed out, jarring his knee. The old woman had gone, her knitting abandoned on her chair. The mangy Pomeranian raised its head for a moment, and stared at them as if it were trying to remember who they were. 'Let's hit the bricks,' said Nathan. Smoke was already starting to pour out of the open window, and it wouldn't be long before the entire house was blazing.

By the time they reached the Amadeus Hotel, a tall column of brown smoke was hanging over Kupa and Izaaka Streets, and they could hear the wailing of firetrucks.

They flew out the following afternoon from John Paul II International Airport. It was a gray day, but a warm wind was blowing from the south-west, and drying up the overnight rain.

Rafał gave each of them one of his bear hugs. He was wearing his spare spectacles, which had very thick tortoise-shell frames, so that he looked more like somebody's uncle than ever.

'I keep open my ears, Nathan,' he promised. 'But from what they say on the news, all of that house is destroyed. The *policja* will puzzle over the bones, of course, and wonder what kind of strange animals were kept there. But we have left no evidence that *we* were there, or of what really happened.'

'Goodbye, Rafał,' said Nathan. 'And thanks for everything.'

'Remember a good Polish saying,' Rafał told him. '*Marz o tym, jakbyś miał wiecznie żyl, żyj jakbyś mial umrzeć dziś.* This means, "dream as if you will live forever, live as if you will die today".'

'Hey, that's so cool,' said Denver. 'How about one for me?'

'Well, here is an easy one you can say to your friends,' Rafał told him, with a smile. "*Moja dupa i twoja twarz to bliźniacy*".'

Denver repeated it, and then again, just to make sure he was pronouncing it correctly.

'That is so cool,' he said. 'I can go back to school and speak Polish. My science teacher is going to be so impressed: he's Polish. What does it mean?'

'I recommend you not to say it to your science teacher. It means "my ass and your face are twins".'

Nathan and Denver had to wait for over an hour when he arrived at the Hahnemann, because Grace had to be washed and then Doctor Ishikawa wanted to run a series of routine tests. By the time he was allowed into her room, the sun was already setting over City Hall, and the sky was streaked with crimson and purple.

He told Denver to keep watch in the corridor outside, and then he went into Grace's room and sat down close to her bed. She was even whiter than she had been before, as if she were a statue, rather than a real woman, and her hand when he held it was icy.

He took out the test tube of optic fluid, and unstoppered it. He had taken it to the Zoo during this morning's lunch-break, and borrowed a corner of his old laboratory so that he could analyze it and make sure that it hadn't started to break down.

As far as he had been able to tell, it was still unspoiled by bacteria. He had also made the discovery that it contained luciferase enzyme – similar to the enzyme that makes fire-flies glow. Each of the basilisk's eyes, in effect, had been like ten million fireflies, giving off a light that could shock any living cell into total paralysis and death.

'Grace?' he said. 'I know you can't hear me, but I'm praying for you now. May God bring you back to me.'

His hands were shaking as he parted her lips and poured a little of the optic fluid into her mouth. Then he stoppered the test tube again, and sat back, and held her hand.

Denver poked his head around the door.

'How's it going, Pops?' he asked him. 'Did you give her the gloop?'

Nathan nodded. 'All we can do now is wait. I just hope I've given her enough, or that I haven't given her too much. I just hope I haven't left it too late.'

Denver came into the room and stood beside him.

'Pops?' he said.

Nathan looked up at him. 'What is it?'

'I don't know. What happened in Kraków—'

'I don't think we need to talk about it yet. It's going to take some time for it all to sink in. Give it a couple of weeks, then we can go for a beer together and chew it over.'

'Patti could come too.'

'Sure. Patti could come too.'

Outside the window, it began to grow dark, and the city began to sparkle. Nathan kept on holding Grace's hand, but he couldn't think of any words to say to her. Denver went and sat in the corner and watched TV with the sound turned right down.

Three hours went by. Denver dozed off. His head tilted sideways and he started to breathe deep and slow, and occasionally to mutter. *'Didn't want to – you can't . . .'*

Nathan was determined to stay awake, but his eyes began to close. He was almost asleep when he became aware that there was somebody else in the room, apart from himself and Denver and Grace.

'Well, well,' said a smug, Germanic voice. 'You think that you have discovered a cure, do you?'

He jolted and opened his eyes. Doctor Zauber was standing so close to him that he could have touched him. He was dressed in black, as usual, and he was looking down at him with one black eyebrow raised.

'You are not the genius I thought you were,' said Doctor Zauber. 'How could you have thought that the optical fluid from a dead basilisk could revive your poor sleeping wife?'

'It worked for me. It worked for Rafał Jasłewicz.'

'No, Professor, your wife is destined to sleep for ever, in the castle of nightmares, surrounded by thorns which you can never cut your way through. That is your punishment for what you did to me, and my basilisk, and my entire life's work.'

'Damn you,' said Nathan. 'Damn you and damn you and damn you.'

He was so exhausted and so disappointed that he started to cry, and tears ran down his face. 'Damn you,' he repeated. 'Damn you.'

Doctor Zauber reached out and took hold of his hand. But then he realized that it wasn't Doctor Zauber at all. Doctor Zauber had been wearing black leather gloves, and this hand was much smaller, and much colder, and it wasn't wearing a glove at all.

'Nate?' said a soft, hoarse voice. 'Nate? Where am I?'

TWENTY-ONE

A Gift from Poland

Five weeks later, Grace came into his study and said, 'You've had a package from Poland. Save me the stamps, will you? They're so pretty.'

She handed him a padded envelope with his name scrawled on it in large letters. The sender was Rafał Jasłewicz, from Kraków. He cut it open, and drew out a red leather-bound book. It was very old, with brown-spotted pages. On the title page, in smudgy black letters, it said, *Kitab Al-Ahjar*, *The Book of Stones*, by Abu Musa Jābir ibn Hayyān, printed Cairo, 1818.

There was a note inside. It said, simply, 'In case you are ever tempted to try again.'

TWENTY-TWO

Under the Ruins

In the darkest crevice of the basement beneath the burned-out ruins of the Murdstone Rest Home, something rustled. Two dim lights shone for a moment, illuminating the soot-stained brickwork, but then they faded, leaving the basement seamlessly black.